THE

Wind

AND THE

Drum

THE

Wind

AND THE

Drum

KATHARINE JOHNSON

— Beaver's Pond Press —

Minneapolis, MN

Edited by Sara & Chris Ensey

ISBN: 978-1-59298-760-3
Library of Congress Catalog Number: 2017912385
Printed in the United States of America
First Printing: 2017
21 20 19 18 17   5 4 3 2 1

Book design by Athena Currier

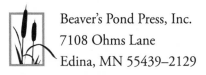
Beaver's Pond Press, Inc.
7108 Ohms Lane
Edina, MN 55439–2129

(952) 829-8818
www.BeaversPondPress.com

To order, visit www.ItascaBooks.com or call
1-800-901-3480 ext. 118. Reseller discounts available.

For more information about the author, visit:
www.katharinejohnsonbooks.com.

For Ada and John

THE FIRST JOURNEY

The Wind and the Drum

I am Tuuli.
Wind brings me breath.
Drum beats with my heart.
Without wind. Without drum.
I do not live.

1

A CRY BROKE THE EARLY MORNING SILENCE. "Kauri's baby is born! It's a boy!"

Tuuli awoke to the news with joy. The winter had been long, dark, and frigid. Even though the sun was peeking above the horizon for short times every day, the reindeer as well as the Saami people still suffered from the cold and shortage of food. Frost crackled in the morning air. But now, a baby was born. Maybe his birth was a good omen. Maybe it signaled that the snows would melt and the cold grip of winter would loosen.

Poppi, too, awoke to the good news. "Hand me my drum," he said to Tuuli. "I will sing to this good fortune. For our newest *siide* member. For a good, strong name that is a sign of hope."

Tuuli watched her grandfather unwrap his drum from a pouch made of reindeer hide that he had brushed until it was soft. He held the drum with both hands and nestled it on his lap. Tuuli heard the excitement of the siide quiet as everyone listened to Poppi singing. Then others brought their drums out, too. Tuuli listened to the gentle *pum-a-rum, pum-a-rum* from the nine drums of her people. Through the skin and birchbark walls of their *goahti*, Tuuli heard everyone join Poppi in singing a *joik* of happiness, of the spring to come, of rebirth for all the plants that had been waiting in the cold earth for the days of light and warmth.

> *Beavi, rise.*
> *Light the day.*
> *Warm the earth.*
> *Welcome new life.*

When Poppi put his drum away, Tuuli ducked low to go out of the goahti they shared. Outside, Siru hugged Tuuli with her one good arm and twirled her around. "Friend, come see the baby. He's so perfect."

Poppi came to hold the baby, too. Tuuli watched as he slowly made his way from their goahti and past the cooking fire, feeling his way with his rowan walking stick. He shuffled his feet and almost stumbled on a tree root. A drop of saliva slid from the corner of his mouth to his jaw. A cloud shadowed the morning sun. Tuuli shivered. *Poppi is old and feeble. The long cold, dark time has been hard on him.* The cloud drifted past the sun. The morning brightened, but the realization of Poppi's frailty still lingered.

Tuuli sat at Poppi's side as he held the newborn. The baby seemed strong and healthy—precious life born on the cusp between the dark days of winter and the coming of the season of unending sunlight. Tuuli gently touched the baby's soft cheek. She uncovered his feet. They were beautifully perfect. She thought of Gabba, her newborn fawn. He was born with a twisted hoof—a bad omen. Tuuli sang a song of thanks as she held the baby's feet because the foreboding omen of the lame fawn had not marked Kauri's baby with a twisted foot of his own.

"I'll sleep for a short time now," Poppi said, handing the baby back to Kauri. Later, when Tuuli heard her grandfather snoring, she stole out of the encampment to where she'd hidden her deer. Ruusu nudged and licked the fawn, urging him to stand. He did. He teetered, but stood on his three good legs. Tuuli steadied him as he took a few steps to get close enough to his mother to nurse. Her new fawn was white, pure white. A good omen, but Tuuli kept him hidden because of his front hoof that knuckled over and was bent to one side. A bad omen. She was sure her siide members would want him destroyed, so she'd found a hollow ringed with stones and dwarf pines to shelter and hide Ruusu and Gabba.

As she ran her hand along the fawn's soft coat, Tuuli thought of Siru, who had been born with a limp arm. She worked as hard with her one hand as any who had two good ones. And Poppi had been blind for several seasons. His blindness had not taken away his goodness. He was still loved and cared for, yet she was sure he would tell her to kill the fawn. He would remind her how its sinews would be tender, easy to chew, strong for sewing. Their people could crack the bones for rich marrow. It had been a long, cold winter, and they all would feast eagerly on a simmering stew.

While she warmed her bare hands in Ruusu's thick fur, Tuuli heard a sled pulled by reindeer grinding over the pebbled snow. As it neared the camp, Tuuli's heart thumped. A chill ran up her spine. The crunching of snow and snorting of reindeer grew louder, then stopped. Many times, the wind had whispered to Tuuli foretelling change, danger, and men in coats as dark as night. The wind had also told that a traitor would lead the strangers.

The strangers had arrived. And the traitor, too.

"*Bures. Bures.*" The wind carried greetings as her people met the strangers. There were so many voices all at once Tuuli couldn't make out the words, but she heard the warmth of her people's welcome. Why were her people so friendly? Strangers meant trouble. Curious, she crept to the top of a hill and hid within a small copse of trees looking down at the encampment.

Through branches, she saw one large sled and four harnessed reindeer. Four men in long black coats stood with their backs to her. Almost everyone from her siide surrounded the strangers. Even Poppi, awake from his nap, stood in the circle, leaning on his walking stick.

The voices Tuuli heard were a mixture of her language and another—a strange tongue. How could anyone make sense of what was said? Then she noticed. One—the shortest of the newcomers—listened to the strangers speak and then spoke Saami words, the words of her people. It was he who was warmly greeting all her people, calling many by name. Some put their hands on his shoulders and clasped his arms. *The traitor! Who is he?*

Her people gestured for the newcomers to sit. Siru's mother offered food. Some youngsters carried more wood for the fire. Soon warming flames danced high. The wind carried their words to Tuuli. The strangers did most of the talking, but the short man turned their strange words into Saami. He told of a god and a new way of life. He said his god was more powerful than any they'd imagined.

"We have been hungry for many seasons now," Siru's father said. "Can your god feed us?"

"If it is his will."

"Impossible," some of the herders said together. "How could any one god be stronger than the wind and the sun? How could any one god be more powerful than the god of the trees, the god of the waters, and the god of earth?"

"You are hungry and you have lost many deer. Your gods have not kept famine and disease away." The young man translated for a tall stranger who smiled a lot, but even from the distance, Tuuli could see that his smile did not reach his eyes.

"That is true," said one of the herders. "But how can a god hand us food when we're hungry? The deer, the waters, the plants, and the forests give us food."

One of the strangers held up something black, square, and thick. He opened and showed it. He thumbed through while the traitor said, "All answers are here. All you need to know is here."

"We have drums to tell us what we need to know," said Utsí.

"That's exactly why we're here. We've come for the drums."

Tuuli gasped. It was as she had heard whispered by the wind.

The short man who spoke Saami encouraged the people to touch the black thing. Some were afraid and stepped back from it, but some held it and repeated its name cautiously, unsure how to say the strange word. It was so different from their drums. Some came forward to tap it. "It's not like a drum," they said. "It doesn't vibrate." And they tapped it again. "Nothing," they said again and turned away.

Good! Why would we need something black and ugly when we have the beautiful drums? Their drums told the story of their lives. Poppi had the ancient Drum of the Four Winds. The hands of many ancestors had held it. If Tuuli's mother had lived, Poppi would have passed it to her. But now, when her grandfather died, it would become hers. She would lay her hands where Poppi had laid his, and she would join the long line of *noaidis* who wove her people with the spirit world through the power of the drum. Ever since she was a young child, Tuuli had sat on her mother's lap watching as Poppi taught them how to pat rhythms on the drum. He showed them the different rhythms needed so he could fall into a trance as his spirit traveled to another world to find the knowledge he needed to cure illnesses or to divine the future.

Wanting to get closer, Tuuli crawled away from the copse and down the hill until she crouched behind her own goahti. Her people's gods gave them wisdom and everything they needed to survive. They had sent the warm winds Tuuli had asked for to end the cold season. The strangers' god could never be better than that.

Closer now, Tuuli heard the short man say, "You must give up your chanting of the charms and singing of the songs. You must give up the drums. You might think that they are the source of good, but they arouse the spirit of evil and cause great harm to your people."

Her heart chilled. Poppi's drum was in their goahti. She was not going to let the strangers have it. Not the Drum of the Four Winds. Poppi used it often for healing his people of frostbite, of cuts, of fevers. It brought him the honored wisdom of their ancestors.

But then she remembered Poppi had also used it when jagged sheets of ice had swept her mother into the roiling freezing waters of a river. Poppi did his best to save her after he'd found her lying on the rocky shore, far from their siide. He had carried her, his only child, all the way back. He wrapped her in fur robes, lit a fire, soaked lichen and mosses in hot water, and packed them around his daughter. He sent Beto, Tuuli's father, to bring in rowan. He laid the branches upon her. He made hot drinks of roots, leaves, and berries for her to sip, placed rocks around the fire in the goahti, and, when they were hot, he'd sprinkled them with mashed aromatic grasses. The goahti had misted densely with steam. Beto mixed blood and milk from a healthy reindeer for his wife to drink. Day turned to night and back to day while Poppi ceaselessly chanted joiks of healing and beat his drum. The next night, a golden orb with a cloudy tail glowed in the dark as it passed over their camp. Tuuli and her father had held her mother's hands and felt her spirit flow to the highest skies as she closed her eyes for the last time.

Soon after, Poppi's eyes turned as white as doe's milk, and he could see no more. Many said it was because he'd strained them searching for Tuuli's mother, staring into the cold waters of the river with the sun reflecting and burning sight from his eyes. Others said when his daughter died, Poppi blamed himself for not seeing the danger so he punished himself with blindness.

Tuuli missed her mother every day, but she kept busy caring for Poppi, her dog Kulta, and Ruusu. Even now, relentless grief tormented her to the deepest bone in her body. Every day, Tuuli wove patterns of her mother into her thoughts as she picked berries, skied to the deep lake to catch salmon, dried and smoked venison with the women of her siide, and gossiped with her friend Siru. Even now, after two autumn gatherings had passed since her mother died, hot tears slid down her cheeks. Angry, she closed her ears to the whisperings of the wind.

I will not listen. The wind did not warn my mother of the rising, rushing waters.

After her mother died, Poppi insisted Tuuli sit at his feet when he took out his drum. "Listen to the wind and learn to speak to the drums. You will have to be the next noaidi. You should have had more time to learn the ways of a noaidi, but your mother is gone now. She was a wind listener and a skillful healer. I still miss her. When I die, it will be up to you to make the journey to the Mount of Four Winds. You'll carry this drum with you."

Tuuli's father, Beto, scolded Poppi, saying, "Don't expect so much from her. She's too young. If the drums really talk, why didn't they warn my Iiri that day? Why didn't they call out the danger? Tell her to get away from the slippery banks? And the wind didn't whisper either. If it did, my wife would have heard, and she wouldn't have been beaten so brutally in the rocky waters."

Sad and no longer believing in the power of the talking drums or the whispering wind, Tuuli's father left the encampment and traveled to the towns of the south. Since then, Poppi had cared for Tuuli, and she for him. No word—if her father lived or died—had come since.

Tuuli thought now of her father. She wondered if he was following the ways of strangers and their black book. She thought of her friend Hánas and wondered where he was and why he no longer came to the falling-leaf gatherings.

Tuuli shook all those thoughts from her head. She needed to get to Poppi's drum. Keeping out of sight, she crept into their goahti. The drum quivered in her hands as she slid it under her doeskin coat. Peeking out to make sure no one was watching, she saw Kauri cradle her baby to her breast. The strangers still spoke their strange words. Some people no longer seemed friendly toward them. Others had slipped away from the circle, but still a few remained, listening with interest.

Tuuli crept quickly out of the goahti. Her heart raced. Sweat ran down from under her arms. When she was sure no one had seen her, she ran back to where Ruusu and Gabba were tied. Out of breath, and with her heart thumping fiercely in her chest, she dropped onto her knees to rest.

She bent to put her ear to the ground, but she heard no footsteps coming closer. She felt for the drum. It was still safely tucked beneath her coat. She dared not take it out until she found a hiding place. She wondered what the strangers would do if they found she had taken the drum. After her breathing returned to normal, she dug a hole between the twisted and dwarfed roots of a spruce tree. She held the drum high. It was a small drum. Small enough to hide under her coat. Smaller than any of the others she had seen, but also more ancient. Then she carefully packed mosses around the drum, put it in the hole, and covered it with twigs, boughs, and flat stones.

2

AFTER HIDING THE DRUM, TUULI CREPT BACK to the camp. When she got close, she heard angry voices, so she crawled into the copse of trees again. Her people stood in a line at the far side of the camp. They shuffled their feet and frowned; their heads hung low. All signs of welcoming were gone. The strangers, except the short one who had translated earlier, were waving their arms and shouting at the people. When they stopped, the short one spoke softly, saying that his traveling companions wanted them to point out all who kept drums and to name their noaidi.

No one replied. No one pointed. The strangers shouted and scowled. Some of the Saami turned to leave, but the strangers pointed their gun-sticks and barred the way.

Finally, the young man approached Poppi and said, "I remember you are the noaidi and have one of the drums. Bring it to us, and tell your people to bring all they have. You no longer need the drums and the wind to help you."

Poppi stood, unmoved, silent as though he were deaf as well as blind. Finally, he asked the young man, "You say you come with good hearts? What about the words we have heard at the falling-leaf gatherings that your strangers have burned whole encampments and have tortured our people? If that's what you mean by good hearts, we will have none of it."

Tuuli edged to the side of her goahti and knelt behind some small bushes to get close enough to see the young man who changed the strangers' words into her language. Her heart turned to ice as she looked at his back. *Who is this traitor?* He was worse than Aiko, the noaidi who betrayed the Deep River Siide. His people expelled him because he had played tricks with his skills and powers when he should have been helping those in need. As bad as Aiko was, Tuuli could think of no greater evil than bringing the strangers into their midst. Strangers who demanded taxes on the land they said belonged to their king. To the Saami, the land belonged to the reindeer, and the people just followed them on their migrations. The strangers now insisted they give up their sacred drums. The very drums that, along with the deer, were the center of their lives. The traitor had brought strangers who spoke of a strange god in strange words. Strangers with the power to destroy their siide. The traitor must never be forgiven!

Then Tuuli's heart beat wildly, and her bowels twisted. What if she were to blame for the strangers coming? She hadn't killed the lame fawn. She hadn't even told anyone about it because it might portend bad things to come. She'd even closed her ears to the whispers of the wind when it carried messages to her. Now strangers had come. What would happen to her people if the drums were taken from them? Was she to blame for everything?

Tuuli's heart wrenched as she looked at the back of the traitor. There was something familiar about him beyond the language he spoke. Something about his posture. When he spoke again, he turned sideways to her. She almost gasped aloud. The traitor was Hánas! Hánas, her favorite childhood friend. Stunned, Tuuli almost shouted his name aloud.

Then she looked again to be sure. Yes! It was Hánas. She could see his eyes now. They hadn't changed, but his voice had. It was no longer the voice of the child she had known, but that of a man.

Hánas and his family had been from the Broken Birch Siide. They were one of the many clans that came to the falling-leaf gathering. Even as toddlers, she and Hánas had played together. Through the seasons, they had looked forward to meeting again. They had even promised each other that when they got old enough, they would run the courtship race. She promised to tell him before the race which direction she was going to run so he could follow and catch her for his wife.

Tears ran down Tuuli's face as she listened to Hánas explain that the new way demanded the drums be destroyed. "They raise the devil spirits," Hánas said. "They must no longer be used. All you will need is this book we bring to you."

Tuuli's head ached. She felt faint. Even in her worst dreams, nothing this bad had ever happened. At first when the wind whispered to her, all this seemed far away. Tuuli had thought her siide would be safe because their encampment was so far north.

Poppi turned to his people. He stood among them, touching shoulders as he felt his way from one to the next. In a low droning voice, he implored that no one give up the drums. He asked that no fingers be pointed at drummers or wind listeners. He pleaded, "Our ways must not be forsaken. They are more ancient than our ancestors one hundred times over. From the beginning of time, these things have been important to the Saami—our people."

The people touched Poppi back. They whispered to him, "Fear not, Poppi. We will stand strong for our siide, for our ancestors."

"We need the messages from the drums and the wind. They led us here, to the icy north, to the reindeer that give us all we need," Poppi beseeched as he finished his circle among the people.

Hánas stood at the far edges of the circle, listening. He did not translate for the strangers. It was only after one of them gruffly barked at Hánas that he stood before Poppi and asked for the drums again.

Poppi stood as tall as he could while leaning on his stick. In a voice stronger than Tuuli had heard him use for a long time, he said, "I see no drums."

Tuuli was proud of her grandfather for standing up to Hánas, but she couldn't help but remember her earlier friendship with Hánas. She hadn't seen him for several years. Now Hánas was here—a stranger.

Hánas put an arm out to Poppi and said, "Respected aged one. You are blind. Of course you don't see drums."

Poppi remained silent. Tuuli held her breath. She saw her people stand stiffly, wondering what was going to happen.

"The Deep Lake people and the Hollow Hill people have already given up their drums. We know this siide has many," said Hánas. "Do what is best for your people."

One of the strangers spoke to Hánas again. He spoke back, rapidly and angrily, in the language Tuuli could not understand. *Hánas is like a branch that breaks and falls from a tree.* A broken branch is no good to the tree. Hánas had fallen away from the Saami. Even his clothes were no longer the clothes given to their people by the deer, but made by strangers. And, worst of all, he used their language as a weapon to help strangers come and make demands.

"Please give up your drums," Hánas urged. "I don't want anyone to get hurt."

Unable to control her anger anymore, Tuuli leaped from her hiding place and stalked right up to him. "*Broken Branch!*" She spat the words and glared at him.

Startled, Hánas looked directly at her. Then his eyes softened. "Tuuli," he said. "It has been a long time."

"Not long enough," Tuuli said, holding his eyes with a steady, piercing look. "*Traitor!*"

Hánas held both hands out to Tuuli. "I hoped I'd find you here, still with your siide and not yet taken as a bride."

Tuuli ignored Hánas's hands and was about to spit at him when the strangers closed in. They clasped Hánas by the arm and led him to the edge of the clearing. Poppi leaned on Tuuli. She led him to a log to sit. "Poppi, what shall we do?"

The people gathered around them, whispering. "We are many, and they are few. We can chase them away."

"How can we? They have those gun-sticks that roar and kill."

Poppi coughed. "We'll think of a way." Poppi's voice faded.

Tuuli felt his whole body tremble. Tuuli looked at those gathered around. Their faces were gray and gaunt. Tuuli felt tears swell in her eyes. She looked down to hide them. No one said anything. No one offered ideas. Many turned to go to their own goahtis shaking their heads, unconvinced that there was a way to get the strangers to leave.

Tuuli, feeling Poppi's thin and quivering body leaning against hers, no longer held her tears back. Bitter bile filled her throat, and she cried.

3

A DARK CLOUD BLOCKED THE SUN, and a chill settled in the air as the strangers demanded everyone circle around the campfire. Hánas came to stand by Tuuli, but she turned and stood between Poppi and Siru. The strangers spoke loudly and waved their arms. Hánas came to stand in front of Poppi. He held his hands out in friendship and respect even though he knew Poppi could not see him. "I'm sorry. I didn't think they would threaten this," he said, "but they will kill, stampede, and scatter the reindeer herd unless you give up the drums."

"Don't let them do that," Poppi answered. "You know we need the deer."

"Yes, I know, but they know it, too." Hánas pointed to the strangers. "That is why they threaten the herd. They will use their guns. Even if they kill just one deer, the noise will scare and scatter the rest of the herd. I'm sorry, but to save your deer and people, you must give up the drums and your gods. It is the only way."

Everyone turned to each other and murmured angrily. Poppi said to his people, "They threaten our deer. Tell me, should we give up the drums? We can make new ones when these strangers leave."

Hánas stood silent. The people of the siide buzzed among themselves, trying to decide. Give up the drums? Never! The drums were their past and their future as they had been held by their mothers, fathers, and many before them. And the deer? Their lives depended on the deer.

One spoke up. "We are barely making it through the harsh seasons with the help of the drums. What will happen without them?"

Another countered with, "We can do as Poppi says. We'll make new drums when the strangers leave. We must protect the deer."

Hánas walked to Tuuli and implored, "You do not want your deer killed. The drums are nothing but things. They do not bring you food or the words of your gods. Tell your people to give them up."

Tuuli backed away from Hánas and said, "I do not listen to you. You! You are no longer Saami. You don't wear our clothes. You don't follow our ways. No one should ever speak your name again."

Hánas's eyes welled with tears. He reached to Tuuli, but she turned her back. Bitter gall filled her throat.

"*Broken Branch!*" she rasped.

The people argued among themselves. How could they live without their old drums? New drums would not hold the spirit of their ancestors, yet the deer needed to be protected.

Poppi listened and then held up his hand until they came to a hush. He hesitated and then said to Hánas, "Our people cannot live without the reindeer. Tell your strangers they can have the drums. Take them, but then you must promise to leave and never come back. And take your book and gods with you."

Those who owned drums reluctantly brought out fur pouches. The tallest of the strangers opened the pouches one by one and tossed the drums into a pile. Everyone in the camp gasped at the rough treatment. They circled close, wanting to be near, but not daring to pick them out of the pile. When the last drum was unwrapped, no one said a word. No one moved. Eight drums. Tuuli saw the people silently count them over and over. She could feel her people hold their breath when they were sure there were only eight. One was missing.

18

4

TUULI, TOO, HELD HER BREATH. She heard everyone's heart beating with fear as they looked at the drums and wondered about the ninth. Did the strangers know there should be another? She shut her eyes tightly and whispered, "Blow, Wind, blow." At that moment, a stiff wind blew into the camp. It caught everyone's breath and blew away unspoken words so the strangers would not hear them thinking about the missing drum.

As Tuuli silently praised the wind, she heard Poppi's buried drum vibrate. The wind swooshed and swirled about, covering the telling beat of the hidden drum. Who else had heard it? She looked at Poppi. He had turned his head quickly with his one good ear in the direction of his drum. And then he quickly turned away. Hánas, too, seemed to be listening and nodding in rhythm with the drum.

The silence broke when one of the strangers demanded, "Where is the noaidi's goahti? His drum is not here!" This time, Tuuli's people did not need to have the words translated. Poppi pointed to his skin- and bark-covered dwelling. Two strangers entered. When they came out, their hands were empty.

More strange words spat from the tall man's mouth. Hánas looked at Poppi and said, "Where did you hide your drum? Your people say you can sing a broken leg whole, a bleeding wound healed, and a baby safely born. But your people have been hungry through the long, dark, cold of winter. You might as well give up your drum."

Tuuli spun to face Hánas. "Traitor, what reason do you have to bring strangers to disrupt our lives? You were born Saami and know our ways are good."

"Tuuli, I only put their words into Saami words so you can understand. These men bring a message so your people can be saved."

Siru's father stepped forward. "Saved? Saved from what? We have heard of your ways. You burn whole villages. And you dance upon the ashes of the drums you burn. You scatter herds of reindeer. You torture and burn people alive if they don't give up their drums." Before he could say more, two strangers grabbed him and twisted him to the ground.

Siru flung herself at the men holding her father. One grabbed Poppi's walking stick and struck her hard. Siru fell. She yelped in pain. Tuuli and others ran to help her. When she got up, she beseeched Poppi, "Give up your drum. They'll kill my father if you don't."

Hánas stood in front of Poppi. "My fellow travelers have never done things like this before. I don't know what they will do now that they are angry. Do not defy these men. Nothing good will come of it. Where is the drum?"

Poppi wobbled without his stick, but in a strong voice said, "I don't have it. Your men looked in my goahti; it was not there."

The strangers snarled and grabbed Poppi by the arm. They dragged him toward the goahti they'd taken as their own.

Tuuli pushed past Hánas and ran toward her grandfather. "Poppi!" She wanted to tell him she had the drum and would give it up.

He raised one hand to her. "Go. Go. Go and be as the wind." And then he raised his other hand.

Tuuli felt the wind calm. Poppi wanted her to be still and not reveal the drum. She touched his arm so he'd know she understood. A stranger shoved Poppi and Siru's father into the goahti. A second one pointed his gun-stick from person to person. Another stranger piled an armload of wood onto the cooking fire. When the fire crackled, he tossed the drums one by one into the hot flames.

"No!" Tuuli screamed. She ran to the fire and pushed the stranger, but he was too strong for her. Warding her off with one arm, he shoved her to the ground and tossed the last of the drums into the flames.

Tuuli looked for Hánas to beg him to stop this, but he wasn't there. She screamed again. Frightened, everyone in the siide moaned and cried as the drums began to burn. The wind, the trees, and even the dried grasses moaned with them.

Leaping flames engulfed the drums. Tuuli jumped into the middle of the fire to stomp it out. She heard the strangers laugh over her own choked cries. Siru's father pulled her from the fire as the flames licked at her boots. The wind swirled. Tuuli held her hands to her ears but could not block out the crackling and the splitting of the drums as their life was burned from them. Then as quickly as it started, it was over. The drums were ashes.

The wind swirled the ashes in all directions, leaving Tuuli covered with the flakes from head to foot. Her boots and leggings were blackened and scarred from the fire. The wind swirled again and flung the ashes to the north where the nightlights danced in the sky, to the south where the warm airs came to melt winter snows, to the east where Beavi rose each morning, and to the west where the mountains rose to majestic heights. Except for those that covered Tuuli, the ashes were carried by the four winds to the skies. The drums were gone.

5

THE TALLEST STRANGER LAUGHED AS HE SAW THE DRUMS crumble and ashes swirl to the skies. Birds flew from the trees, escaping the ashes. Everyone surrounded Tuuli, touching the ashes that covered her. With their fingertips, they brought the ashes to their own hearts.

"Look at your boots and leggings," they said through their tears. "They're charred from the flames." When the people tried to leave the campfire, two strangers signaled for them to stay.

Tuuli headed for the goahti where Poppi was, but the tall stranger wouldn't let her in. She looked for Hánas again, but he was still nowhere to be seen. Bitter spit flowed into her mouth. Her whole chest felt like it could break into two. Her friend Siru came and stood by her.

"Do you think the strangers are right when they say that the drums bring evil to us?" asked Siru.

"No. They are wrong. The drums are good." Her words were jagged from the smoke that had singed her throat.

"They say when Poppi chants, evil seeps into all of us. When he drums up magic, it blinds us to real goodness; and if we follow him, we also become evil."

"Evil?" said Tuuli. "Not you, not me, not anyone. Especially not Poppi. Even as his hair grows thin and gray, and his teeth fall out, he has always been good to our siide. He sees to it that we all share the work and the food. He holds the children tenderly. He sits with the ailing for hours, cooling their foreheads, singing joiks of healing. Our wild herds are never neglected, and our tame deer are carefully tended to."

"What if the strangers are right? They say their god brings light to our long, dark times. We almost starved this past winter in the cold," Siru persisted.

"Don't worry. It's the season of light now, and the sun will shine all the time, making the dark and cold go away. We'll be warm, able to fish, find nuts and berries. We'll have plenty to eat. We don't need their ways."

"Yes, but winter will come again. Then we'll freeze and be hungry if there aren't enough berries and fish to last the winter. We dare not slaughter too many deer. Their numbers grow fewer. So many grow thin and die from the sickness of not enough food."

"Are you beginning to believe what the strangers say?" Tuuli shuddered to her very core.

"I don't know. It doesn't hurt to listen to them, does it?"

"Look. They burned our drums. They threatened our deer. And at this very moment they're holding Poppi in their goahti. They might be hurting him. They even struck you." Tuuli sounded brave as she said this, but when she reached for Siru's hand, she felt it limp in her own. A heavy burden seemed to weigh her own shoulders down as she remembered the fawn with the twisted foot. *It's my fault that the strangers are here!* She could not shake the thought.

Siru took her hand out of Tuuli's. "I was hungry every minute of the long, dark, cold winter. I never had enough to eat. I dreamed every day of something—something that could save me and all the rest of us from our hunger."

"The strangers cannot take away the cold and dark," Tuuli said, but she wondered, *Could they?*

"Well, I'm going to keep listening to them. And others are listening, too." Siru turned and left Tuuli standing by herself.

Tuuli stood in the same spot. Stunned by what Siru had said, she wondered, if Siru was beginning to question Poppi and the drums, how many others were? Kulta ran up to Tuuli holding a stick in her mouth and whining. Tuuli was glad for the interruption. "What do you want, little dog?" Tuuli asked. Kulta wagged her tail and dropped the stick at her feet. Tuuli threw the stick for her dog to chase as Siru went to sit by her mother.

A cloud passed over the sun. Tuuli shivered. She had not seen her deer since the day before, yet now wasn't the time to go. She had to see Poppi.

A stranger stood outside the goahti where her grandfather was kept, so Tuuli entered her own. Kulta followed. She smoothed Poppi's bedding that had been tossed during the search for his drum. Their little goahti seemed empty without him. Kulta whined as she sniffed Poppi's bed robe. "You're right," she said to her dog, ruffling her soft red fur. "Poppi belongs here with us." With that, she went out again. Hánas stood near the spot where the drums were burned.

"Coward! You brought trouble but didn't stay to watch."

"I'm sorry," he said. "My whole body trembled and ached when the drums were thrown in the fire. Every hair on my head pricked. My heart felt like it would stop. My hands and feet burned like they were on fire themselves. Even the nails on my fingers and toes throbbed. My stomach lurched and twisted, so I had to go into the woods to be sick."

"How long are they going to keep Poppi?"

"They say until the drum is handed over."

"I need to see Poppi and bring him food."

"You won't be allowed. I'll be sure that he gets food and water."

"I need to bring him his robe. He's old and needs it to wrap himself against the cold."

"Yes, bring it and I'll give it to him now."

"No, I'll give it to Poppi. I must see him." Tuuli turned back to her goahti to get Poppi's fur robe. When she returned, Hánas was no longer outside. She wanted to talk to Poppi, to know if she should return the drum. When she was close, she heard Poppi say, "You searched my whole goahti. If there were more drums, you would have found them." He must have known she'd hidden the drum.

Then Hánas translated the stranger's words, "You are the drummer much spoken of throughout many siides. We know you have a drum, but we found none in your goahti. Even I remember many telling about your ancient drum, the one they call the Drum of the Four Winds."

"Why are you helping these people?" Poppi asked Hánas.

"They took me as their son when my own parents died. They gave me a home, food, and clothes. They taught me to understand and to speak and read their words," Hánas answered.

"But don't you see how cruel they are? They don't care who they hurt. What kind of people torture, kill, and burn? And they do these things in the name of their god, yet say our gods are evil. What have you become?"

A loud voice overrode what Poppi and Hánas were saying. Tuuli could hear Hánas trying to calm him. Perhaps he was trying to help Poppi. But if he was, why did he still insist that Poppi give up the drum?

The harsh voice bellowed out again. Tuuli shivered and pulled her coat closer around her. A sharp slap rang out. She heard Poppi's cry. Without thinking, she pushed her way into the goahti.

"Oh, Poppi!" She flung herself on him and wailed, "How can you endure this?" Tears stung her eyes.

The white-haired man with fur hat and crooked front teeth pulled her from Poppi. He laughed and pawed at her. She did not understand his words, but she certainly understood his rough ways. Hánas stepped between them. "Go, Tuuli," he whispered.

Before she could, one of the strangers slapped Poppi again. He slumped and groaned. Hánas grabbed the man. "Stop!" He held his hand up to the man. Then he turned to Tuuli and said, "Go. Go. Go now!"

Knees quaking, she left. The wind was cold, and black clouds gathered in the sky. There was no one outside in the camp. Everyone in the siide hid in their goahtis ever since the drums were burned. Tuuli felt very alone. She was afraid even to go to the oldest, most trusted ones for advice. She no longer knew where they stood. Some, she suspected, were ready to do anything to save the deer. Some didn't trust Poppi's skills anymore. They wouldn't trust her, especially not if they knew for sure that she had the drum and that she'd hidden a lame fawn. They would blame her for putting everyone in danger.

She wanted to dig up the drum and bring it to the strangers, but Poppi hadn't asked her to get it when he had the chance. She ran through the grazing grounds and then headed toward her deer. When she reached the hiding place, Ruusu and Gabba were bedded down. The mother licked the side of her fawn's face. Tuuli buried her face in Ruusu's soft fur. The fawn startled and struggled to stand. After the third try, he rose, favoring his lame foot.

"Gabba, you will be a fine, strong reindeer," she told him through her tears. "You will learn to walk and run." Then the wind blew, but it didn't speak to her, so she called upon the wind.

Come, Wind, whisper to me.
Brush my cheek.
Cool my forehead.
Come, Wind, whisper to me.

Often Tuuli closed her ears to the wind, singing to herself, wishing not to hear the murmurings. The wind of the north and the wind of the south had always been stronger in Tuuli's ears, and she hadn't been able to block them out. The wind of the sunrise and the wind of the sunset had been gentler.

Sometimes the wind spoke in murmuring tones, just like her mother's voice. Tuuli liked to pretend she was hearing her mother. Once she had asked Poppi if it was her mother speaking on the wind.

"No," he'd answered, "your mother was a strong woman and a smart one. She listened to the wind and could understand. She used all four winds. But in death, she is not the wind."

Now the wind calmed. It was so still not even the tiniest twig moved. No words came to her ears. Gabba stood still as though listening to the wind himself. Tuuli patted him. Her stomach ached with hunger, so she searched the pouch she always carried at her side. Finding a few dried berries and a withered mushroom, she popped them into her mouth.

Still petting her deer, Tuuli thought of the hidden drum. She'd held it many times and felt it quiver in her own hands. When Poppi had gathered all the young people of the siide around him to learn about the drums, she had been reluctant to hold the drum, not wanting others to see how strongly it vibrated for her.

"It's a most powerful drum," Poppi said whenever he placed the Drum of the Four Winds in her hands. "Remember, use it only for good and for celebration. It will bind your heart to Guovza, the bear, just as the wind binds your breath to the life spirit. When you are noaidi, you'll need to be as strong as Brother Bear."

Gabba and Ruusu lay down, so she knelt by the rocks she'd piled over the drum. She opened her hands wide over the stones. Even though the evening was raw and chilly, warmth rose from the drum through the mosses, branches, and stones and into Tuuli's hands.

The drum resounded in long, slow beats. Birds sang. The woods around her quaked. The very earth beneath her feet trembled. From between the crooked branches of a small pine, a misty figure stepped into the glade. Tuuli's heart ached as she saw her mother come close.

Yes, Tuuli, keep the drum. It is yours.
Use it when you sing for the reindeer to birth,
to keep wolves away from the herd, and
to break the long days of darkness with Beavi's rays.
You were marked from birth
to be wind listener and drummer.

Tuuli stood. Raising one arm to where the sun would rise in the morning and the other to the treetops of the north, she vowed, "I will save the drum." More warmth arose from earth to the top of her head as she made her promise.

Poppi had taught Tuuli the names of all the noaidis in the family who had come before him. Some could listen to the wind as her mother had. Some had the gift of talking with the sacred drums, as Poppi, but in all the generations, not since Sanna, had there been one who could do both, as could Tuuli.

She reached out to her mother to ask her how she, Tuuli, had been marked at birth. Many times while her mother lived, she'd been told, but now she wanted to know the whole story of her own birth. The image of her mother ebbed and flowed before her eyes. Tuuli trembled. Ashes from the drums shook from her hair onto her eyelids.

The warmth and excitement she felt soon gave way to an ache in her chest and a deep sleepiness. She needed to find some way to free Poppi, but her burden weighed heavily. She would be the eighteenth noaidi since Sanna—she was supposed to be powerful, but she felt powerless. She wished for more time before she must be noaidi. Leaving the drum hidden, she decided to return and demand that Hánas let her enter the goahti to see Poppi.

Even though there was no wind to hide any sounds, Tuuli was so deeply entranced in thought about Poppi she didn't hear footsteps come up behind her.

"Got you!" Rough hands grabbed her shoulders and pulled her to her feet.

6

Tuuli jolted to reality. She turned to see who'd grabbed her. It was Utsí.

"Did I scare you?" he asked, still holding on to her.

Even though she was relieved it wasn't one of the strangers, she shrugged against Utsí's grip. "Yes, now leave me alone. Get away."

Fully awake from the reverie about her mother, she was glad she hadn't been digging for the drum when Utsí came upon her.

"What are you doing out here alone?" Utsí tightened his grip on Tuuli's arm.

"Tending to my deer." As soon as the words were out of her mouth, Tuuli was sorry she said them. She didn't want Utsí paying attention to her deer. Thankfully, Gabba was lying down next to his mother, so his deformity didn't show.

"Oh, I see that old deer of yours gave birth. Why haven't you told anyone? And it's a white fawn. A good omen. Do you think it will be good enough to help Poppi get away from the strangers? Speaking of Poppi, you should be tending to him instead of lolling here with your deer. If you know where the drum is, you'd better exchange it for Poppi, or they'll kill him."

"Why would they kill him? He's too old to be a threat to them," Tuuli sounded surer than she felt.

"Is that what your dear Hánas told you? Hánas—whom you call *Broken Branch* and *traitor*?"

"Never mind Hánas. He is nothing to me. I don't need him to save Poppi."

"You think *you* can? What good are you? Just a girl? You need my help to get Poppi away from them."

Tuuli didn't like Utsí, but she asked, "Do you think there is a way?"

"There might be. If I could get Poppi free, you might be so thankful that you'd run the courtship race at the gathering, and then I could catch you, and you'd come to live in my goahti. But on the other hand, if I free Poppi and he lives, you'd have an excuse not to race. You'd have to still take care of your blind old Poppi. As long as he lives, you don't have to race. I need to think about this. If they kill him, you'd be alone, and the whole siide would demand you join the race. You're old enough. It must be more than fourteen or fifteen gatherings since you were born. You know I can catch you." Then Utsí laughed a laugh that contorted his whole face into a menacing sneer.

"Don't talk to me about racing. Siru told me you'd promised to race for her."

Utsí's face darkened. Then, shaking Tuuli by the shoulders, he asked, "Do you have the drum?"

"Let go!" Tuuli spat. "Watch out. I might just give you a crippled foot with one look of my eye." Tuuli moaned to herself as soon as she said the words. She was so angry with Utsí she was saying things she shouldn't. Utsí might wonder why she said *crippled foot*. Out of the corner of her eye, she glanced at the deer. They were still lying down. She had to get Utsí away before they stood.

"Ha," Utsí rasped, "that's a good one. And that's the only way you could slow me down so I couldn't outrace the others who'll be chasing you."

"Enough about the courtship race. I'd never let you catch me. Tell me, do you have any ideas how we can free Poppi and send the strangers away?"

"I might. Maybe I could shapeshift into a great bear and chase them away. But I won't help unless you agree to run the race this time. Or is it your dear old friend Hánas—that traitor—you want to catch you?" With that, Utsí spun on his heel and left.

Tuuli's heart beat harder than the drum ever had. Utsí was the fastest runner of their siide. Last year, she'd hoped that he would race and catch one of the other girls, but he had chosen not to run. Shapeshift? Only a rare few of her people had ever been able to do that. They needed the magic of the spirit world and help from the brother and sister animals to do that, and she didn't think Utsí had either.

Slowly stroking Ruusu's soft fur, she waited for her heart to slow its beat. A thin slice of moon was already rising, pointing in the direction it rose, so it was a growing moon. The gray of twilight was coming. Soon the days and nights would blend into one long day, and they would be able to see the sun peeking above the horizon even in the middle of the night. Then the moon would be so faint, it would be hard to see it at all.

"Bures, Tuuli," Hánas said, stumbling over a tree root as he entered the glade.

Tuuli, not pleased to see him, looked away. When she didn't reply, Hánas said, "Tuuli, remember me for who I was, and still am. Your friend. I was sick and couldn't stop them from burning the drums. I know how much they mean to all the Saami. I want you to know that I came here because of you. My new father wouldn't let me travel alone, so he arranged for me to join these men. I'm sorry now that I showed them the way here."

Tuuli still said nothing.

Hánas pointed to her charred leggings and boots. "You are brave. I heard you stomped on the fire, but it was too strong. I don't believe in the drums anymore, but I do not want your siide to suffer because of me."

Tuuli looked hard and saw the light in the dark eyes of her old friend. It had been five gatherings since she'd seen him. In the winter, Hánas's siide camped farther to the south than hers, but they'd always been eager to see each other when the leaves fell. She and Hánas had often gone sledding behind the reindeer if there was snow at gathering time. They played catch with a ball made of hide and stuffed with moss. They'd watched the older unmarried people race for mates. They'd chased each other, pretending to be running the courtship race. At night, they sat together, listened to willow pipe music and joiks, and danced while sparks from the campfires crackled to the dark sky.

Hánas and his family hadn't come to any gatherings for a long time. Hánas explained now, "My father died. My mother wanted to travel back to her family's encampment. On the journey, she weakened."

"I had heard your father died, but not your mother. I'm sorry."

"On the way, she got sick. One day when she could go no farther, the noaidi who was expelled from his siide came upon our resting place. He helped me build a circle of stones for a fire pit. We made a bed for my mother above the hot stones and sprayed water on them to make a healing steam for her to breathe. He tried everything to cure my mother, but his pouch of herbs and mushrooms was almost empty. He dug for roots in the stony tundra until he found a few he could use, but no brew of leaves or mixes of roots was strong enough. He had no drum to call the spirits, but he sang all the healing songs he knew for three days. My mother died anyway. Jabemeahkka came to take her breath. Her bodily warmth seeped away, just as the stones cooled after the fire was gone.

"There we were, alone in the wilderness. I cried. My spirit was broken. The noaidi held me close until I had no more tears. He helped me build the fire on which to burn my mother. We collected all the dry wood we could find in that rocky and barren land. It wasn't enough, so the burning wasn't complete. I didn't want to leave her like that, but he said Brother Bear would come and scatter her ashes among those who had gone before.

"I was afraid to be alone. He started to take me to my mother's family even though he said he would not be welcome there. A raven followed us as we traveled together. A few days later, we met some strangers. They offered him some food if he would let them take me.

He refused, but that night one of the strangers carried me away. He tied a band around my mouth so I couldn't cry out and tied my waist to his. We traveled tethered that way during the day. At night, he tied me to a tree and treated me badly. I counted. It was more days than all my fingers and toes. It was an eternity. I was always afraid. Finally, we reached his home in a town far away to the south. There, he took money from another man and handed me over. That man took me home to his wife. I was to work in his warehouse. He wife was good to me. She treated me like a son. They didn't try to understand my words, but they taught me theirs. I missed my dead mother and father. I tried to keep from crying, but when I lay down to sleep at night, tears filled my eyes for a long time."

Tuuli felt like crying as she thought of her friend so alone, but she dug deep to rekindle her anger and said, "So that's how you became a traitor to our people and our ways. How could you?"

Hánas said, "Tuuli, my friend, the old magic is not real. It did not save my mother. My new family taught me about their god. My new father calls me Gregor. He heard me sing joiks of mourning for my parents. He said a very holy man from long ago sang plain songs, too, and his name was Gregor, so that would be mine in my new land with my new family."

Tuuli watched the light in Hánas's eyes soften and blur with tears as he told his story. She knew his pain was like what she felt when her mother died. Poppi's songs and herbs and drum hadn't been able to save her, either. Then Tuuli's own father had left. At least she still had her grandfather and the siide. Without a family of his own, Hánas had become part of a stranger's family.

"But why bring these strangers to poison our people?"

"They would have come anyway. They are determined to bring saving words to all the Saami camps. The world is changing, Tuuli. And change will come here, too. The Saami have lived in this cold far north as long as their stories have been told. They are alone, apart from other people, apart from the world. The ways of my new family are good ways. Your ways are good, too, but they are strange and frightening in the eyes of others. They think your noaidis contact satanic spirits to learn magic. People try to destroy what scares them."

"I can't believe that," Tuuli protested. "Look what your strangers are doing to Poppi. And what they did to the drums. We have heard that strangers burn whole encampments when the people refuse to accept their ways. Many die. Many are left without shelter and food. Is that what you call 'the good ways'?"

"I, too, have heard that some who bring the message mistreat the Saami and burn to death those who resist. Or if a whole camp resisted, a fire was set to scatter reindeer herds."

"That's exactly what they have done here—taken Poppi, burned our drums, and threatened our deer. Why do you take part in anything so murderous?" asked Tuuli.

"Not I," said Hánas. "I never would, but yes, there are some who are dangerous."

"You are a broken branch," Tuuli said. "You divide our people—one against the other—when we most need to be strong and work together to survive."

Tears sprang up in Hánas's eyes. "Tuuli, it is you I came to see. I have missed you, and it was easier to travel with these men than to travel alone. I didn't know these men were so dangerous. I traveled two changes of the moon to get here. I was hoping you had not already run the race and been caught. I was hoping we might run it together this autumn."

Hearing him say this, Tuuli felt herself soften; it was what she'd always hoped for. But it was too late. Hánas was now a stranger who no longer was of the wind and the drum. She wished Beavi would burn hot in her heart to destroy what she'd felt for Hánas just as the fires destroyed the drums. Tears welled in her eyes, "So you've already said, but now I vow never to run the race with you!"

Hánas reached up to brush ashes from Tuuli's cap. Even though she shrank away, he held her arm gently. "Tuuli, I didn't come here to argue with you. I bring you words. Some of your people are angry. They think you have the drum. They want you to give it up so Poppi will be set free and they can leave when the herd migrates."

Before Tuuli could answer, the little reindeer stood.

Hánas saw the thick and bent hoof. "So this is why you hide here. Your fawn is a bad omen. You must kill it."

"Now you speak of omens. I thought omens weren't part of your new belief."

"They're not, but it is what your people would say."

"*My people?* You really are no longer a part of us."

"In my blood and my bones I am, but my life in another world has changed me."

"I won't kill him. Look, he is white. That is a good omen."

"But a lame foot. He won't be able to keep up with the herd. The migration is going to start soon. It's a wonder wolves haven't gotten him yet."

"If that happens, let the wolves take him. Then they will be satisfied and will not eat one of the healthy deer," she said.

"Your people will think he's a bad omen. Slaughter him now. Everyone could enjoy a fresh stew even with the little bit of meat on him. This autumn at the gathering, his hide will have great trading value."

Tuuli stomped her foot. "Quit talking about the fawn. I'm not going to kill him. I want you to get me to see Poppi."

"I'm afraid for him, too. He is weak. His blind eyes seeps. He won't live much longer. If you have the drum, give it up. When Poppi dies, I'm afraid they will start killing the reindeer or punishing others from your siide. Maybe even you."

"Hánas, if our old friendship means anything to you, take those strangers away from here. And if you have any goodness in your heart, don't tell about the fawn."

"Tuuli, do you have the drum?"

She hesitated, and said, "The drum? I haven't seen it for days, and I don't have it." Tuuli used a word for *don't have it* that had a double meaning of *I don't have it right here*. She hoped Hánas had not used the Saami language for such a long time that he wouldn't remember the difference.

"I've heard that you are going to take the noaidi's journey. Is that why you keep the drum?"

Not wanting to get trapped into admitting she had the drum, she carefully said, "I need to see Poppi."

Hánas looked her straight in the eyes, nodded, and said, "I'll get you in to see him. Come with me."

7

EVEN THOUGH THE DAYS GREW LONGER and would continue until the sun showed itself every hour of the day, these were dark days for Tuuli. She worried about Poppi. The next day, the strangers still held him. No one was allowed to see him. The wind turned again, bringing more cold and crusting the snow that had started to melt.

The strangers went from family to family. They tossed cooking pots, food baskets, and sleeping robes out of goahtis as they looked for the last drum. They searched everywhere at least twice. The strangers kicked, twisted arms, and yanked hair while trying to persuade someone to tell where the drum was. Screams and cries pierced the air.

That morning, the people of the siide sat around the open cooking fire roasting one little hare and some fish that Utsí and Siru's father had caught. From inside her goahti, Tuuli heard the people talking among themselves in low murmurs. Although she heard the words, she couldn't make out who spoke what.

"Useless old drums," said one. "What's a drum? Just a thing."

"It's more than a thing," argued another. "It comes alive when Poppi holds it in his hands."

"You're right. Besides, what is that book of theirs?" asked a third. "It's just a thing, too."

"Poppi's old. Have you seen how few teeth he has? His powers are leaving him," the first spoke again. "New ways are beginning to sound good to me."

"Don't listen to the strangers. We must keep the ways of the drum and the wind. They are as our fathers and their fathers lived."

"Kah! I no longer have any use for the drums. No use for the wind. No use for the chants. They do no good. We starve. Our herd is weak. Just like the strangers say, Poppi with his drum can't stop people from the south from plowing the grazing land to grow crops the deer won't eat. More deer will die. We will, too."

"But our songs have always comforted and healed."

"There will be new songs to sing."

"And what about Poppi? We need to free him from these strangers. Then he can sing the strangers away, and we can go with the deer."

"We can't risk being beaten or worse anymore."

"My arm still feels like it's been wrenched from my shoulder, and I have big bruises where they kicked me. I won't give in to anyone who treats us like worthless beings."

"We all have long walks ahead of us, and Poppi is almost finished with his. He is old and tired. Tuuli hasn't taken her journey yet, so there isn't a noaidi to take his place."

"Let's ask her to leave right away. Then she will be ready to lead us with the drum and the wind when she returns to the gathering of siides during the leaf-fall. We can celebrate and live our ways."

"The strangers have words that are magic, too. Maybe they have more power than the drums. Maybe they can tell us how to ward off starvation this winter."

"I doubt their words have more power than the wind."

"They talk about something as unseen as the wind, but more powerful."

Tuuli's mouth puckered dry as she listened to her people argue back and forth. She got up and took her water basket off its hook. She hesitated because everyone would quit talking as soon as she stepped out of her goahti. Whistling to Kulta, she opened the flap.

The first people she saw were Siru and Utsí sitting with the strangers. She asked Siru if she wanted to go for water with her. When Utsí held her by the elbow, Siru lowered her head and said, "No, not today."

After returning from the river, Tuuli saw the strangers had gathered everyone around the central fire. Siru and Utsí sat as close as they could to hear the strange words Hánas transformed into their own. "If you give all their troubles to the new god, you will be relieved of your burdens. Follow the good book and all good will come your way."

If it were only that easy, Tuuli thought as she listened to Hánas. He spoke so well. Over the past few days, many had sought him out, crowded around him, asked him questions, touched his coat. His coat—a coat woven, not a skin or fur like her people wore, but one like those worn by the traders who came to the gatherings. Tuuli reddened with anger because for so many years she'd dreamed of being his wife. Worst of all, the strangers closed the gathering with a challenge. "If your drum has so much power, let it show itself and how powerful it is by turning one fish into many so you no longer go hungry."

The challenge quieted everyone. As they turned to leave the circle, those who had listened most closely to the strangers shied away from Tuuli and would not look her way. Utsí pulled Siru to stay in the circle. Later, Tuuli saw her going to the river for water. She raced after her and asked, "How can you follow those men? Look what they are doing. They beat and kick people. And they keep Poppi away from all of us and won't even let me in to bring him food."

"They're not that bad. They apologized to my father. They thought he had a drum," Siru said, and then she added, looking Tuuli in the eyes, "If you have Poppi's drum, Tuuli, give it up. We don't need it. What good is it doing us now?"

Tears sprang forth in Tuuli's eyes. How could her friend have changed so much in just one day? She went back to the camp alone and sat by the fire. She looked for a chance to enter the goahti where Poppi was kept, but there was always a stranger guarding the entrance.

Two women brought her a bowl of broth. They sat on either side of her and whispered, "Tuuli, start your journey now. If you have the drum, take it with you and keep it safe. Some are planning to overcome the strangers so we can free Poppi and be ready to leave with the deer. We'll take care of Poppi for you. Go, now, while you can."

Just then, Utsí came and interrupted them. Standing with his hands on his hips, he asked, "What are you whispering about?"

"We're sharing a sip of broth," said the older woman. "Come join us." She patted a spot next to herself.

"Why are you being nice to her? You should be scolding her. She probably hid the drum but won't give it up. I think that she has brought all these troubles to the camp. What if the deer leave and we can't follow?"

Tuuli's heart beat heavily, and her stomach tightened. She could not look at Utsí. Hot tears filled her eyes. Maybe it was true she had brought trouble to her people. She went to her goahti to lie on the bed of soft mosses covered by her robe of fur. She let her tears run freely and thought of Hánas and how he told of crying when he was alone without a family.

She felt alone. Sad. Guilty. Hánas, Utsí, Siru, and so many others were listening to the strangers. Her own clan family was breaking apart. It would be so much easier to join the strangers. She could give up the drum and follow the new ways. Then she would not have to travel the long journey alone. She would not have the worries of feeding her people through the long, cold winters. Nor would she have to listen to the wind or bring the drum to life with the spirits of another world. She would not have the weight of being noaidi every day.

Outside, the wind blew softly. Tuuli tried to block out the sound but could not.

Be strong.
Your journey is long.
Poppi's is short.
Be strong.

She pulled at her hair and dug her fists into her eyes. She rocked back and forth on her knees. The wind persisted.

Be strong.

She cried. She covered her ears. Kulta squeezed through the opening. She whined and licked Tuuli's tears from her cheeks. The wind blew the flap open. Tuuli looked at the central campfire where her people used to be happy as they sang, cooked, and shared stories along with food. Now it was where the strangers had burned the drums.

Be strong.

The campfire circle was empty. The happy laughter had died.

Tuuli cried, "Wind! Free Poppi! Send the strangers away! Blow me in the direction I must go!"

8

HÁNAS PEEKED INTO HER GOAHTI and motioned for Tuuli to follow him quietly. They crouched and made their way close to where Poppi was held. Signaling Tuuli to stay hidden, Hánas walked up to the stranger who guarded the entrance and talked to him. In a moment, Tuuli saw the man leave, and then Hánas waved her to come quickly. An evening bird sang as she bent to enter.

Seeing Poppi, Tuuli gasped and held her hand to her heart. Her grandfather's milky eyes were sunken. He was pale. His hair hung in thin strands. He had weakened greatly. She bent and cradled him in her arms. They hugged and crooned together. Hánas stood guarding the entry flap. From time to time, he peeked out. When a thin ray of light entered through the flap, Tuuli saw worry on Hánas's face, and once she saw a glint of a tear when he glanced at Tuuli and Poppi.

"He's sick," Tuuli said. "How can you treat an old man like this?"

Hánas signaled her to lower her voice.

Still rocking Poppi in her arms, she said, "You know what he means to my people. He has done good for many years."

Hánas looked out the flap and again signaled her to speak softly.

Poppi whispered into her ear, "Do not scold Hánas. He has treated me well even though the others watch him constantly."

"Poppi, Poppi." Tuuli still held on to her grandfather.

"I am old and dying. Each day, it is harder for my legs to hold me, and there are more aches in my bones. My mouth has fewer teeth than fingers on my hands. I will not live until the cold, dark days of next winter, not even until the falling leaves. Not even until the warm season. No one can hurt me now. Listen carefully to what I say. You must begin your long journey right away. It will be a burden greater than anyone so young should have. But you can do it. Take the drum. My old ears still hear it calling."

Poppi's voice faded to a whisper as he said, "If I die before you leave, take my ashes along with your mother's. Climb to the very top of the Mount of Four Winds. From there, toss my ashes and those of your mother to the winds. Breathe them in, let them fall upon you, and let them be carried far, far away. As far as the winds shall blow. Even to other lands."

"No, Poppi. Don't leave me. And I won't leave you as long as you live."

"You must go. And you must listen to what I say," Poppi wheezed. His whole body shook with a spasm as he moaned. Tuuli felt his energy seep from his body into her chest, her arms, her hands. Afraid to defy Poppi again, she asked, "How do I find the mount?"

Poppi answered, "Cross three rivers." He reached for Tuuli's hand. His voice was but a rasp as he added, "And follow the three sacred circles of stones."

Tuuli trembled as she thought of leaving Poppi and her people for the long journey, but if she was to return to be noaidi, she would have to go.

The chilling idea returned—it would be much easier to follow the ways brought by the strangers and Hánas. She would not have to journey alone. Her friend Siru and others already seemed to be following along easily. She could unburden herself of so much if she accepted their ways.

Poppi shuddered. She held him closer. Softly, she stroked his hand. She could see the veins through which his blood flowed. His skin was thin and as brittle as a dried leaf. Brown splotches mottled his face and arms. Tuuli wiped away a tear and asked, "Poppi, what if you die while I'm gone? Who will sing for you? Who will prepare your death burning? Who will collect your ashes and bring them to the mount?"

"My dear Tuuli. Do not worry. Jabemeahkka is coming for me soon. Then I will join with my family in the world beyond. The winds will pick up my earthly ashes and blow them to the high cliffs to join those that waft forever on the winds. Someday, no matter how far away you travel, when you breathe deeply, you will take me in, and I will be with you as you walk your way."

Tuuli held Poppi close, and lifting her head, she sang. Hánas came and sat with them. Tuuli watched as he mouthed the words of her chant; no words were heard from his mouth, but his breath reached Tuuli and Poppi. Together, they sang nine times.

> *Wind, breathe breath.*
> *Bear, give strength.*
> *Sun, shine warmth.*

Poppi whispered again. Tuuli bent her ear close to hear. "Be careful of Utsí. Don't make any promises with him. He wants what he cannot have, and he wants to be what he cannot be."

Tuuli held his hand to her cheek. His skin felt cool, too cool. She touched a bruise on his face. It spread with the color of blueberries. Why hadn't Hánas stopped the strangers from hurting her grandfather?

Poppi's whole body shook as with cold. His voice quavered as he said, "There is one who will help you."

"Who is that, Poppi?"

He closed his eyes and seemed to sleep.

Hánas knelt by. "You have to go now. If you make Poppi a broth, I'll bring it to him. But no more songs. No more chants."

Brushing aside her strangle of sadness, Tuuli gathered strength and answered, "I will sing whenever I want. I will listen to the wind if I like. And my own heartbeat will be the beat of the drum that serves my people for as long as the moon shines and the sun warms." This said, she rocked Poppi in silence until Hánas again said she must leave before the stranger returned.

In her goahti, Tuuli built up a small fire. She melted snow in a birch burl and stirred in pieces of dried fish and seeds she'd picked the summer before. Tuuli dropped dried mushrooms into the mix, too.

After giving Hánas the broth for Poppi, Tuuli stretched out on her fur robe. She nodded and soon fell asleep. She awoke to hard rain mixed with bits of sleet pounding the skins and birchbark that covered their homes. Kulta whined at the entrance. Tuuli opened the flap. Her dog came in and shook, showering her with wet. Without scolding the dog, she pulled her pet under her fur robe to dry off. Soon Tuuli slept again. Not even the blustering wind and rain kept her awake.

Wild dreams drowned out the howling winds. In one, a cloud of mosquitoes attacked Tuuli's people. Everyone whirled their arms above their heads, swatting uselessly as the buzzing swarm dove to sting and suck their fill of blood. If one was swatted and killed, red blood spurted from its sated belly, and many more took its place.

In another, all the red foxes and red squirrels of all the lands proudly fluffed their red fur. The squirrels held their tails high. The foxes preened their beautiful fur. Then a shiny flickering apparition hurtled toward them. Foxes and squirrels banded into a pack to protect themselves. The phantom burst into flame. Sparks shot in every direction. Blinded and frightened, the swarm of red ran toward a roaring river engorged with rains and melting snow. The waters spun and tumbled over rocks and banks and crept across the land. Heedless, the foxes and squirrels sped toward the rushing river and ran into its depths and were swirled away by the churning waters.

In the last dream, a white wolf wound his way around Tuuli's goahti. Then a gray wolf came and it, too, circled. Together, they loped around the whole camp. Together, they jumped into a lake of blue and swam toward the distant shore. Only the gray wolf climbed onto dry land.

Tuuli awoke haggard from her troubled sleep. She wondered what the dreams meant. She wanted to describe them to Poppi so he could tell her. Kulta licked her face and whined to be let out. Slowly, the blanket of sleep lifted, and she realized the wind was now just a sigh and the steady pelting rain was gone.

Opening the flap, she was much relieved the bad weather was over. Kulta bolted out of the goahti, and Tuuli scrambled after. It felt good to stretch in the cool morning air. Others came out, too. A slash of sunray knifed into the camp. Tuuli blinked in the bright light. The herders' dogs all leaped and bounded. The people laughed and called to one another.

"Hilde had her baby last night. A handsome boy, and so strong. Two babies in so few days! A good omen. Surely the births mean that better days are ahead."

"It was so cold last night that we rolled all the little ones into fur hides to keep them warm and dry. Not one of them complained."

"Did you hear the wind? I thought it would blow our goahti over."

"Ours shook like it would come down!"

"That thunder was the worst ever."

"Really? I couldn't hear a thing over Pallo's snoring!"

"Snoring? I thought he was farting!"

"Thankfully, the sun is warm. The ice will melt, and we won't slip and fall."

"Like Makko did yesterday? Did you see? He looked like a salmon flopping on the ice."

"Well, you're not so graceful yourself. Remember when you stumbled over your own feet and fell face first into some mud?"

"I remember that. You were *so* handsome with mud covering your face."

"The rain and melting snow will make the rivers rise. I hope they won't be too high and fast for the deer to swim when they leave."

Tuuli, too, joined in the laughter and playful passing of news. "The rains make for good mosquito weather. We'll suffer yet!"

"For sure. If we had as many reindeer as mosquitos, we'd never have to worry."

"Last melt season they were so big, when I slapped one, it slapped me back."

"That I'd like to see. You need a good slap once in a while."

"Maybe we should bite them back. Roast them over the fire. Then we wouldn't be so hungry all the time!"

The talk about food must have made the dogs hungry, because then Kulta and the other dogs chased out of camp to hunt whatever small creatures they could find. Amid gossip and news, a small cloud passed over the sun, and a chill quieted the people. Tuuli looked to where the strangers kept Poppi. There were no sounds from inside. No one stirred.

9

Tuuli ran to the goahti. No one stood in her way. The strangers were gone. Hánas, too.

Inside, Tuuli knelt and put her ear to Poppi's chest. Others followed her. Poppi still lived, but he was weak, his breathing halting, his heart slow. Tuuli breathed on him, her lips and nose touching his mouth and nose. She held his hands in hers. Poppi's eyes were closed; his hands cold. Tuuli sang:

> *Poppi, oh, Poppi.*
> *Your life blood flows in me.*
> *My bones are made of your bone.*
> *My marrow is of yours.*
> *Poppi. My life.*
> *Hei-la-laaa.*

Siru's mother brought milk that she mixed with blood she had just taken from one of the deer. Others brought warm water infused with dried leaves and grasses for Poppi, but he refused all of it—his voice but a raspy breath. Siru's father swabbed a bit of sweet from the summer bees on Poppi's tongue. His oldest friend offered some dried mushrooms to speed him on his next journey. These, too, he refused, shaking his head.

A gentle breath brushed Tuuli's neck; the small hairs stood on end. She heard the soft voice of her mother.

Daughter, Poppi will soon be with me
and my mother and all the mothers before us.

Poppi raised one arm. It trembled. He drew Tuuli to his lips and whispered, "My time here was borrowed. Now I must give it back. I am just one tiny person—like one snowflake that falls in a whole storm. Here on earth I have no more steps to take, but there is a place for me in the distant other world. There I will shine like a star. Do not be afraid for me. I go. It is my time."

All the siide people came, one by one, by twos, carrying their little children. They laid offerings from what little they had of dried berries. Even those who had listened to the strangers and doubted Poppi's powers as he grew older came and put their hands upon his chest, touched his rowan walking stick, and sang songs of healing, songs of thanks.

Once more, Poppi raised his hand to Tuuli, so she bent close. "Go, go seek the Mount of the Four Winds. Swirl my ashes to the winds along with those of your mother. The white bird will soar high, protecting you. It is your mother's spirit bird."

Tuuli pressed her fists into her eyes to stop the tears that welled. She did not want Poppi to die. She did not want to go on any journey. As much as she wished Poppi to live much longer, she heard how his breath rattled and how he struggled to talk.

Poppi closed his eyes. Tuuli placed her hand on his chest. She felt the drum give a final beat. She gently placed her hand upon his nose. The wind within blew no more. She nodded to those who surrounded her. Some left the death goahti to carry the news to those who waited outside. "Jabemeahkka has come for Poppi," they said.

As the women and men gathered around, wailing their songs of mourning and their songs to the spirits that came to gather Poppi to their world, a cry pierced the air.

"The deer are restless. They're raising their heads to the winds and snorting. They'll be leaving soon." Herders quickly packed their belongings to be ready.

Tuuli smoothed Poppi's hair with her hands. She stroked his wrinkled cheeks. Her tears flowed and her heart ached all the while she sang to the spirits so they would welcome Poppi as Jabemeahkka led him from this world to the next.

> *Huuu Taiii Yeee Yaaa*
> *Huuu*
> *Huuu*
>
> *Huuu Taiii Yeee Yaaa*
> *Huuu*
> *Huuu*

The wind stirred. It howled and swirled. The hides covering the goahti flapped. One tore from the pegs that held it to its cedar frame. An old chant Tuuli had heard Poppi sing many times during a windy storm surged from her throat. She went out into the storm, raised her arms, and sang out:

> *Wind. Wind.*
> *Calm yourself.*
> *Wind. Wind.*

The wind did calm. And it whispered

> *Tuuli, Tuuli.*
> *Draw in air so pure.*

Fill your lungs with strength.
Long, long journeys are yours.
Fill your lungs with courage.
Fill your heart, your core
with will—the will to overcome those who threaten.
Tuuli. Tuuli.
Breathe in air so pure.

10

A HERDER ARRIVING AT THE CAMP just then said, "The herd is gathering. Hurry, we need to build the ritual fire to burn Poppi and get ready to leave when the herd goes. It will be soon, before the sun gets too high."

By the time a high bier had been built, Tuuli heard the deer pawing the ground and snorting. *Earnk. Earnk.* Many ran to the herd hoping to calm them, but the migration started. The clicking of their hooves filled the air as the deer left their winter grounds and headed as one toward their summer pastures. There would be no stopping them.

The herders and their families ran to follow. Those who stayed behind entered Poppi's goahti. Tuuli knelt by his head and started to sing the death chant.

Aiii Yaiii Yeee Yaaa
Aiii
Aiii
Whey Maiii Yeee Yaaa
Whey
Whey

Several mothers with small children, the old, and the ill stayed to help Tuuli get Poppi's body ready for the burning ceremony. After, they would hitch tame reindeer to sledges, load their belongings, and follow the deer at a slower pace.

One woman folded Poppi's large fur sleeping robe. Handing it to Tuuli, she said, "Yours now." Tears welled in her eyes. Another picked up Poppi's rowan walking stick and said, "This, too, is now yours. It will protect you on your journey."

Tuuli laid her cheek on the robe and ran her hands along the length of the stick. With a start, she thought of the drum. It was hers now, too. A loud sob escaped her. The women patted her back and head, letting her mourn deeply with body-shaking moans until she was ready to finish getting Poppi ready.

After pulling her grandfather's boots onto his feet, Tuuli dripped a bit of honey into his mouth. "Boots to keep your feet warm. Honey to give you strength for your journey," she whispered as she smoothed his hair. Her chest heaved. She choked on her own breath as she tried to suppress another sob. Finally, she let her tears fall freely onto Poppi's cheeks as she held him one last time.

She couldn't linger, so she signaled for others to help lift Poppi. He wasn't heavy; he was just skin-covered bones. After they laid him on the wood, two children handed her a basket with birch shavings. They, too, swallowed hard and tried to hold back their tears. Tuuli struck her flint and lit the bark. Smoke curled skyward, and soon the tinder was aflame, and then the larger pieces of wood caught fire. More smoke swirled around Poppi's body. Flames crackled. The fire slowly claimed all that had been the earthly man. While the fire turned him to ashes, women mourned by rocking and crooning. The old men joined the mourning and sang.

Whey Maii Yeee Yaaa
Eeee yai yai yai
Yaiii-iii
Yaiii-iii

Whey

Whey

Just as when the drums were burned, ashes from Poppi spiraled to the sky, and then some spun earthward. They fell on Tuuli, covering her. She held out her hands and caught more, then cradled her face with ash-laden hands.

The woman next to her said, "Tuuli, you are to be the next noaidi. Make your journey and return to us at the gathering when the leaves begin to fall."

"Yes," the others agreed. "We cannot forget you were marked at birth to be a noaidi with great skills. Make the journey."

Tuuli dug through the circle of piled rocks for the pouch where her own mother's ashes lay. She held the pouch to her heart and with a finger traced the drawing—a chrysalis. It was her mother's mark, showing she was born on the day the butterflies became free.

It was time for the rest of her siide to leave, to follow the deer. "Go," she said. "I will stay until Poppi's ashes cool enough so I can gather them."

Looking at them, Tuuli felt a great sadness and a deep aloneness. It was the first time in the fifteen migrations of her life that she would not be going with them. She went to each one, embracing them in long, tight hugs. Her father's sister whispered to her, "Go in peace and safety. Know that you are not alone. Look to the sun, the moon, and the bear, and listen to the wind. We'll never follow the beliefs of these strangers. Many of us hope you kept the Drum of the Four Winds from their fires. If you have it, keep it safely with you. May the wind that goes with you always be but a gentle breeze."

Tuuli replied, "Thank you. The wind will guide me and keep me safe. I will return to you." She tried to sound brave, but her voice cracked at the end.

Tuuli looked to her friend Siru, who helped her own grandmother onto a sleigh. As she stood near her friend with arms raised to embrace her, she hoped to see a sign of their old friendship, but Siru looked down and away. "The time for wind listening and drum talking is past," said Siru quietly. "Utsí says the strangers have promised us a new life in a new belief. We will learn from their book. I have promised Utsí that I will help him teach our people in new ways. When you come back, you'll see there is no need for the wind and the drum. Utsí and I will be leading our people."

Tuuli's heart felt pierced by a sharp sliver of ice. She moaned and wiped her eyes on her sleeve. *Is Siru right? Will there be no need for the wind and the drum?*

The sun was low in the sky when Tuuli finished gathering Poppi's ashes. She drew his mark on a pouch—Beavi partially blocked by the moon—chosen because he had been born in the middle of a warm day when the moon darkened the sun.

She whistled for Kulta to follow, and headed to the copse of trees where her deer hid. She felt heavy, as though crushed by a huge rock, chilled by the thought of the journey ahead. All she really knew was that she needed to reach the Mount of Four Winds. She would be away from her people throughout the fullness of summer. That was a long time.

11

TUULI UNCOVERED HER DRUM AND TUCKED IT under her coat. As she untethered Ruusu, she said to her dog and the deer, "Tomorrow, when we start our journey, Beavi will shine warmth upon us."

Even as she said these words, she realized they were to calm herself as much as the deer. She already was anxious at being alone for such a long time. Her journey would last long enough for her moon-blood to flow four times. When she returned, the cold would start creeping into the land again.

Drained from worrying and mourning, she wrapped herself in Poppi's fur robe as soon as she got back to her goahti. She pulled Kulta close and buried her nose in the thick scruff of her pet's neck. Tuuli slept fitfully, yet dreamed much. Many dreams were of Poppi. A shimmering specter, he rasped his words in a strange tongue. Tuuli shivered in her fur blanket and wished she could understand what he said. In her dreams, Poppi was sometimes alive and sometimes in the land of those gone to the beyond.

In another dream, she lived in an ancient land, so ancient only the stars, the moon, the seas, the rivers, and pure icy air existed. Floating among the stars were the ghostly shapes of her ancestors. She floated, too, but not among the stars. She swam with the fishes of a big water.

When Tuuli awoke, she went outside to relieve herself. Birds twittered in the early morning. The wind blew gently through the trees. Closing her eyes, she enjoyed the beauty of earthly sounds. Beavi was not fully up yet, so Tuuli saw only gray ethereal shapes. Kulta was hunting already, her nose to the ground. Tuuli untied her deer and whistled for Kulta. Even though it was early and the day still dim, they needed to get to the river for water and then on with their journey. She put Poppi's pouch of mushrooms into her own birch basket of dried meat and berries. Then she tied the pouch that held her flint and knife to her waist.

Taking a last glance around the winter goahti where she'd lived with Poppi, she saw her mother's hat hanging from a peg. She put it on her head. She tied Poppi's sleeping robe and his fishing net into a bundle. Finally, she slung the bundle, as well as the two pouches of ashes, onto Ruusu's back.

She knew the land well and had watched how Poppi made his way in his dark world. Now, in the faint light, she could find her way. Using Poppi's walking stick, Tuuli felt for mosses under her feet. She also checked for familiar stones along her path. She went slowly, careful not to stumble.

Tuuli reached out to feel for the biting spruce needles and then the spindly branches of a young birch. The spring vegetation was still sparse, but she could smell the pungency of some emerging plants and the sweetness of others. Each new smell guided her toward the river.

When she reached it, the sun rose, breaking the darkness with a pink glow, slivers of red, and finally sheer silver and blue. Shafts of golden light pierced the gray and dappled the waters in front of her. Tuuli fell to her knees and gave thanks to Beavi, the giver of light and beauty. The river before her ran cold. Its snow-melted waters splashed over the banks of its ancient bed.

She stood on a water-slicked stone, carefully bending toward the rushing waters to scoop a handful to her mouth. Cold water soothed her throat. The waters foamed white, silver, gray, and gold, gleaming and reflecting in the morning light. Next, she took off her hat, washed her face and hands. She loosened her hair. With her fingers, she untangled the knots. As she twisted her hair back on the top of her head, she watched Kulta and Ruusu drink, too.

A flock of geese flew overhead. A white bird, too. Kulta followed a scent trail. She came back holding a mouse in her mouth. Tuuli relaxed as she watched Kulta toss it in the air, play with it, tease it with freedom, and then catch it again. She laughed and called to her little dog. She watched a flock of birds circle and land. They alit on tree branches to peck for bugs that came out in the warm sun.

It had been a long time since either Poppi or her mother had traveled to the Mount of the Four Winds. Poppi had told of sweet grasslands, wet bogs, a rocky land of black stones, and high hills she would encounter. She would have to look out for dangers in the harsh land. Noaidis, and those who wanted to be, had to travel through that desolate land that few others dared traverse. Tuuli stood. It was time to go.

12

Tuuli's people told stories around the Saami campfires for countless generations. They told of monsters that lived in the frozen north and threatened all who dared enter. Bieg was a monster so huge that if you walked right up to him, you'd think his big toe was a high hill to climb. He was nicknamed Wicked Wind Man. At one time, he wielded two huge scoops that he twirled above his head to swirl the wind into a tremendous force. Then he scooped snow from the far clouds and dumped it upon the land. No living thing had ever dared enter his realm back then. The land he ruled was one of bitter cold-black rock and frost-white snow.

But then, it was also told, that once amid his fury, one of his scoops broke. Since then, the wind had abated and less snow fell. Living beings dared trespass upon his lands but still feared the mighty storms he conjured. Even with only one scoop, Bieg could show his anger with a violent fierceness and bury a traveler in deep snow. Thinking of this, Tuuli sang a joik asking to be invisible to Bieg so he would not notice her journeying on his lands.

Then, too, she had to be wary of the monster Stallu. It was told that he was short and squat and slow but so persistent that one rarely escaped him. He was most dangerous when looking for a young woman to add to his flock of unwilling brides. Tuuli shuddered to think of him.

And there were flying rocks, roving evil spirits, as well as Aiko, the outcast. He was not a monster but a banished Saami noaidi who wandered the far north, playing tricks on the few who dared traverse the lands of Bieg and Stallu.

Kulta whimpered and looked back toward their home. "No, Kulta, we go this way," Tuuli said. She, too, felt the tug to follow her people, so she sang for the wind to lead her.

> *Wind,*
> *Show my path.*
> *Wind,*
> *Blow all clouds away.*
> *Wind,*
> *Show my path.*

Using Poppi's rowan walking stick, she quickened her step. The wind blew gently on her back. She urged the deer forward. Kulta whined and then, with her head and tail down, followed.

Going was slow because old Ruusu stopped to rest often and to nurse her fawn, Gabba. He, too, tired easily. He struggled to walk, putting his bent foot down carefully to steady himself. Hobbling, he always kept close to his mother.

At times, Kulta was playful as though they were on a great adventure. Other times, she zigzagged off the path sniffing the ground, stopping to look and listen, only to return quickly to Tuuli's side. Tuuli petted her when she was close.

"Good Kulta. What do you smell? What do you hear?"

The dog stopped and cocked her head to the side and listened, both ears up. Tuuli laughed and scratched the dog's ears. Kulta looked to Tuuli as if to say, "Don't you hear?" Then she stopped, too, but didn't hear anything other than birds singing and could only smell duff beneath the twisted trees.

When the day got long, Tuuli stopped to rest. Her basket of dried venison, mushrooms, and berries would not last long. Later in the season, there would be many tender roots, leaves, berries, and mushrooms, but for now, she would have to fish.

The roiling mists, rush, and roar of the river thrilled Tuuli. She walked slowly along the banks, keeping away from the swirling waters. She didn't want to die as her mother had. Finally, she found a place she could safely stand to toss her fishing net into the water. After several throws, she felt a tug on the net. When she gathered it up, a fish with a huge back fin struggled, tangled in the knots. Her mouth watered in anticipation—a grayling. She tossed her net again and again until she had caught three fish.

Carrying the graylings in her net, she went back to the deer. Kulta trotted ahead, nose to the ground, excited by smells of fox and otter and the many animals that came to drink. Nearby, in a glade, they found a towering circle of rocks. Tuuli was sure the spot was one of the sacred places her people talked about. She trembled in its presence.

She wondered about who had come this way and piled the rocks, and from where they'd been carried. Kulta sniffed and scratched at the stones with her paws. Just beyond the rocks, Tuuli found a small stand of fir and cedar trees. An even smaller glade was hidden in the middle. It was a perfect shelter for the night. Fresh water was nearby, and she had fish. New fern fronds poked their heads through the duff.

She slid her knife down the belly of the graylings and scooped out the innards. She admired the beautiful fins on their backs. No other fish had such colorful fins. With her knife, she cut down three slender birch branches and removed the bark. On these, she skewered the fish and set them to roast over a small fire she'd built with bark and small twigs. While the fish roasted, she stretched until her joints cracked. Then she cut cedar boughs to spread Poppi's fur robe on top.

Next, she went back to the circle of stones and found new shoots of fern fronds she could eat right away. Their freshness stung her mouth. It had been a long time since she'd had any fresh plants to eat. The late day was quiet. No wind rustled the branches. Tuuli's mouth flooded with saliva, anticipating the fish's soft roasted flesh as she pulled it from the skewers. Even as Kulta ate the fish entrails that Tuuli tossed her, the soft twitterings of birds kept the dog's ears swiveling from one direction to another. The deer lay quietly nearby, settled for the night.

The sun barely peeked above the horizon. Tuuli would have the advantage of long days on this journey. It gave her comfort that she wouldn't have long, dark nights alone in this wilderness. Tomorrow, she and her animals would cross the boundary from the familiar into the unknown. The land would be rugged, food scarce, and dangers many. Her biggest obstacle would be her fears and her aloneness.

Before lying down for sleep, Tuuli raised her arms to the darkening sky and sang praises to the setting sun, the wind, and the bear—just as Poppi would have done.

The sun is my father.
I dance alive in my father's warming rays.
Without my father, my bones would chill and my skin wither.
The light of my father brings good to me and my earth-home.
The sun is my father.

The wind is my mother.
I dance alive in my mother's breath.
Without my mother, my will would tremble and the light in my eye
would die.
The breath of my mother brings hope to me and my earth-home.
The wind is my mother.

The bear is my brother.
I dance alive in my brother's earthly footsteps.
Without my brother, my body would shrivel and turn to ash.
The strength of my brother brings nourishment to me and my earth-home.
The bear is my brother.
He walks the earth with me.

There was a moon that night, just a sliver, but it gave enough light so every time Tuuli awoke, she saw shadows stretching across the glade. Black on silver. Silver on black. The trees wavered eerily in the thin light. Tuuli reached out to Kulta, who snuggled close by. She gladly shared Poppi's fur pelt with her. It wasn't the warmth that comforted her but the dog's slow and measured breathing, and she could feel Kulta's heartbeat—strong, like a drum.

13

THERE WERE FEW GRASSES AND LEAVES, so in the morning, Ruusu pawed through the remaining thin layer of crusty snow and ate lichen and mosses. They had plenty to eat that day, but as they journeyed farther into the barren north, there would be less. Before going too far, she needed to catch more fish and maybe a willow grouse or two to carry along.

She'd hunted for eggs of the grouse with Kulta many times. They weren't far from a bog where dried sedges and low-lying brush provided good hiding places for the grouse. Tuuli carried Poppi's walking stick. She used it to balance as she stepped from sedge tuft to sedge tuft on the soft bog. In the winter, it would be frozen hard, but now it was thawing. Water and mud oozed between the tufts of bog grass. She watched each step. Rich odors arose; she liked the smell. Poppi always said it was the smell of dying that fed new life.

Tuuli watched Kulta. The dog could smell a bird before she could see it. Before long, Tuuli saw her dog's nose twitch and her whole body stiffen. Tuuli whistled softly for the dog to stop. She wanted to get close to the nest before her dog scared the bird. She crept forward in the direction Kulta looked. Tuuli held the stick over her head. A sudden burst of fluttering wings warned her. The grouse flew right at her, but she was ready. She struck it down with one blow. Picking the stunned bird up by its feet, she whistled to her dog, who zigzagged through the bog until she came to the nest. Kulta already had an egg in her mouth when Tuuli caught up with her. She collected the nine tiny eggs carefully.

The grouse roasted; melting fats crackled as they fell and sputtered in the flames. When it was done, Tuuli poured the last of her berries and mushrooms from their basket onto her sleeping robe. She filled the birch container with water from the stream. Then she took hot rocks from the fire and dropped them into the water with the eggs. While they cooked, she ate the wings and legs, and then sucked each piece to the bone. She wrapped the cooked eggs in mosses with the grouse back and breast and put them in the basket with her berries and mushrooms.

With food in their stomachs and their thirst slaked, they were ready to travel. Tuuli looked to the hills. There were lowlands to cross, rocky grounds, and rivers before they got to the fells, and finally to the Mount of Four Winds.

Lonely, Tuuli thought of her people. She missed the talk and laughter as they made meals over fires at the end of a hard day traveling; she missed the passing of babies from arm to arm. And she missed the teasing and playing while picking berries and nuts.

When the deer stopped their migration, her people would set up summer dwellings. It would be a time of warmth. The deer would take care of themselves, fattening on summer grasses. Her people would fish, hunt, pick berries, tell stories, play games, mend and make clothing, and weave birch baskets for storing food. They slaughtered deer for food and for their furs and skins—everything to get ready for another cold, dark winter. Fawns would be born. More deer would be tamed and trained to pull sleds. Maybe they would meet with another siide following their herd.

Tuuli wiped the tears that ran down her cheeks. Then she turned her back to the sun and headed away from the land she knew, toward the unknown.

14

THE SUN SHONE ON THE LITTLE TROOP. They walked slowly so the deer wouldn't tire. Tuuli marveled at the minute beauty found in the harsh land. Delicate pink buds braved the rough and rocky ground ready to bloom in the long days of sun. Little stars of flowers pushed through the mosses. Meandering vines clung to flat rocks, winding round and round. A blue butterfly, rarely seen, flitted in front of Tuuli and landed on a branch.

For several days, they walked through rock fields or skirted boggy lowlands, crossing one small river on their way. The land now was laden with rocks and roots. She kept stubbing her toes. The deer slowed. Ruusu urged Gabba to keep walking when she stumbled. Finally, Gabba lay down and lowered his head.

Tuuli moaned. It was wrong. It was unnatural to bring the deer with her. They should be migrating to the nourishing grasses they needed to strengthen their bodies for the long, hard winter ahead. Tipping her head back, she sang to the skies:

No bird sings.
For a long time

No bird sings.
My heart is sad.
It beats alone
In this wilderness.

The land was hard and hilly. Gabba refused to get up, so Tuuli carried him for a long distance before putting him down. Later, when they came to more rough terrain, she had to carry the fawn again. It was hard work, so she tired quickly. They traveled more slowly and rested more often, so didn't get very far each day.

The sky and all below it were gray in the morning drizzle. There were very few buds for the leaves yet to come. The farther they traveled, the fewer trees there were, and those were scrubby and stunted. How else could they be, growing in such hard, rocky ground on land that had been scraped and frozen since time eternal?

15

THE NEXT DAY, HEAVY RAINS FOLLOWED BY steady drizzles slowed their way even more. They slipped on wet round rocks. Thawing bogs sucked at their feet. The air, land, and sky were such a deep gray that it was hard to see any distance ahead. When Tuuli was completely exhausted, they stopped. The fawn seemed reluctant to walk. Ruusu, too. Tuuli found a few roots and mushrooms. She ate them along with a few scraps of meat. Soon she would have to catch another grouse or veer back to the river to fish again.

Before settling down for sleep, she stretched her arms to the sky and asked the rains to stop and the winds to blow away all traces of their travels so Bieg would not rage against them. The deer sniffed the air before lying down, and Kulta circled three times. She, too, sniffed the air. Tuuli was uneasy, but she needed sleep. Her head hurt as though river gravel swirled inside.

Time passed. Finally, the rain stopped. Tuuli silently thanked the wind for blowing it away. The moon was but a faint sliver. Stillness, deep silence webbed earth to sky. Eerie, so eerie was the silence that Tuuli turned from side to side just to hear any small sound.

Later, when Tuuli awakened, the wind had picked up, breaking the quiet. She listened. Was that a growl brought to her ears on the wind? A wolf in the woods? Kulta dreaming? Bieg? The trees bent to the wind as it blew harder.

Alarmed at the sudden fury, Tuuli chanted.

> *Wind, be gentle, keep us safe.*
> *Blow all Bieg's strong powers away.*
> *Let no danger find our camp.*
> *Wind, be gentle, keep us sound.*
> *Wind, be gentle, keep us safe.*

The deer snorted. Kulta whined. The deer shivered as they huddled under the rambling branches of a small evergreen. Kulta and Tuuli—fully awake—turned and turned again. Instead of bringing day, the sky darkened. It cloaked itself in gray, then darker gray. Not a streak of gold or white slashed the sky. Branches above them swayed and then snapped and cracked. Tuuli's basket with dried berries and mushrooms swung back and forth on its branch. The wind blew harder.

Then the wind roared. Tuuli pulled Kulta to her. The two shivered under the fur wrap as the wind swirled. Rain pelted through the sheltering branches. The air chilled. Rain changed to hard pellets of sleet and snow. Was the great monster Bieg trying to scare them out of his territory?

The deer huddled together, their eyes wild with fear. Snow and ice coated their fur. In the winter, reindeer had thick wooly coats under their guard hairs, but Ruusu had been losing her thick undercoat for summer. Chilled, Tuuli moved her fur robe and Kulta closer to her deer so they could warm each other. The cold sharpened with the wind. Tuuli pulled her hat lower over her face.

The wind never lessened. Snow fell constantly. The sky blackened more. There was not even a hint of the sun. The deer stirred, but just barely. Gabba nudged Ruusu to stand. Cold and hungry, he tried to nurse, but his mother didn't budge.

Tuuli's stomach growled. Unwillingly, she reached one arm from beneath her fur robe to get her basket. A few berries and the pouch of mushrooms remained. She ate only half of the berries and gave some to Kulta. It wasn't enough, but if the storm rampaged all day, it would be all they could have until it ended. They could eat snow to slake their thirst, but it would be cold and make them shiver even more.

Tuuli shook herself. She must not let Bieg win. She and Kulta could survive if they ate one of the deer. But Ruusu and Gabba were her pets. How could she slaughter them? And which would she kill? Ruusu, who was old and would die a natural death soon, even sooner in this rough country, or Gabba, who was crippled and depended on Ruusu, yet was sapping his mother's strength? Ruusu needed the green grasses of the south to keep producing milk for her fawn. She would go dry soon. The fawn would die, so killing Gabba now would help the rest of them survive.

Tuuli pulled her knife from its pouch at her waist and felt its blade along her thumb.

> *Felt its sharpness, its fine edge.*
> *Felt the bite along her thumb.*

The wind bit sharply, and beads of snow pelted her back as she knelt by the fawn. She stroked his head and back. "You are young, but it is not meant that you are to live long days." Tears sprang and ran down her cheeks. She looked deeply into the fawn's soft eyes, rimmed in pink.

She ran her finger along the carved lines of her knife. Poppi had shown her how to care for it when he'd given it to her. "This was your father's," he explained and showed her the symbol of a bear her father had carved into the leather handle.

"I can't do it!" she cried to the wind as she slid the knife back into her pouch. She pleaded with the wind to end the storm. Then she crawled beneath her robe again and curled around Kulta, the two of them shivering. The storm never lessened. The sky never changed. It was dark all the time.

Tuuli had never felt so hungry and cold. She had been through bad storms before, but she'd always had her family and her siide nearby. She was so alone.

As the snow swirled and fingers of ice crept beneath Tuuli's robe, stealing precious warmth, her mother floated to her on a golden ray of sunshine. Her mother held out a broth of summer berries. When Tuuli reached for it, her mother floated away into blinding sunrays.

Tuuli longed to drink deep swallows of hot broth. Her teeth chattered. Kulta's warmth and her fur robes were not enough in the buffeting wind. With no food and no drink, Tuuli shivered to her very core. Drowsy and hoping to see her mother and the warm rays of Beavi again, she shut her eyes and curled as tightly as she could.

Then Poppi stood in front of her wrapped in a robe of white wolf skins. He was barely a silhouette against the snow. She reached out to him, but there was no Poppi, only two wolves. One white and one gray. They, too, dissolved into a mist.

Tuuli no longer could feel her toes. She rubbed her hands together in her mittens. Her belly felt hollow, her mouth dry. She sucked a handful of snow. It chilled her more. Tuuli felt her eyes sinking into their sockets. She needed something warm. Then her mother appeared again. And Poppi. She no longer knew what was real. What was a dream? When was she awake? When asleep?

Hungry, Tuuli reached for her food basket. Her hand fell on the pouch of Poppi's mushrooms. Mushrooms he used to see visions. Mushrooms that brought the spirit world to him. She shook out a few small withered caps. She put the mushrooms into her mouth and savored them as juices swelled in her mouth.

Her hunger remained, but a welcome warmth crept throughout her whole body. A bright light, brighter than the sun, danced around her. She felt warm, too warm. Tuuli stood and shook off her cover.

Snow and ice fell from the branches above her. She watched the ice melt and flow away in rivulets that joined streams of sparkling blue waters. The bright light spun and twirled. It turned from red, to violet, to yellow, and back to red. She was so warm she shrugged off her coat. From under the fur robe, Kulta whimpered. "Come, my little dog. Come dance with me. It is warm here in the light." She clapped her hands for her dog to come. Kulta kept her eyes fixed on Tuuli and backed away.

Tuuli looked to where the deer bedded down, snow heaped high. Kulta woofed and dug at the snow mounds. The snow quivered. When Ruusu stood, she broke through the crust, clumps of snow and ice falling as she tossed her head.

Like Kulta, Ruusu snorted and shied away from Tuuli. She pawed at the snow that still covered her fawn. After a little prodding, the fawn wobbled out of its bedding. Tuuli watched both deer. Ruusu's udder was flaccid. There would be no milk for the fawn. Tuuli reached out to pat them, but they lowered their heads, flared their nostrils, and snorted. Kulta whimpered.

Warmth surrounded Tuuli but did not lessen her sharp pangs of hunger. How long could she endure without eating? Already, she felt herself wavering between sleep and wakefulness, the living and the dead. She wondered what it would be like to meet Jabemeahkka, the spirit of the world beyond. Would her mother take her by the hand to enter the death journey, or would it be Poppi? What was the realm of the dead? Was it watery and warm? Did you rock and float as on gentle waves? Or was it airy? Would she fly freely as an eagle on wafting winds?

Thoughts jumbled and tumbled as Tuuli hung between a numbing drowsiness and prickly wakefulness. She felt a deep warmth; she was so warm she tossed her hat to the ground and tugged at her leggings.

Pangs of hunger stabbed throughout her whole being. Tuuli pulled the knife from her pouch. She had to kill the fawn now. Feeling herself lift away from her earthly self, she chanted:

Brother Bear.
Earthly Brother.
Come to me. Warm me. Feed me.

As she said the words, she looked down at her own slumped, starving, and freezing body.

Then she felt herself swoop down and lunge toward Gabba. Her hand swiped at him. Lights swirled before her eyes. What she saw, she could not understand. It was not her hand, but a great paw with one long claw. One more swipe and Gabba fell. With the long glistening claw, she slit the fawn's throat.

A thundering heart quickened within her as the heartbeat of the fawn faded. Tuuli stared at the great furry paws and strong legs that were now her body. A warmth like a glowing flame cradled her as she watched red blood from the white fawn spill onto white snow. Then, little by little, she felt herself shed the fur, claws, bones, and flesh of Brother Bear.

Sharp tinglings of cold picked at every part of her as the bear-strength and warmth left her. Shivering, she pulled on her mittens, leggings, hat, and coat again. To live, she must get warm. To live, she must eat.

She shouted above the winds, "I will not let Bieg win!"

With her knife, she slashed the belly and the chest of the fawn. She removed the heart, held it in her hands, offered it high to the spirits, to Jabemeahkka who had not come for her but had taken the fawn instead. Then she brought the soft warm heart to her mouth and bit into it.

16

THE SUN SHONE AGAIN. BEAVI FAVORED THEM with warmth and chased Bieg back to his stormy cave. The winds blew warm. Water trickled as the snows started to melt.

Even with the sun shining, Tuuli still felt a deep chill in her bones. Although weak, she dug through the snow to find lichen to start a fire. She found small strips of birchbark for tinder. She built a circular outer ring with lichen and small twigs. Her hands were stiff and sore, but she whittled some wood into shavings that would catch fire from the bark. It took her a long time just to get wood of different sizes ready. All the while, she chanted.

Beavi, giver of life.
Beavi, giver of light.
Beavi, giver of warmth.
Enfold my world.
Charm my ways.
Share your fire.
Guide me. Keep me.
Beavi, Father Sun.

While entreating the sun, she carefully laid lichen and tinder for the fire and thought of all the times she had watched Poppi build fires even when it was stormy and wet. A gift from the sun, fire was sacred for her people. It provided warmth and heat to cook life-giving food. Fire warmed the body, especially hands and feet. One could lose fingers and toes if they got too cold. The lichen and birchbark strip caught the first spark she struck with her flint. While feeding that tiny dot of light with more strips of bark, Tuuli shielded her small flames from the winds that would blow them out.

Focused on building up the flames and leaning over it to warm herself, Tuuli thought of fire, sun, wind, deer, and the waters. They were all she and her people needed. They did not need strangers coming to tell them how to live and what to believe. Even mothers and fathers and children from as long ago as nine generations nine times knew a deer was as important as a person. Water was as necessary as fire. Without Beavi's warmth, there would be no life. Nothing.

When the fire threw off waves of heat, the old reindeer, Kulta, and Tuuli huddled close until warmth seeped into every bone of their bodies. When Ruusu strayed to find lichen, Tuuli laced strips of Gabba's liver on a stick and roasted them for herself and Kulta.

Two days after the little fawn was killed, Tuuli carefully skinned the pelt from its carcass. After severing the legs and the head, she cut the ribs into pieces. She set the ribs close to the fire to smoke-dry. Tuuli's hands were clumsy and stiff, so each task took longer than it should have. Sores blossomed on her hands from the deep cold she had suffered. She rubbed Gabba's soothing fat on them. Later, she would look for roots and leaves to make into a balm for healing.

After scooping the brains from the skull, she boiled them with the round bones that held rich marrow. She scraped pieces of meat and fat from the inside of the skin while the boiled mixture cooled. She set the fat aside, little that there was. Then Tuuli scooped out every piece of solid meat. These she licked from her fingers and threw some to Kulta. When the water from the brains and bones cooled, she drank some and then offered some for Kulta to lap. While working, she rested often. She sang joiks for Gabba—thanking for his tender ribs and loins—thanking for his beautiful white coat. And she sang thanks to be alive. Thanks that Bieg's storm had died down. Thanks that she and Kulta now had meat to eat.

Each day, Kulta gathered strength, as did Tuuli. Her dog nibbled at little bits of the remaining snow. They both gnawed on the rib bones. Tuuli tossed sticks for Kulta to chase. But Ruusu did not recover as quickly. She often lay down after digging for lichen and pulling green shoots that poked through the remaining thin crust of snow.

Tuuli sang a joik to the Brother Bear who saved her.

> *Guovza. Thank you.*
> *Guovza. Long life to you.*
> *Guovza. I owe you my spirit.*
> *Guovza. Thank you.*

When the pelt was dry, she held it to her breast and sang for the young fawn whose skin she tanned, whose blood she drank, whose bones she chewed, whose flesh she ate.

> *Gabba, fawn of crippled foot.*
> *I hid you. I saved you.*
> *And then you gave your life*
> *So I could live.*
> *Your good meat feeds me.*
> *Your pelt warms me.*
> *I am one with you.*
> *Gabba, deer of white.*

17

WHEN TUULI FELT STRONG, WARM, AND FED, she took stock of her food basket. There were a few mushrooms left but no more berries. As summer came on during her journey, she could find more. She had meat from the fawn. She needed to fish or hit down another grouse as she traveled.

Before packing the food basket, she held Poppi's drum to her chest and felt its gentle rhythms. She wrapped it into the bundle with her bed robe, Gabba's pelt, and the pouches of ash to Ruusu's back and took the first steps to continuing her journey.

The snow had completely melted by the time she reached a branch of the river where she could fish. Sunlight glanced off the rushing river, almost blinding Tuuli. She threw her net to the middle of the stream, but the force of the current almost dragged it from her hands. On her second throw, she held the net tightly and brought in a fish. As soon as she tossed it to the shore, Kulta picked it up and threw it into the air again and again.

"You're no help at all, little dog." Tuuli laughed. She felt renewed warmth while standing in the sun on the rock, fishing for food. Her heart lightened to see her dog playing, while Ruusu browsed on green shoots of grasses.

The sun lowered in the sky as Tuuli cleaned the fish, gathered firewood, built a fire, and cooked the fish. Then she lay to rest on the cushion she made of mosses and her robe. A gentle breeze whispered. Tuuli let her mind wander to her siide and wondered how everyone was. Was the migration going well? Were the deer finding enough to graze?

Then Hánas came to mind. Her heart leaped when she thought of him. She pinched herself, saying, "Heart, do not leap at Hánas's name." She was angry with herself for thinking of how good-looking he had become. Her heart thudded hard and with sadness. Tuuli looked skyward to keep tears from spilling. The sun still peeked above the horizon as it would for two cycles of the moon, so the stars—those points of light that fascinated her in the winter—didn't show. She shook her head, chasing Hánas from her thoughts.

To keep her mind from returning to him, she considered her journey. She'd already crossed one of the rivers. In the morning when she crossed this branch, it would be the second. There would be one more to cross. She'd only passed one circle of sacred rocks. She needed to find two more before coming to the Mount of Four Winds. Poppi and her mother had never encountered one of Bieg's fierce storms on their journeys, but Bieg had already done his best to send her to the land beyond the living. She had survived his tempest, but there would be other challenges she would have to overcome with her strength and wits. She wondered if the monster Stallu would show his ugly face and what she would have to do to conquer him.

Kulta ran up to Tuuli and sat beside her. "I have my own monsters—monsters inside my heart and my head, that I have to conquer, too," she said, stroking her dog. "And you, are you missing your dog friends?" she asked as she laid her cheek on her dog's head. A white bird flew overhead, and a raven perched nearby.

18

In that season when the sun shone for long hours, the earth warmed quickly. Little plants shot their stems and leaves above the ground, turned green, bloomed, and formed berries in days. It was as if they knew it would not be long before the sun grew faint and left them again. Tuuli laid her bedding next to little plants that poked up from the earth all around her. Scented buds teased her nose. Waxy red berries grew close, so she reached for a handful and popped them into her mouth. Birds twittered in the trees. Green sprouted everywhere. New leaves unfurled. All the earth shrugged off the cold winter.

Warmth spread through Tuuli's body as Kulta snuggled close. Tuuli fell asleep holding the drum. That night, her mother again came to her, held her, rocked her while she slept, and whispered sweet words to her.

The night before you were born, the moon beamed gold.
In the morning, the sun gleamed silver.
You were born as blue as the sky,
and as cold as the first rains,
but the wind blew breath into you,

and Beavi, the sun, warmed you.
And Poppi, fearful that you might die,
beat his drums until your heart leaped into rhythm with them.

And on that day when the wind blew breath into you,
and Beavi warmed you,
and the drums beat with your heart,
Guovza, the bear, circled our goahti three times.
Each time he circled, you became stronger,
until on the third you cried out
and turned from blue as the waters
to pink as spring flowers.
It was then the whole siide knew you lived,
and we sang with joy.

When Tuuli opened her eyes, her mother was gone. A shimmering light enveloped Tuuli. A sharp chill permeated the early morning because Beavi was still low in the sky, but she felt comforted in the glow. Poppi and her mother had always told her she was marked from birth to be an extraordinary noaidi. She had thought the round patch of mouselike fur on her shoulder that itched before it rained was what they meant by marked, but now she knew the sun, the wind, and the bear had chosen her.

When Tuuli awoke the next morning, a little flower bloomed next to her cheek. Its delicate fragrance scented the air she breathed in. Lingering on her fur robes, Tuuli could still feel her mother's lips at her ears and hear her crooning, softly singing the story of her birth.

Before rising, she sang the story of her own birth three times so she could remember her mother's words. Airy sounds flowed from her mouth. Her voice surprised her. It was not at all like it had ever been before, but ethereal, as if she were drifting in the sky and not rooted to the earth.

Plants were more plentiful now. Tuuli often stopped to dig for tender roots and eat fresh green leaves. She tucked half of what she found into her basket, not wanting to be caught without food again.

Small streams made catching fish easy. Bright red berries ripened, and Kulta sometimes caught a nesting grouse or hare.

Days later, the ground grew rougher. There were no more bogs and fewer lakes. They walked well into the deep north. Each day when Beavi was at its highest, Tuuli held her drum high to the sun, to each of the four winds, and then asked Bieg and Stallu to sleep deeply during the rest of her journey.

On some days, memories of songs and chants her mother and Poppi had sung to her seeped into her consciousness. They rose easily from her throat as she traveled and as she made her bed during the twilights that never gave way to darkness. She sang to her earthly brothers and sisters, joining herself to the land around her.

Coyote.
Bear.
Silver Salmon.
Soaring Eagle.
Serpent.
Fox.
Pike.
Willow Grouse.
Brothers and Sisters All.

At those times, she felt heartened. It wasn't wrong to take the drum or to hide the deer. She was sad Gabba was gone, and she noticed Ruusu was walking slower, usually with her head held low.

When she felt weary, she lay upon the ground, letting warmth soak into her until she felt nothing between herself and the ground upon which she lay. She was one with all—especially her mother, Iiri, and her grandfather Poppi. As she felt absorbed into the earth and the rock upon which she leaned, a deep silence cushioned her. The birds stopped singing, no mosquitoes buzzed.

As a noaidi, she would be relied on for so many things. She would carefully set aside the mushrooms that brought visions and allowed the noaidi to travel to the spirit realm. She would also be the story keeper of her people. That part would be easy. She had listened to Poppi's stories and repeated each one until it was firm in her memory.

On cold, dark nights, Poppi had asked her to retell the stories. With Kulta cuddled by her side under her fur robe, she would recite each story exactly as he had told it. Poppi would nod in approval and then fall fast asleep. When he was gently snoring, she would tell the story to herself one more time.

Her favorite was how her clan became the people of the deer. For more dark times than one could even count on their fingers and toes, or even on the fingers and toes of all the people in their clan even back to the eighteenth generation, her people had wandered. Tired of carrying their skin tents on their backs and hunting for food every day, they stopped close to a body of water where game came to drink. There they set their camp circle. But soon, a strange tribe would find them and threaten them with clubs and stones. They couldn't under-stand each other's words, but it was plain they would have to fight for their new land or leave. The Saami did not believe in fighting or in harming another human, so they tied their belongings to their backs and wandered once again.

Finally, after many full moons, even more full moons than one could count on their fingers and toes, or even on the fingers and toes of all the people in their clan back to the eighteenth generation, her people found a frozen land where no other tribes lived. In that cold land, they found a giver of life—the reindeer. Even when Beavi was hiding for three full moons at a time, the deer gave them milk and meat to eat, and warm furs to wrap around themselves.

When the land and waters were frozen, they strapped deer ant-lers to their feet and skated on icy lakes and rivers. When the snow was deep, they carved long feet for themselves from the trees so they could travel on top of the snow. For many generations, her people had dwelled in that far north, where the earth was beautiful white crystals all winter and a glorious green with delicate flowers and berries all summer. No one chased them out with clubs and stones. They found all they needed in the forests, the streams, and from the deer.

As Tuuli finished telling the story to herself, she wished for the days when strangers did not enter their land to demand skins and furs as taxes to allow the Saami to live on the land that had been their own for so long. And she yearned for a time when other strangers did not burn down their forests and plow up their grazing lands. And when still more strangers did not come, demanding the drums and burning their encampments.

Rested, she piled all her belongings onto Ruusu's back and tied the pouch that held her knife and flint about her waist. Then she picked up her walking stick, whistled for Kulta to come, and headed for the fells. As they journeyed, the trees became fewer and fewer. Low bushes held a few berries, but mostly the ground was covered with rocks, more rocks, and yet more rocks.

As she walked, she thought of her mother. Even though she'd been dead for two migrations, the people still talked about her with great affection. How she'd cured their newborn. How she'd stopped the flow of blood when young Aslek fell onto a sharp rock and tore open his arm. How she'd pressed mosses onto the burn that Makko had gotten when he stumbled into the campfire. And she'd sung the healing song. Would she, Tuuli, ever be that skillful? Or would she be tempted to use her skills for her own good, as Aiko, the cast-out noaidi, had?

Her thoughts about the strangers were troubling as usual. They, like mosquitoes, would keep coming—perhaps coming in even greater numbers. It was a thought that shook her from head to toe. Would the strangers ever leave them alone to live their lives the way they always had?

19

WARM BREEZES FOLLOWED TUULI, KULTA, AND RUUSU as their path left lowlands of many lakes and boggy marshes and rose to treeless plains and hilly vistas. At last, they climbed steeper trails with rocky cliffs, mighty rivers, and small rills. All the land was bathed in color. Rich reds of alder and berries. Greens nearly yellow and greens dark as black clad every bush and shrub. Waters murmured blue and silver. And the sweet aromas of delicate flowers wafted in the air. So much vivid beauty filled Tuuli with a heady wonder. She held the drum high and dropped to her knees often, awed, at the splendor of this land.

After two full moons passed, the day arrived when in the dimness of late travel, Tuuli heard a humming and saw a mist swirl above a rock cliff that rose higher than any of the hills—unmistakably it was the Mount of the Four Winds—the most sacred place of her people. The place where the four winds swirled together.

Even though she tingled with excitement, Tuuli forced herself to stop for a night's rest. When a thin shaft of light shone on her face the next morning, she roused her animals. After a small meal and a drink of springwater, they got on their way. The sun was already low in the sky, and when they neared the mount, Kulta's ears perked. She stopped to listen. Ruusu, too, twisted her ears from side to side, listening. The winds of the north, the south, the east, and the west sang in perfect harmony. Their whispers, their swellings were unlike any sound Tuuli had ever heard. It was more beautiful than all the birdsongs put together. Even more beautiful than a baby's coo. The swirling pulsated with her heart and filled her with a deep sense of reverence as they approached.

When they arrived at the base of the Mount of Four Winds, Tuuli fell to her knees. With joy, she let the concordance of the winds envelop her, tingling the roots of her hair, the tips of her toes, and the depths of her bones. Happy to finally be at the farthest reaches of her journey, Tuuli spread her bedding and enjoyed the magnificence of the early evening.

After resting, Tuuli built a fire of dried mosses and carried water from a nearby spring that bubbled up between two rocks. When the water was warm, she peeled off her clothing. Shivering a little in the thin sunlight, she scooped water onto her face, shoulders, breasts, stomach, legs, and feet. Then she loosened her hair from its braids and dipped handfuls of water onto her head. She stood and let the winds breathe upon her skin. Tuuli felt her feet sink into the earth as roots of a tree seek to become one with its mother. After dressing, she leaned against a large rock to dry her hair. The sun was as low as it would get that day, and she faced its weak warmth full on.

Tuuli placed two mushrooms on her tongue. Holding Poppi's drum close to her chest, Tuuli invoked the names of the noaidis who had held the drum before her, the men and the women, her grandfathers and grandmothers:

Juuti, Loppi, Elki . . .

As she said each name, an image came as a vision before her.

Jukka, Pekka, Veli . . .

In their hands, they each held a gift.

Ossi, Riga, Rasio . . .

A feather, a seed, a flower, a branch, a rock, a spark.

Tuoni, Lukka, Kyrre . . .

Each one passed his or her gift to another until all the gifts were stacked high in the hands of her mother and Poppi.

Lemmi, Ukka, Hupi . . .

The gifts were from those that made her who she was. The feather was a gift of knowing; the seed a promise of more generations; the flower of kindness; the branch for belonging to family; the rock of strength; the spark of breathing with the wind and feeling the beat of her heart.

She named each again, ate a few berries and another mushroom, and sipped cool water from the spring. Then she smoothed her hair and braided it high on her head. Kulta crept onto her lap. As she stroked her dog, she slouched in complete relaxation. The dog swished her tail, but Tuuli did not feel the silky fur. A white bird swept the sky above her, but Tuuli did not see it. Her eyes closed in deep sleep.

Kulta growled. Tuuli awakened just as a hand grabbed her shoulder. "Yeeooow!" Tuuli shouted. Swiveling to see who it was, she saw no ordinary hand, but one with scales like a fish and talons like an eagle. Looking up she saw a broad, squat creature. A monster. A monster with warted skin, slanted eyes, and a mouth that gaped showing sharp teeth. *Stallu!* She jumped up. A claw tore her coat, but she slipped free. A croaking and a cry coarser and louder than that of the raven sounded in her ears. *Grrronnnnk!*

As she leaped to a flying run, she looked back to see Stallu stumble over Ruusu and swipe a claw at her head. Then he turned to Tuuli and flung himself straight at her. In a strange land and in faint light, she had no idea which way to run, so she swerved away from the monster and fled straight ahead. She slipped on wet mosses, caught herself, and glanced back to see that Stallu was frightfully close. He was clumsier and more horrible than the stories she'd heard.

Terrified, Tuuli was angry with herself for not remembering to guard against Stallu, the great, ugly monster. His reputation for capturing young girls to be his brides made him feared by all in the far north. Again, she looked back to see how close he was. Kulta was running next to Stallu, biting at his legs, slowing him down. Stallu roared and swung at the dog, but she kept right on.

Good dog, Kulta! But a worry crept into Tuuli's mind. One kick or swat from Stallu, and her dog would be injured and unable to help her. *I have to outrace him. I have to get away from him.* She heard him roaring louder and closer. She yelled to the skies:

Wind,
Blow on my back.
Hurry me along.
Wind,
Blow on Stallu's face.
Slow him down.

Tuuli's heart pounded in her chest. The thundering of Stallu's feet echoed in her ears. The icy cold wind sliced into her chest. She breathed it out fiery hot. She ran along a stream and then up a rocky slope, all the time whispering:

Rocks,
Clear my path.
Rocks,
Make Stallu stumble and fall.

Fire burned in her legs. The thundering of Stallu's steps resounded in her ears. They raced when the shadows were long, and when the shadows shortened, they still ran. Soon there were no more plains, no more rocks, no more hills, just steep mountains ahead.

Behind her, Tuuli heard an awful snort as Stallu bellowed, "Oh, it's to be the top of the mountain where I catch you. Good. The whole world will see me take you for my bride."

Stallu thundered right behind her. She could smell and feel his hot, putrid breath. There was no way but up.

Her breath stung in her chest, icy and fiery at the same time.

Wind.
Be my friend.
Speed me.
Wind.
Do not let Stallu catch me.

The wind whooshed and whoooed. It cooled her forehead as she ran on up the mountain. Just as Tuuli reached the top, Stallu grabbed her coat. She shrieked.

"Jump," snarled Wind.

"I'll fall!" Tuuli screamed.

"I'll catch you," Wind whooshed.

"I got you," Stallu cackled.

"Jump to me," Wind whispered. "I'll swirl you high into the sky for all to see that you are free from Stallu."

Tuuli jumped. She yanked her coat from Stallu's grasp. Looking back, she saw him stumble and sway and finally fall down the mountain. The wind lifted Tuuli high into the northern sky. She danced on silver air. Her skirt and coat and scarves swirled. She danced on the wind like the night light of the far north—free from the monster Stallu.

Then the wind, cradling her, lowered her back to the earth, back to her fur robe. Tuuli landed with a jolt she felt throughout her whole body. Kulta jumped onto her lap and licked her face. Her heart pounded as fast as when she'd raced up the mountain. Was it just a dream? Had she really outraced Stallu? Did he lie dead deep in a chasm, or would he rise again to terrorize her more? She put her hand to the shoulder of her coat, where Stallu's claw had been. A tear. From Stallu? Or had it been there before and she hadn't noticed?

Little by little, her heart slowed and her face cooled. Then she remembered Ruusu. Her old deer lay a distance away—unmoving. At the same time, Kulta ran to Ruusu, sniffed her from head to tail, and circled the still deer three times before lying down next to her. Tuuli ran to the deer. The deer was hurt; an open wound bled freely. Tuuli stuffed the injury with mosses and carried water to her. Ruusu raised her head to drink and then lay down, closing her eyes. The deer lay still, too still. Tuuli patted her head; the deer didn't move. She held her hand by the deer's nostrils. A gentle breath touched her hand, but it was too soft, too slow. She put her nose next to Ruusu's and breathed deeply for a long time, trying to instill life into her, but the deer's breath weakened. She put her hand on her deer's heart. The beats were far apart and soft.

Tuuli tapped her drum firmly. "Please, Drum, bring strong beats for Ruusu's heart." But the deer's heart slowed more. Refusing to give up, she took Poppi's rowan walking stick and waved it over the deer. Then she brushed Ruusu's fur with her hand. Kulta stood nearby watching. The deer rasped a deep breath and closed her eyes.

Tuuli called to the wind; it swirled around the two of them, but soon no breath came from the deer. She put her hand to the deer's chest and gently kneaded a rhythm, demanding a pulse. But soon no beats came. She called to the sun, but Ruusu's body cooled. She cried and massaged her tears around the deer's eyes, but no light came from within.

For a long time, Tuuli wept. She lay beside the deer, running her hands along its neck through thick fur. Kulta nudged her, urging her to get up. She said, "Little dog, it's just the two of us now." Kulta sniffed the deer and gave a sorrowful whine deep in her throat.

Tuuli waited for all the life-warmth to go out of the deer that had been her pet for all the years of her life. Lovingly, she stroked it, admiring the beauty of Ruusu's fur. Her heart jolted as she thought of the many times she'd sunk her hands into this same fur to warm them during the cold winter. Her tears flowed, wetting her face as a gentle rain might.

Tuuli sang mourning songs to Ruusu until her eyelids drooped. Kulta rested with her head on her paws. As long as her dog was not sensing any danger, Tuuli felt she could sleep. Tomorrow, she would not only have to tend to Ruusu's remains, but she would carry the ashes of her mother and Poppi to the top of the mount. She looked to the sky. A white bird flew overhead. This time she saw it. Then she fell asleep.

20

THE NEXT MORNING, TUULI AROSE WITH a mourning song already in her throat. With a heavy heart, she began to skin Ruusu's pelt. Just as she had done with Gabba, she cut the ribs in two and tossed one to Kulta, and then she put the rest over the fire. When they were roasted, she ate the meat and gnawed at the bone. As she worked, she sang:

> *Save the sinews for the sewing.*
> *Tan the doeskin for some clothing.*
> *Put the skull in a birchbark basket.*
> *Stew it in steaming water.*
> *Soak the hide to make it supple.*
> *Save the bones and crack for marrow.*
> *Make a soup for tomorrow.*

Before setting out to climb the mount, Tuuli placed a mushroom on her tongue. She called for Kulta to follow. As she climbed, the winds whistled and whooshed around her. Tuuli, thrilled with the sound, loosened her hair and let it swirl with the winds that wound round and round her.

As the trail steepened, she clung to rocks, small birches, and rowans whose roots seized into the cracks of hard rock. The four winds twisted the air around her, harmonizing a celestial song. At the top, she took a handful of Poppi's ashes and another of her mother's. As she spun on her toes, the winds picked up the ashes, churning and mixing them with the air she breathed. Tuuli stood tall and inhaled deeply, taking them into her lungs to become part of her. Now Poppi and her mother would always be with her. The winds swirled ashes to the high skies; they mingled with the stars and became part of the world above. They would fall back to earth with the rains of summer and the snows of winter and be with her and her people. Wherever the migrating deer went, the winds would carry the ashes to them. When she had but a small handful left in each pouch, she quit.

Tuuli bent and spilled the remains of her mother's ashes on the ground and covered them with a flat stone she'd carried with her. Then she covered the remainder of Poppi's ashes with the other, conjuring images of his life in flashes of light and color. Poppi drumming. Tending to the reindeer. Carrying her on his shoulders before she was old enough to walk. Singing ancient songs. Telling the stories of her people and at the end, lying on his robes, dying.

A white bird flew overhead as Tuuli chanted:

Wind I know,
Drum I hear,
Sun I feel,
Earth I am.

The wind replied:

Whoosh, swoosh.
Hush, hush.
Be so still
And watch
And hear.

Breathe it in.
Breathe it out.
Be one.

Be the bear; be the deer,
Be the sun and the wind,
The life and the death.
Be the birth; be the whisper,
The root; the wing,
The strength; the promise.
Be the grandparent of old; be the grandchild to come.
Be the song; the word,
The dark; and the light.
Be the all.

All—all warm and glowing, flowed into every pore of Tuuli's being. Ancient songs sprang from her deepest heart to her throbbing throat, past her tongue and lips to vibrate with the life airs that blew high over the hills swaddled in the clouds.

The four winds lifted her from her earthly footing. A soft swoosh filled her ears as she floated high in the sky. Above all earth-beings, she swayed and swung through a swash of blue sky, and the winds sang with her.

Hei la lo la
Fei la lo
Mei la lo la
Eeei la lo-o-o
La lo la
La la la

Swallows swarmed to sing with her and the wind. She swept through gleaming ribbons of silver sun. Spreading her arms, she tilted and soared, joining with a great white bird. Tuuli saw the whole of the land, the land that was hers, the Saami's, through ages and ages.

She saw her past. Her own birth, the blueness of her lips until the wind blew breath into her. The death of her mother as roaring waters took her strength and she weakened until there was no return to her earthly life. And finally, Poppi losing his sight and his teeth. She saw visions of her mother, her father, Poppi and her other grandparents, and their parents, and theirs, and theirs, and theirs, and theirs. The stories Poppi had told her were those he called "nine two times"—the family. And it was up to Tuuli now to remember. She was the root of the past and the wings of the future.

Soaring, she saw herself walk the lonely trail that had led her to the mount. She had been but a small speck in a big land. Lost, but not lost. Alone, but not alone. Comforted, she saw the filmy fires of her mother, of Poppi, of her grandmothers, her grandfathers of the near and far past. She looked hard at the fires. She did not see Beto, her father. He must still be counted among the living.

Still soaring, she saw herself in the time yet to come. She saw herself join the long line of her people who had made their journey here. She saw danger for her people's way of life and danger for herself. She saw herself with her own people, but she also saw herself leave and go with strangers. She saw herself floating on a great water and walking in a new land. She saw herself with another people who faced the same challenges from strangers who came to their hunting grounds. Who took lands and destroyed their way of life.

Then she saw the future eighteen generations beyond herself. Huge birds flew in the sky. They didn't sing lovely melodies but roared earsplitting dirges. Some dropped flames, melting everything on the earth beneath them. Lines, thin like sinew but impossibly long, crossed the skies, making lights at night that were not stars or moon. Herders gathered their reindeer by riding on noisy sledges that spit out acrid, stinging smoke. Loud, ugly sounds crackled and splintered the air from all directions, so the breezes could not be heard. People sealed their ears with little plugs that filled their heads with strange noises. They no longer took time to listen to the wind whispering or to sing joiks.

Tuuli's eyes filled with tears and her heart pounded against her chest. *Is this truly what is to become of my people?*

Seeing no more, she slowly folded her arms to her body and followed the great white bird back to the earth. She must return to stop the strangers—to stop the changes.

As she landed, she felt the reality of sharp rocks beneath her. Running her hands from throat to toes, she checked to see if any bones had broken in the hard fall. She felt the roundness of her breasts. She felt the softness of her thighs and the tingling of her inner self. She knew she was no longer the girl too young to be noaidi for her people but was becoming a woman. She would face the meeting of noaidis at the gathering. She was a woman, a wind listener and a drum talker, and keeper of her people's story.

Tuuli stood straight, determined. *I can do this. I must return to my people. I will stop the strangers.* The winds strengthened, but Tuuli held still. What she needed to know was all wrapped up in the noaidis who had gone before her. Her skin prickled. She felt they were all there with her, yet she was the only living one. It would be up to her to have children, to pass to them the essence of herself and her ancestors. That was how her people would survive and live as they had always, with their reindeer, the winds, and their drums.

Picking up her drum and holding it to the sky, she felt it jump to life, vibrate, and join the throbbing of the skies with her own throbbing. Tuuli raised her arms and began to dance. She could face the strangers. She had seen herself going with them, but she fiercely resolved not to let that happen. She would stay where she belonged—with her people.

21

IN THE DAYS THAT FOLLOWED, TUULI CLIMBED to the top of the Mount of Four Winds several more times. She felt free as she gave herself over to the swirling winds of the north, the south, the east, and the west. Kulta enticed her into games of chase and hide-and-seek. They swam in a small stream and ate plenty to get strong for their return journey. But always in the shadows of Tuuli's mind was her worry about the long trek ahead. She no longer had the pouches of ashes, but she still had many things to carry and no deer to help. Nothing could be left behind.

On her last day, she climbed the mount again. She twirled with the four winds and sang.

I perch high
As the eagle
On the mount.

I fly high
As the eagle

Finding the currents
Of life.
I seek low and I seek high.

As the eagle
There is the past
And there is the time to come.
Above and below.

Then she twirled with the winds one last time and said good-bye, wondering if she would ever return. Or if the next time she came, would it be as ashes carried by another?

Back at the foot of the mountain, Tuuli made Ruusu's pelt into a pack for her back to carry the drum, her sleeping robe, Gabba's pelt, and the net. Her knife and flint were tied in a pouch at her waist. In her hands, she carried the walking stick and basket of food packed with venison, berries, roots, and mushrooms. Ready to leave, Tuuli broke a small branch from a tree and swept the ground where she had eaten, slept, and walked, erasing all signs of her stay.

Walking with Kulta, who was full of energy, and not having to wait for or worry about the deer, she was able to enjoy the beauty of her surroundings. The land that now was so rich with flowers and berries would soon turn cold. A frost would nip the plants; they would darken and die. The sun was starting to rest for short times. Soon it would be falling-leaf when the nights would last just as long as the days.

After full days of walking, they stopped to rest. Kulta found sticks to bring to Tuuli and begged for her to toss them so she could chase after them. Tuuli enjoyed the games. She laughed at her little dog. They ate, swam, and played until it was time to sleep and they curled together on their sleeping robe. Tuuli didn't feel as lonely knowing she was on her way back to her people. All would be good now if the darkness of the black-coated strangers didn't hover always at the edge of her awareness.

22

ON THE DAY THAT TUULI HEARD WATER TUMBLING and roaring, she said, "We are nearing a river we must cross. I had hoped for a quiet one—shallow enough for us to wade." Kulta perked her ears and whimpered as though agreeing with her.

At the river, Tuuli walked the steep banks in each direction. No matter where she went, the current ran swiftly. Great rocks protruded from the foamy waters. Ragged tree branches caught on the stones. Swirling eddies caught leaves and branches at every turn.

At a high cliff next to the river, she looked for a trail to the top. It sloped sharply and was rocky. A sharp rock sliced through the sole of Tuuli's boot, biting the bottom of her foot. She stopped to check the bruise. Kulta limped to sit with her. She, too, was footsore from walking on and climbing rough, sharp rocks. Tuuli's skin boots were torn in more than one place. She would have to make herself new boots from Ruusu's hide before climbing the cliff so she could see if there was a good way to cross.

As Tuuli carved an awl from one of Ruusu's thin bones, she sang:

> *Sharpened knife with a stone.*
> *Carved a needle from a bone.*

Made it flat.
Made it strong.

Used some sinew for the sewing.
Laced it into needle's eye,
Then sewed till almost night.

With her knife and her bone needle, she sewed four skin boots for her dog and two for herself. After finishing the boots, she bit a design into each one. For the dog's booties—a fish on each. For her own, she bit a sun and the moon for light to follow her day and night.

Kulta nipped and tugged at her booties. She couldn't get them off, so she finally took a step and then more, shaking her feet. She whimpered at Tuuli, who only said, "You'll like them when you get used to them. Your feet will heal."

In the stillness of the next morning, with Kulta leading the way, they climbed the cliff. At the top, Tuuli stood on a ledge overlooking the river. All she could see were more steep, slippery, rocky banks, and a swift current. Even though there was no good safe place to wade or swim to the other side, they would have to.

Hungry, Tuuli ate a strip of meat with a handful of mushrooms and berries. Then she closed her eyes and envisioned herself flying over the river as Sister Bird. She rose on her toes and flapped her arms in the air, but no lightness lifted her high over the rushing waters. She held her arms to the wind. "Swish and swirl. Carry me over the river to the other shore," she implored. No wind, just mosquitoes swirled round and round. Swatting and scratching, she turned to her dog. "Come, let us cross," she said, trying to sound brave.

Tuuli stood on the edge of a slick rock. She judged the distance to a boulder. If they could leap to that, and from there to the next, the waters looked calmer near the far bank. They could wade through that part. They had to try. Tuuli leaped to the first. She slipped on its wetness but kept her footing. Then she jumped to the next. Secure there, she turned to call Kulta.

The dog made it to the first rock. "Stay," Tuuli commanded. She herself had to wade or swim to the shore so there would be room for the dog on the second boulder. She tossed her walking stick to the other side. Then she pulled her bundle from her back. As she heaved it to the opposite bank, she heard a splash. Kulta was in the water.

The dog yipped. Tuuli cried, "Swim, Kulta, swim!" The dog sank under the swirling water. She needed to get to her dog. The booties were weighing the dog down.

"Swim, Kulta, swim!" she called again. The little dog pulled itself to the surface and paddled furiously, but she was caught in a fuming current. Finally, the waters spun past a log. Kulta banged into it and then jumped onto it, and from there to a big rock. There she was, stuck in the middle of the churning current. Kulta yapped and paced on the rock.

"Stay still," Tuuli called. But Kulta slipped into the dangerous water again. Tuuli heard her yodel a hollow howl as the swirling waters swept her away again. Then an eddy current pulled Kulta under.

Without a thought, Tuuli plummeted to the roaring river. She hit—nose first. Then she felt herself slithering through the water. She gave a mighty surge to surface for a breath. When she did, the air stung. Tuuli looked down at herself and saw a shining, scaled fish—a silver salmon. Plunging back under, she swam, swaying her body back. She flipped her tail, darted back and forth in the river, looking, searching. When she spied her dog, Kulta was fighting to get out of the underwater swirl. Tuuli angled her fins and swam to the dog.

Reaching her pet, she nosed Kulta, nudged and pushed, until she managed to get the dog out of the whirling pool. Tuuli kept pushing the dog upward until she surfaced. She hoped Kulta would have enough strength to swim cross current to the shore, but the dog coughed and sputtered. Her legs flailed weakly in the fast water. Finally, Tuuli was able to nudge the dog to the rocky shore. Kulta dragged herself onto the bank.

"Thank you, Brother Salmon," said Tuuli as she slowly shed the scales and fins in the waters and became herself. She pulled Kulta beside her. Her dog lay listlessly. Hoping all hadn't been for nothing, Tuuli turned the dog over and gently squeezed her chest to force out water the dog had breathed in. Kulta coughed and spewed water.

Tuuli cradled the dog, brushing water out of her coat. The dog didn't try to lick herself dry. Her head hung limply to one side. First Gabba, then Ruusu, now Kulta. Tuuli saw that Kulta's eyes reflected no light, and she felt limp and boneless in her arms. She must have been seriously hurt banging against the rocks.

She held Kulta, warming her on the sunny rocks, petting and crooning. Remembering how ice-cold swirling waters had stolen life from her mother, she sang healing songs, hoping Kulta hadn't been in the water too long.

After a while, Tuuli put the dog on mossy ground so she could stretch. The dog shivered. Tuuli, too, was getting chilled. She needed a fire to warm them both.

From the mossy bed, Kulta gave a little woof, stood, shook herself, and stretched. Tuuli gave her a big hug. The dog lay down and curled up again. "Good. Stay warm," Tuuli said to her. She pulled her knife and flint from her waist pouch. She gathered some lichen and small branches for kindling, struck the stone with her knife, and got a little fire going.

With a small fire crackling, Tuuli gathered bigger twigs. Within a short time, her fire was burning enough to send off heat, so she moved Kulta closer to it. As Tuuli huddled over the fire, she thanked it for its flame. From the corner of her eye, she saw a dark shadow. When she turned to look, nothing was there, but the darkness persisted. *Is it Jabemeahkka coming for Kulta?* She drew the dog closer to herself.

As she cuddled her dog, she thought about returning to her people as noaidi. "It's not fair," she said aloud. Too much depended upon her. Many of the families had several children. It was never up to just one to carry on. And as far as she knew, neither Poppi nor her mother had shifted shapes, as she had done on this journey—to bear, to bird, to fish. And whom would she marry? She was old enough to bear a child, and she should run at the gathering and be caught, so she would have a husband and children—someone to succeed her. The life of her people was precarious, and she shouldn't wait to marry. If only Hánas hadn't become a broken branch, separate from the Saami, a traitor to her people. Holding her hands to her chest, she felt its quickened beat just from thinking of Hánas.

23

As the sun sank low, mosquitoes attacked furiously. Tuuli waved her arms frantically trying to ward off their whines and bites, but it did no good. Wave after wave of the stinging menace dove at her. Kulta didn't snap at them. She didn't even shake her head when mosquitoes landed on her. Despite the onslaught, Tuuli felt the dog's ears and nose. They were dry, too dry, and warm. Her heart ached, and tears did fall. Her deer. Her dog. Her throat tightened as sour bile rose.

Taking out her drum, Tuuli bent her knees to ground. She sang to all the holders of life—trees and animals—pleading with them to share their life with Kulta. Even as the wind blew gently and the drum throbbed, Tuuli saw a shadow hover over Kulta. She reached to stroke her pet. It was the season of warmth, but Kulta was losing hers. Tuuli hugged and wrapped her in the sleeping robe and held her close. The dog whimpered but allowed Tuuli to stroke her.

Tuuli sang to the sun. She sang for rays to caress her dog. Beavi shone on Kulta, turning her red hair shining golden.

Sun,
You are warm.

Warm my Kulta.
Drum,
You do beat.
Beat rhythm into Kulta's heart.
Wind,
You are breath.
Fill Kulta with healing.

Kulta closed her eyes and slept. Her breathing was deeper than it had been. Tuuli laid her ear on her dog's chest and heard her heart beat slowly, but firmly. Tuuli's cares eased, but she kept singing.

Seeing her dog sleeping peacefully, she spread her clothes and boots to dry. Then she picked some berries and ate them by the handful along with another strip of venison. She scooped handfuls of the cold river water into her mouth and lifted Kulta onto her lap.

She held her dog close to her chest and crooned as the sun lowered in the sky.

Can you hear the sound of roaring waters?
Can you hear the wind in the trees?
Can you hear my heartbeat against your ear?
Can you stay the path of life?

If Kulta died, the only thing she'd have at the end of her journey would be the drum. But the drum was the center of her problems now. It had brought the strangers, who would do anything to get it. So hungry were they for the drums they would destroy the Saami and their encampments. But it was also the drum that had talked to Poppi. In his hands, it had sent healing messages, calmed storms, and brought the warmth of Beavi. It would be the drum that would tell her the way to lead her people.

She lay close to her dog and covered them both with Poppi's sleeping robe.

Tuuli rested another day on the riverbank with her dog. Although Kulta was still weak, Tuuli decided they must start their journey again.

She could carry her pet if she had to. Traveling would be slow. Eager to be with her people, Tuuli left their little camp by the river and started for her clan's gathering grounds. She guessed she had a nine-day trip ahead of her, maybe longer, depending how much she had to carry Kulta.

After the first day of walking, Tuuli was tired and ready to stop when the sky dimmed. Kulta moaned in her sleep at first, but soon quieted, so Tuuli slept. She didn't waken until Kulta stirred beside her. Her own stomach felt hollow, so she sat up, ready to fetch food from her pack.

To her surprise, three rows of rocks surrounded their sleeping spot. They had not been there when they bedded down. Someone had circled the rocks while they slept. How? Why? Rocks in a circle were sacred, like the *seidas*. They were also markers for ashes of the dead. A chill ran through her. Was someone was playing a trick on her, or was it a warning? Angry and puzzled, she got up and kicked the rocks away. How could anyone have crept into her camp to do this without her or the dog waking?

During their travels that day, Tuuli stopped often, not only to rest but to listen for footsteps, snapping branches, any warning that someone was following them. She heard nothing other than animals. She saw birds and a hare and once spotted a fox, but no trace of a human. And no trace of the white bird. Nervous and tired, Tuuli stopped earlier than usual for the night.

At first, she stayed awake, listening for sounds, and hoping whoever had circled them with stones was gone. When exhaustion overcame her, she slept. She woke to a deluge of water pouring down on her. At first, she thought it was rain, but it had started and stopped so quickly that it couldn't have been. She jumped up and looked for whoever had done it. No one was there. No sounds. No footsteps. She put her ear to the ground and listened. Even then she couldn't hear any pounding of feet running away.

Kulta licked at her wet fur languidly, but she made no sounds. Tuuli's heart was racing, so she gave up the idea of sleeping and fixed some food for them. She carried her dog to drink from a small inlet of the river, where the water ran smoothly. After packing her bundle and slinging it on her back, she started her journey in the dim morning light.

Again, Tuuli watched, listened, even backtracked to see if she could catch whoever was playing tricks on them. It had to be someone who followed them during the day. Again, she only saw one raven and other small animals. That night, Kulta curled up to sleep right away as though nothing had happened. Tuuli tried to stay awake. Her ears perked at every sound. An owl hooting. A hare running through the woods. A fox and its kits drinking at the river. She managed to stay awake for a long time, but in time, weariness won.

When she did awaken to a shaft of sun spearing between branches, she was relieved. She was dry, and there wasn't a triple ring of rocks around them. Hungry, she reached for her food basket. It was gone. Tuuli looked again. It wasn't on the tree branch where she'd hung it. She looked all around her camp.

When she finally realized it was truly gone, she felt for her knife. It was in the pouch at her waist. Her drum, net, and walking stick were safely tucked under her sleeping robe, where she kept them every night.

Her travels would be slowed now. Without the food basket, she would have to pick berries and catch fish along the way. Kulta was no longer interested in chasing hares and mice, so she would also have to fish enough for her dog. Without Kulta's help, it would be hard for her to flush a grouse. When Tuuli tossed her net several times into the water, she only caught one fish. This she roasted and shared with Kulta before they started on their journey again.

24

Beavi shone in a clear sky. Tuuli picked ripe berries right into her mouth as she followed a well-worn animal path. At the height of day, she saw a ragged figure that moved like a leaf dancing on the wind. When she got closer, Tuuli saw that it was a man who was as thin as a sinew. As he stepped, a melody like that from a willow whistle swirled about him though he held no whistle in his mouth. He was dressed in skin clothing like she was. A floppy hat partially covered his long hair that looked as fragile and silvery as a spider web in sunshine. He carried a coat flung over his narrow shoulders and walked with only a small bag at his side and a crooked rowan stick.

"Bures, bures," the man called out when he spied her.

Tuuli felt curious, but uneasy. She adjusted the pouch that held her knife. "Bures," she replied.

"What's your name?" he asked.

She wasn't sure who this was, but among her people, it was impolite to ask a person's name. He should have waited for her to offer it or at least offered his first. Caution overcame her. If she told her true name, he could use it to have power over her, so she answered, "Otta. My name is Otta. What is yours?"

The man ignored her question.

"Who are your people? What are you doing out here alone?" His questions tumbled from his tongue. Tuuli listened to his words and voice. He wasn't from one of the clans by the far rivers like her people.

Even though it was rude, Tuuli answered him with her own questions. "What is your name? What are you doing out here alone? Who are your people?"

"Hah! If I told you, then you'd have power over me."

A sudden thought came to Tuuli. "Are you the banished one? The one whose name no one speaks?"

"Hah! Such a wise tongue for such a young one."

"Then you are the evil one."

"So some say. But, no, I'm not evil. I'm just misunderstood. I endure without a home. I have been chased out of my siide and am cursed to wander forever with no one to call me to the cooking fire."

"Then you are the outcast who plays tricks. Have you been following me and playing tricks to frighten me?"

"Maybe yes, maybe no. But now you must tell me who you are. I think you are not called *Otta* by anyone. Who are you?"

"Just a traveler going home," said Tuuli.

"You're not just a traveler going home. I think you have been to the Mount of the Four Winds. I think you are the one the ravens told me about. If that is so, I know your name, and I know your lineage, too."

Tuuli was struck he would know about her, and to have been told by the ravens? She didn't think so. She would have to be very careful. *Aiko*, she thought. Yes, that was the name of the banished one. He had strong powers. He was rumored to be a wind listener, a drummer, a healer, and a shapeshifter, as well as a player of tricks. His gifts were the same as hers, but he had had more years to sharpen them. He must be the one Hánas spoke of meeting when his mother was dying. He'd helped Hánas; maybe he wasn't all bad. But she had to be careful.

Tuuli couldn't think of any way to answer him. Lying wouldn't work, so she said nothing. Kulta was heavy in her arms and whining, so Tuuli put her down. The dog crept a short distance from her feet.

Aiko circled her and the dog, examining them. "You're just a wee one, aren't you? Too young to be so far from your people. What sent you on your journeys? Has the old noaidi of your siide died? Have you brought his ashes to the Mount of the Four Winds?"

Again, so many questions. He did not believe in one at a time. Tuuli didn't want conversation with him. She shouldn't even be talking to the banished one. She needed to leave now.

"Kah!" he said. "So I'm not good enough for you? Aren't you even polite enough to talk to a fellow traveler? We could exchange stories about where we've been and who we've seen."

"It's time for us to leave," Tuuli said. She turned to pick up her dog, but Aiko quickly stepped between them. Then he started to run circles around Kulta, teasing her with his stick. Though weak, the little dog snarled. She chased after the stick even though Tuuli called for her to stop. Kulta did stop, and then she fell to the ground. Tuuli ran to get to her, but Aiko stood in her way.

"What's in the bundle on your back? Trade me something for your dog. Then I'll go away," he demanded.

Having so little, there was nothing Tuuli wanted to give up from the bundle. Bundled in Ruusu's hide, she had Gabba's pelt and her sleeping robe. They were packed on top of her drum and fishing net. She would have to give up one of the furs.

First she offered Ruusu's hide, hoping he would be satisfied with it. She was eager for him to leave so she could go to Kulta, who lay panting, her tongue out, almost touching the ground.

"No, no, I see with my mind's eye you are holding something back that is more precious."

Now Tuuli knew it was not going to be as easy as just offering him another of the furs. To save the drum, she would have to trick him into thinking one of the furs was the most valuable thing she had. If she offered Gabba's pelt next, the trickster would probably refuse it and ask for something even more valuable.

So Tuuli thought of a plan to trick the trickster. She slowly opened her pack. Turning away from him, she hid Gabba's pelt under her coat. Then she slowly pulled out Poppi's fur sleeping robe that was larger and thicker than any other in her whole siide. She handed it to the trickster, pretending to be unwilling to let it go, and at the same time she held Gabba's white pelt tightly under her coat.

The outcast handled the sleeping robe, felt its thick fur, saw how well tanned and how large it was. He knew it was of great value— thick and warm—but he had seen Tuuli hiding something. He feigned interest in the robe. She pretended it was the best thing she had, leaving the rest of her pack carelessly on the ground as though there were nothing good in it.

"Look how beautiful this robe is," she said, rubbing her fingers through the fur. Aha! The trickster mulled over what he should do. Tuuli watched him scratch his chin while he hatched another ploy. She hoped he was falling for her ruse and would ask for what she was hiding under her coat. Then she would reluctantly take out the white pelt. The trickster would see the rare fur and greedily snap it up thinking it really was the most valuable thing she had.

But the outcast had earned his reputation well. He could never do anything straight out. He came up with another tactic. He spread the big sleeping robe on the ground before himself. Tuuli walked awkwardly holding the fur she'd hidden under her coat from falling out. The trickster watched her from the corner of his eye.

She wanted to help Kulta, who hadn't moved except to breathe in short, panting gasps. "Hurry and take the robe. I need to help my dog," she said.

"Oh, yes, the dog," he said. "What happened to her?"

"Just take the robe. Let me help my dog. I will miss the robe. It will be a long time before I can get another one. Our deer have been dying. There has been starvation. Their fur is not as good. This is the best, from better days when our deer had plenty to eat and had thick warm fur in the winter. Take it and leave."

Tuuli didn't like the way things were going. She was talking too much. The trickster no longer seemed interested in the robe. Tuuli wanted to be far away from him.

Aiko laughed. He stooped and leaned back on his heels. It was seldom he met up with anyone on his wanderings that he could capture for a while. "Come, now, there is no hurry. Let us sit and enjoy a bit of food while I ponder if there is some way I can help your dog. Surely you have something there in your pack to share, and I have a few wonderful berries and mushrooms here in my pouch. I picked them just yesterday."

"Thank you, but I have to be on my way, and my poor dog needs help. I don't think you can help my dog." She didn't want to admit she had no food, and she remembered he had not succeeded in keeping Hánas's mother from going onto the next world. He probably couldn't help Kulta.

"Look," Aiko said. "Let's have some mushrooms. Then we can become coyotes or ravens. We can fly, leap, or run. We can break the rules of the earthbound and have a good time."

He held her eyes with his as he spoke. Tuuli had trouble shifting her eyes from his. They gleamed; they invited her to forget her troubles and to have a bit of fun.

"No," she said. "I just need a drink. So does my dog. Let us get back to the river."

"Huh, the great noaidi-to-be is afraid," Aiko said, coming toward her.

That shocked Tuuli, but she tried not to let it show. How did he know about her? "Let me be," she said. "My dog needs me."

"Yes, you need to attend to your dog soon. I'll help you. Tell me, do you have a drum?"

"The strangers burned them." Tuuli hoped that he wouldn't realize she wasn't really answering his question.

Aiko eyed the rich blanket on the ground and the bundle she was standing away from. He watched to see where Tuuli's eyes went. Her hands still held something close under her coat, but her eyes only went to the dog and to the large robe.

Aiko thought to himself, *Ah, she still holds her hands to her coat; the thing she values most is what she hides there.*

"Tell you what," Aiko said, kicking the sleeping robe away. "I think you have something more valuable than this fur, as wonderful as it is. You are hiding something from me, and that is what I want."

A trickle of sweat rolled down Tuuli's side. She did not let herself shift her eyes to the bundle on the ground with the drum. She must fool the trickster at his own game.

"Please," she said. "I need to tend to my dog. Take the robe."

"I would rather have what is under your coat."

"There is nothing of value under my coat," Tuuli said. "Take the blanket and let me help my dog."

"No." The trickster was getting impatient with his own game. "Open your coat and let me see what is underneath."

Now Tuuli knew she was in control. "Make a choice," she said. "You can trade the dog for what is hidden under my coat, or this wonderfully warm and beautiful fur. But you cannot have both, and you cannot change your mind once you choose."

Aiko thought a moment. He was sure she had tucked something under her coat. He hadn't seen what, but it had to be more valuable than the fur on the ground. But what if he were wrong? He would be passing up the chance to own this warm robe.

Tuuli forced herself to be calm as she gazed at him. "Make up your mind," she said.

Aiko had a sly thought, another trick. "I want what's under your coat," he said.

"No," Tuuli said. "You must choose what I *hid* under my coat. I know your tricks. You would get all of me that is under my coat. Say the words right. You choose what I *hid* or the blanket you see before you."

"Oh, you're so smart," he said. "All right, I choose what you hid under your coat."

"Agreed. I will give it to you, but only when I am standing with my dog."

The trickster watched her carefully as she moved to the dog.

Without looking at her bundle, Tuuli moved to stand next to Kulta but between the bundle and the trickster. All the while, she held on to Poppi's walking stick in case she needed it to protect herself and Kulta. Then she pulled out Gabba's white pelt.

"Aha! *Vuoi, vuoi,* I knew it!" Aiko grinned with pleasure as Tuuli handed it to him. "A white fur! This is a good-luck omen. No wonder you did not want to give it to me. Now it's mine."

Tuuli played the role. She cast her eyes and head downward. She had wanted to keep the pelt from the little deer, but now she was glad the little skin did not show that Gabba had been lame-footed. The pelt did finally bring her good luck.

"Oh, the things that I can make of this." Aiko danced wildly. "I can make a hat. Or mittens. Or a shawl. I'll make something I can wear all the time, and good luck will follow me. I chose right. I knew it. I saw you hiding something."

"Good-bye," Tuuli said to Aiko. "Be on your way now and have safe journeys."

"Good-bye to you, too. I hope your dog lives. And be careful. You are destined for long journeys." With that, Aiko slung Gabba's fur around his shoulders, and he danced off into a thicket of rowan trees laden with red berries.

Tuuli quickly rolled her sleeping robe and tied the bundle to her back. She knelt next to Kulta and held her dog's head. Kulta's eyes were open, but no light reflected from them. Tuuli massaged her dog and sang a healing chant. Tears clouded her eyes when she saw a darkness hover over Kulta. Her beautiful red dog would soon die.

Kulta sighed deeply. Oh, how Tuuli wished to hear her howl and yodel again and to see her chase the Arctic hare and frolic with the reindeer. Tuuli lay next to her dog and nuzzled her ears and fur. "Do not die," she whispered into her ear. "I need you so I won't have to travel alone. I have a long way yet to go. I remember when you were born. It was during a time when the sun was still fighting with the dark. The snow lay deep. Your legs were so short you had to leap from one footstep of mine to the next. You followed me everywhere."

But the songs did not reach the ears of Tuuli's little red dog. Her heartbeat and breath faded slowly. Then she gave one last sigh and jerked as Jabemeahkka took the last light from her eyes and spun to the skies with it.

Cold as snow.
Cold as ice.
My heart grieves.
I am alone.

Nearby, Tuuli heard the outcast still dancing and singing joyfully. Tuuli cradled the body of her little dog. Then she faced the sky and sang the same death chant she had sung for her mother so long ago and for Poppi not so long ago.

While she was still crying and holding Kulta in her arms, she heard quick footsteps coming near. She quieted for a moment. Looking up, she saw the outcast, still dancing, wearing Gabba's white pelt wrapped around his narrow shoulders.

25

"IF YOU HAD A KIND BONE IN YOUR BODY, you would not be frolicking while I am sad," Tuuli said to the trickster as he approached. When he saw her holding the dog, that it had no light in its eyes, he sat and keened with her until her tears came no more.

Then he looked at Tuuli with seriousness this time, for the first time. "I'm sorry about your dog, but I came back because you must know—you are in danger."

"What do you mean?" She still held her dog close.

"There are those who would do you and your people harm. There is also one who seeks you, and there is one who awaits you."

"I already know those who would harm my people, but who is the one who seeks me?"

"Now I don't know, but I think he does not mean good for you. Perhaps he does not want you to return to your people."

"I am so sad now, and you bring me new worries. Yes, I am who you thought. My grandfather died just before the migration. I must return to my people to be the new noaidi, but there is so much more than knowing when to fly with the birds, when to swim with the fish, and when to hunt with the bear. Our people suffer, yours and mine. They have been starving for many winters. Strangers push into the grazing lands of the deer. They burn the forests and push the reindeer to harsher lands."

"Yes," said the outcast, "I've heard, but I stay far away from them. They go to the autumn gatherings and take the best skins of our deer and furs of our brothers—the beaver, fox, otter, ermine, and wolf. Others call us evil demons and insist we accept their ways. And yet they are the evil ones. They burn whole villages and torture people if they refuse to tell where the drums are."

"They told us the drums are used to talk to dark spirits. They ask our people to point out the wind listeners. They have so many ways to destroy us." Tuuli's tears rose as she thought of what had happened at their camp.

"I can help you protect yourself."

"How?" Tuuli still did not trust this man.

"I can help you learn how to change shape, to be one with the animal world."

"When I desperately needed help on my journey, I was able to do that."

"That's good; it shows you are sister to the animals. Now you need to learn how to change before dangers arrive."

"What can you do?"

"I can change from coyote to raven to bear and back whenever I want. At times I can even be a hare, but I don't want to often. But sometimes it is good to be a hare because everyone just ignores me and says, 'Look, there is a hare. It won't bother anyone.' Whereas when I am a coyote, bear, or a raven, everyone notices."

As much as she didn't want to be, Tuuli found herself comforted by Aiko and what he was telling her.

"You have long journeys ahead and not a lot of time. Which one do you want to learn to change into at will?" he asked her.

"I think the hare, because as you said, no one notices the hare."

"Except when they're hungry," he said, and they laughed together. "There are words that you must learn so you can join yourself with an animal, and there are potions that join you to the spirit world. I make them out of roots, leaves, and dried mushrooms. Here, come into the woods with me. I'll show you where to find the mushrooms and the roots. Then we'll go close to the river to find the leaves."

"First I have to cover my dog. When all warmth has left her body, I will burn her and swirl her ashes to the winds."

Tuuli and the outcast spent the day looking for the right roots and leaves and mushrooms. Some she already knew from Poppi, but Aiko taught her about many more. He told her the best way to dry them so she could always carry them with her and make the potion no matter the season. He told her the most secret words that she must say to exchange her being with that of Sister Hare. He also showed her the secrets of plants that could be used to heal broken bones, coughs, fevers, and ease difficult birthings.

Tuuli found it easy to learn from him. He explained simply and answered her questions patiently. He listened carefully as she repeated the songs and chants he taught her. Some she had already learned from Poppi, but now he told exactly how to combine the words of magic with the right potions.

"A birch basket is the best way to carry everything," he said as he dug some roots with a sharp stone. "Tie it to your belt and keep it with you always. You never know when you'll need what's in it. When it's time to make a potion, you make it faster in boiling water, but if you have to use cold from a river or a spring, you can do that, too, but it takes longer to steep the magic."

"How do I know I can trust you?" Tuuli asked, remembering how he'd tried to trick her.

"You know that I am cast out from my people. I've swallowed too many potions. I could have been a great noaidi as I have heard you show promise to be, but I misused my powers. I could listen to the wind, and I could hold the drum so softly and tenderly that all the tokens jumped and told me the secrets of the spirit world. I should have learned more healing chants, but I was impatient. And I liked tricks. I walked at the edge, and I veered from the circle. I fell from good."

"But why don't you use the powers you have left for good?"

"I try, but I am always tempted. Don't you ever feel that way? Haven't you come across temptations in your travels?"

"I came across you," Tuuli answered with a laugh. "You wanted me to eat the mushrooms that would put me in a trance. I was sad. I was tempted to forget my troubles, but one needs to be with someone she trusts when using the mushrooms."

The outcast laughed, too. "How wise you are. I like the mushrooms. Sometimes my powers are untrustworthy because when I need to think, I can't. But I would like to try. Give me your drum, and I'll see if I can still make it vibrate and tell me what I need to know."

"No. I need to remember you are a trickster and I can't trust you."

He dropped his head and then raised his eyes full onto Tuuli's. "On this you can. I know of the plight of your people—my people, too—even though I am no longer welcome at any of the campfires. The wind is telling me who you are. It also told me that you hid the Drum of the Four Winds from the strangers' fire. Now I know *you* tricked *me*. You got me to think the white pelt was the most important thing you have with you, but now I know it is the drum. I will not take it from you."

With that, the trickster sat and laughed. Then he added, "You are the only one I have been honest with for a long time, but you are right—don't trust me."

Tuuli sat and laughed with him. It felt good to have someone to talk to and relax with after so much time alone, with so much sadness.

"Where are you going?" she asked. "What do you do all alone? Don't you miss your people?"

His eyes glinted in the sunlight. He closed them, and after a long while, he sang.

I am alone.
Beavi spreads his rays day and night.
No home fire comforts me.
The goose tends her brood.
No one tends to me.

Mother fox watches as her kits,
Playful and curious, stray
Farther from their den.
Playful and curious.
No mother watches as I stray farther
From my people.
When I am tired and hungry
I scratch the thin soil of this earth.
I suck the dry rocks of this land.
I curl upon mosses and leaves.
In this wilderness of beauty
I am alone, but I live.

Tuuli had never heard such a beautiful joik. The outcast sang it from his heart with his eyes closed and his face to the sun. They both sat quietly when he finished. When he finally opened his eyes, he said, "I'm sorry I teased your dog and brought her death sooner than it should have been."

"I think there was no saving her," Tuuli said. "She was gravely hurt and dying. She was underwater for a long time before I was able to change into a salmon and push her to the surface."

"Have you met anyone else on your journey?"

"I met Bieg. That's when we almost starved and froze to death. Brother Bear came and killed the white fawn for me, so Kulta and I would have food to eat.

"Then I met Stallu. I almost lost my courage running from him. Mother Wind came and lifted me high out of his grasp. He fell down the mountain. I flew with the birds. High above the earth, I could see my past, present, and future. That gave me the spirit and courage to continue. But before Stallu chased me, he had wounded my pet deer Ruusu, so she died.

"And now I've met you. Each time I came by a challenge, one of my traveling companions died. Are you one of the monsters, one of the tests I must endure?"

"You have passed the test with me already. You have cunning and can detect cunning in others. This will serve you well when you meet with the strangers who seek to destroy all that you are and all our people have been."

"It seems like too much for me. I am but one person. Some of my people have already turned against the ways of our ancestors and are tending toward the new ways brought by the strangers."

"It is time for you to continue your journeys. Keep yourself safe. Remember that the waters are dangerous. Do not let them call your name."

"Aiko," she said, saying his name out loud for the first time, "if there's ever anything I can do for you . . ."

"I have no right to ask anything. You shouldn't even be talking to me or using my name."

"My name is Tuuli, and I thank you for everything."

"Tuuli. You have given me the gift of your name and of saying mine. Thank you. I must be on my way, and you on yours. Travel well on your many journeys."

"You've said that before. I have but one journey, and that is back to my people."

"Don't be so sure. And don't forget there is one who watches for you."

Tuuli found herself hoping to keep Aiko there a bit longer, so she asked, "What are your journeys?"

"Here, I am plagued with an endless journey. One with no home. Even though you have left the safety of your home fire, you have one to go back to. I do not. I am Aiko, the man without a home. But the wind has told me that a long journey I must take could change all that. I return to you the fawn's pelt. Take it."

"Why? Because you know now the fawn was lame and might be a bad omen?"

"No, because the wind is telling me to return it. I would just use it for my own pride."

"But some of my people will think it a bad omen."

"Then hide it as you did the drum. Charm it. Sing to it. You will see there is no harm in it."

"Can't you stay? Help me burn my dog?"

"No, I must go. My raven friend there at the top of that tree waits for me. Rest yourself. And I wish you well as you go back to your people."

"And you, too," she said as Aiko handed her the fawn's pure white pelt. She watched him weave his way along the rocky ground until he disappeared into the woods.

She packed Gabba's pelt with her drum. Crooning for Kulta, she spread the roots and herbs and mushrooms they'd picked on a rock to dry.

Tuuli spent the twilight time gathering dry wood. After piling it high, she layered pine branches that would burn hot over it. Striking her flint with her knife, she caught a flame on a curl of birchbark. With it, she lit the pyre. The dog's body still lay under the tree near the river. Tears rolled from her eyes as she held Kulta in her arms until the fire burned hot. She crooned songs of mourning as she placed her beautiful and faithful dog on the fire. Tuuli couldn't watch as the body of her dog caught flame and smoldered, so she lifted her face to the sky. Her heart ached as she remembered the soft licks Kulta had given to wake her each morning. Her silent tears turned to open sobs.

She tended the fire, adding wood through the lowering of the sun. She stayed awake as it slid below the horizon. When it started to strengthen again, she let the fire die. When it cooled, she picked rocks from the riverbank, piled them on the remains of her beloved pet, and circled the spot with three stone rings.

In the winter when the dark was deep, she could see a myriad of stars, but now in the season of long days, she could barely make out the brightest, the one constant star of the north. Oh, how her heart ached. She missed her people and her dog. Strangely, she missed Aiko, too, and her heart beat hollow when she thought of Poppi.

With tears still spilling from her eyes, she fished nearby. She caught four graylings. When the sun was high enough to peek above the trees, Tuuli journeyed again.

She traveled swiftly, stopping only to pick berries and to dig for roots to chew. She found springs to drink from and soft mosses to rest upon.

As the sun lowered, she spread her sleeping robe on the duff under a leafy tree. The wind blew.

She sang.

I am so alone.
I'm alone when night comes on,
And alone I'll still be
When the sky lightens with the morning sun.

But then she remembered the words of Aiko. *There is also one who seeks you, and there is one who awaits you.* Chills ran through her body.

26

Nervous as she was, Tuuli stayed awake watching for shadows that moved, even slightly. None did. The shadows she studied so carefully soon mesmerized her, and she slept.

Dreams of dread and deep disturbance came to her. Some were the same ones as she'd had long ago during the late storm when the strangers came. First was the dream of the red squirrels and foxes all running to the flooded river. Then, the dream of hordes of mosquitoes—buzzing, persistent, and causing her people anguish. In the third dream, a wily gray wolf and a beautiful white wolf found a newborn fawn in a rocky field. Together they cared for it until it could care for itself.

A sound—a snap—awoke her. She listened. Only silence. Nothing moved. While awake, she started thinking what each dream possibly meant. Kulta was red like the foxes and squirrels. Had that dream foretold her red-furred dog would get caught up in the river currents and die? If so, she had not taken the warning and been careful enough.

She thought about the persistent mosquitoes that were impossible to get rid of. They were like the strangers. Strangers came and buzzed about the new ways and would not leave. If she swatted one, there were still many more. The dream did not portend well, because just as there was no way to quell the mosquitoes, there seemed to be no way to keep the strangers away. And the two wolves and fawn? What did that dream mean?

Snap! And *snap* again! Tuuli sat up. Her heart raced. The hair on her arms and back of her neck stood on end. She felt chilled to the bone even though it was a mild night and she was wrapped in a warm robe. She shook herself. Was she dreaming?

"Trickster!" she called out.

Frightened as she was, she'd be relieved if Aiko came out of hiding, laughing. "Come out from wherever you are," she called, wishing for him to dance from behind a tree. No one answered.

Who was causing her trouble? Even though she hoped it was Aiko, she could think of no reason he would do it. Could it be the person he'd said was looking for her? Or was it Stallu? Tuuli's heart pounded in her chest. Her ears pricked at any sound, and her breath came so fast that she felt dizzy. She crept in each direction looking for signs of someone who might be nearby.

Looking every which way and jumping at every little noise, she returned to camp to pack. She searched for the things she'd left at the foot of the tree. Her fishing net was missing! All the herbs, mushrooms, and roots she and Aiko had picked were gone. Frightened and angry, she started to panic. Breathing deeply and slowly, she forced herself to calm. *Think.* She'd miss the net but could sharpen sticks to spear fish. Ripe berries were plentiful. She felt her side. Her pouch with the flint and knife was still there. She'd slept with the pouch tied to her waist just as she carried it during the day. She felt under her sleeping robe and was relieved to find Poppi's drum and walking stick.

If Aiko had played this trick, he would have taken the drum or the good robe, but not the mushrooms, seeds, leaves, and roots, because he had plenty of those himself and knew where to find all he wanted. Who could it be?

Tuuli packed all her belongings and climbed one of the stunted trees along the river. From there, she could see if anyone approached. For the remainder of the short night, she clung to the tree. When Beavi started to rise, its rays shone brightly. Tuuli began to relax in the light and warmth. She climbed down and planned to travel quickly that day.

When Aiko told her there was someone waiting for her, was it his way to worry her and to make her wonder who was playing tricks? Were they just tricks, or were they meant to harm?

Could it be Utsí who was waiting for her? Or was it Hánas? They both wanted to run the bride's race with her, but she'd refused. Maybe Hánas wanted to ensure she didn't return to be a noaidi for her people. She might be powerful enough to stop the message he and the strangers brought. Or he might want her to return so he could convince her to give up her old ways and accept the new. Maybe he wanted the drum to give to his fellow travelers. Tuuli couldn't believe he would be forceful in any way, but then he had been with the strangers for a long time and might have changed.

If they met again, she would tell him of her travels and of losing each deer and finally her dog. Tuuli surprised herself. As she was thinking of the things she would tell Hánas, she found herself feeling the same fondness she had before he went away. She gritted her teeth and reminded herself that it was he who led the strangers into their encampment.

27

THERE WAS NO TRAIL ALONG THE RIVER, and the bank was rocky and slippery, so Tuuli moved to the woodlands next to the river. There she walked quickly and ran from time to time when there were no rocks to trip over. Close to reuniting with her people at the gathering, Tuuli began to anticipate joining the festivities.

She'd delight in watching children play games and race. She'd listen to older children gossip and giggle and catch up on what had happened in other clans since they'd last been together. Just as had happened every year, boys would eye girls, and the girls would pretend not to notice, but they would all be wondering—one year, two years—when would he or she be racing? They tested and teased each other—holding their eyes steadily on another's. And the young people who were ready to race would decide if this were the year they'd run for sure. Families worried about letting their daughters go. Other families encouraged their sons to race and pointed out which young woman they thought he should seek for a wife. Healthy and good strong workers were qualities they looked for.

Tuuli picked ripe berries she found along the way. When the sun was low, she stopped, afraid she would stumble and get hurt if she went on. She circled back to where she'd already been to see if there were signs of anyone following her. She found no footprints on the soft banks. She saw no broken ferns, no snapped twigs, and no rocks kicked out of place in the woods. Tuuli bent her knees to the ground, and spread her hands on the earth, fingers wide apart. She breathed deeply, raised her head to the sky, and spread her arms wide to receive the winds. Gentle brushes of the breeze fell on her cheeks and whispered into her ears.

Your journey is not over.
There is much for you to do before you are joined
with that person with whom you will lie down at night
and rise with in the morning.

The message disconcerted Tuuli. It told her nothing about who might be watching or waiting for her or what dangers she might come across in this wild land. Aiko had already told her she would be making many journeys. Now the wind did, too. Were they the journeys she would be taking into this land again with more ashes of her people? That she would not have a husband for a long time was new. It relieved her to know Utsí would not be catching her for his bride this autumn.

Tuuli gathered many branches and twigs so she could keep a fire going through the night. She would not sleep. Then she piled small rocks into the flames. Hot, they could be used as weapons. Then she cut pieces from Ruusu's hide to make a sling. She, Siru, Hánas, and other children used to practice with slings, trying to take down a hare or a willow grouse. Sometimes they were successful, and to the delight of their mother and father, they proudly carried them back to camp to be roasted.

The tasks kept her mind occupied. Fire going, she ate the last of her fish and berries. She sang thanks to the day and praises to all of nature, especially to the earth and waters that had provided her meal.

The moon was up, a squashed-looking moon that was on its way to become fully round. The moon always fascinated Tuuli. Why the moon shone cold, and the sun shone hot. Yet the moon seemed to have a friendly face, and Tuuli couldn't look into the face of the sun without hurting her eyes and seeing red and blind spots for a long time after. Beavi was the sun, the father of all that was on earth, yet she could not look into his face without burning her eyes. She wondered why its heat could be so needed yet be so cruel.

Why was the moon usually silver and the sun gold? She had been born when the moon was gold and the sun was silver. That had been unnatural. Poppi said it was one of the signs that she would become a noaidi with many skills.

She also wondered about Mother Wind, who spoke to her and whispered and comforted her and sang in the trees, yet could whip up a fury and cause damage and great coldness. And Brother Bear, who'd taken such good care of her during the storm Bieg had punished her with, could also be an angry bear.

Moreover, the strangers who promised good were bad to her people. What good could come from such evil? She pondered the contrasting nature of these things while she worked on her sling, cutting and forming the pieces of hide that would hold hot rocks. It was then, when she was most relaxed and deepest in her thoughts, that she heard steps in the forest and felt slight vibrations of the earth beneath her. Someone or something was coming.

She reached for her knife with one hand and for her sling with the other.

Darkness came over Tuuli. She screamed. She kicked! She felt something pulled over her head and shoulders. Before she could reach to pull it off, someone grasped her hands together in a tight grip. Tuuli squirmed to be free, but strong arms held her tightly. She kicked and screamed, "Let me go!"

Then she felt the jolt of a strong push. Losing her balance, she landed headfirst in the cold rushing river waters that swirled, pulling her under. Forcing herself to the surface, Tuuli tugged the cover off her head and took a deep breath before the rushing waters pulled her under again. Her hands tingled with the cold. She kicked hard to surface. Her foot struck a submerged boulder. Pain shot up her leg. She stroked hard as she drew her knees to her chest. Her arms already prickled from the cold. Getting her head above water, she gasped for air.

Tuuli paddled as hard as she could. She needed to get out of the deadly cold water before her hands and legs became completely numb. She remembered what happened to her mother. And Kulta.

Through her strands of wet hair, Tuuli saw a fallen tree sticking out into the water ahead of her. Her hands already prickled. As the swift waters sped her to the tree, she grabbed at one of the branches. It broke. In desperation, she reached for another. Her hands were stiff. Tuuli couldn't feel if she had a good hold. Already shivering, she searched for the riverbed with her feet and felt a rock. Balancing on it, she heaved herself onto the tree trunk. Sharp branches jabbed her. Blood ran down her face and into her eyes. There was no time to examine her wounds; she crawled along the trunk toward shore. With each movement, more branches raked her. She felt the pain of every scratch and cut.

Coughing and shivering, Tuuli used all her strength to roll onto the rocky bank. Even though every breath was painful, she immediately looked around to see if her attacker was nearby. The current had swept her far downriver, so no one on foot could have kept up with her. She was safe for the moment, but she needed a fire to warm by. She felt for her knife. It was gone. And her pouch, too. To make things worse, her drum was far upstream with her rowan stick. She had nothing but the soaking wet clothes she wore.

Poking among rocks on the riverbank, Tuuli looked for another flint. There were many rocks, but it was too dark to pick out one that would spark a fire. For now, she just needed to get warm.

With her hands, Tuuli beat her arms, legs, and body to warm up. She stomped her feet and walked in a circle, looking constantly for whomever had tossed her into the river. Her feet were almost without feeling, and her hands felt like rocks at the end of her arms, so she kept rubbing her arms and legs.

She needed to get to her campsite. Maybe her little fire was still going. Nervous about running into her attacker, yet needing to get warm, Tuuli headed upstream. *Keep moving*, she told herself. Tuuli walked as quickly as she could, but her legs felt like logs. She stumbled. She was getting colder. She nodded. She felt drowsy, but she could not give in to sleep. She had to keep going. Vaguely, she noticed she was getting farther and farther from the river. She no longer heard the rushing waters. She turned to go back, but had no idea which way to go. Lost, she feared she could wander for a very long time and not find her way. Tuuli wished for the sun so she could warm herself, but the sky was still dark. She looked to the pale moon, but it didn't tell her which way to go.

Walking in a circle
Getting colder, colder
Walking farther, farther
From the river
Far from her campfire.

Getting colder, colder
Bleeding
Wounded
Stumbling
Needing rest
Wanting sleep.

Numbness now owned her body. Tuuli struggled to keep walking. "I must stop to rest," she said aloud to the trees. Another part of her brain said, *No, keep going. Move to keep warm.*

Tuuli jolted awake when she stumbled. She fell and tried to catch herself. Her wrist jammed against a rock. A sharp pain roused her. Her thoughts were muddled. She wanted warmth. She turned in circles. Looking. Listening. The wind was silent. Grief overcame her, and she cried out for her deer and Kulta. How had it all come to this? She had come so far, and now that she was close to returning to her people, she might not make it.

Sleep, sleep, sleep was all Tuuli could think of. If only she could curl up right there on the ground and just sleep. Then she would be warm and safe. Yes, then she would be warm and safe. And everything would be all right. Deep down, she knew she shouldn't. She would not be all right if she went to sleep. Ahead, she saw Brother Bear. Was he coming to warm her? She lumbered toward him. She stumbled right into him. Not soft and warm. Hard and cold. A boulder? How had he changed to stone? She shook and tried to see clearly. Bear? Rock? Warm fur? Cold stone?

Her knees gave out, and she slowly dropped to the ground, gave herself to the mossy earth, and then felt herself rise and float. Feeling warm at last, she welcomed rest, welcomed sleep. She saw herself soaring with eagles, swimming with salmon, holding her arms out to the wind, and frolicking with the bear. Kulta yipped and played. They ran together laughing and playing chase.

Poppi was young again. His eyes were clear. He held Tuuli on his knee and sang songs of the sun, of the moon, of the sacred rowan tree, and the reindeer that were their life. She patted his whiskers. His eyes twinkled as he held her close. She was warm in his arms. Her mother, too, came and held her in a tight embrace, breathing endearing words into her ear. Brushing hair from her eyes, her mother held her as they watched flames of a warming campfire leap into the air on a dusky night. Oh, she was so warm.

And Hánas was there. It was a gathering. The leaves were turning. Yellows, oranges, and red—just like flames of fire. Many siides gathered around a hot, blazing campfire to eat and tell stories. She and Hánas played hand-clapping games. She liked the touch of his warm hands against hers. And then they played tag with Siru and Utsí. They ran until they were tired, happy, and sweaty warm.

Her mother took her into a goahti heated by a great birch fire. She threw water onto heated rocks. The goahti filled with steam. Oh, Tuuli was warm, so warm. Her mother washed her hair, her feet, and back. With gentle fingers, her mother combed fat from the salmon to untangle Tuuli's hair. They sang songs about birds that came in the spring and the same birds that left in the autumn. And then mother and daughter wrapped themselves in robes of fur and went out into the starry night to watch colorful lights dance and flash and play across the sky. Warm and pink, they went to their own goahti and crawled beneath cozy furs to sleep.

Nothing hurt anymore. Not the cuts on her face. Not the bruises on her leg. Not her sprained wrist. And the deer and Kulta were there with her. Nudging her. Nestling close to her. She was so happy. Nothing could be better. She was warm, so warm.

Then sounds came to her from far away, like thunder before a summer storm reached their camp—distant, yet persistent.

And they got louder and louder.
And the sounds did get louder.
And the thundering shook her.
She tried to turn away.
She wanted to sleep.
To stay wrapped in warmth
with her deer, Kulta, Poppi, and her mother by her side.
All snuggling and warming her.

But then her mother, Poppi, Kulta, and the deer all turned and moved away. "Don't go!" she cried, reaching for them. The warmth she'd felt was being taken away.

"We must," her mother said. "We are from the other world now, but you must stay."

A sob caught in Tuuli's throat. "No! I want to go with you."

Her mother and Poppi and her little dog joined a long line of people who appeared in a glowing light that was as blue as the waters. They surrounded her, smiling and telling her that someday she would join them, but for now she was still of the earth. The long line passed by; they were the ancients, the people from whom she'd sprung. Even as she stretched her arms to them, wanting to become part of their glowing warmth. Soon they faded to shadows and disappeared.

"Wait. Wait for me." Tuuli sobbed and then slept.

28

A CHILL STABBED THE AIR. The nights were now as long as the days. Many siides, those of Many Rowans, Lake of Owls, Bending Birch, Hawk Hill, and others, gathered at the circle of rocks that marked a sacred spring. Clear waters bubbled up from the ground and flowed over mossy rocks toward the river. Beavi shone upon the spring, sparkling its waters so brightly that everyone shielded his or her eyes as they bent to drink. The sweet waters were a gift from the earth to the people and the animals that lived upon it.

The soft orange autumn moon grew larger each night. Soon, when it reached its fullness, the Saami of all the gathered siides would celebrate. Siru jumped up whenever a new clan arrived. After greeting them, she asked if anyone had seen Tuuli. She missed her friend even though they'd disagreed about the strangers and their ways. She hoped Tuuli was safe, and each day of the gathering she'd waited for her arrival. She had so much to tell her.

Two days before the celebrations, another group entered the central campfire area.

"Bures, bures." Everyone greeted the newcomers. Siru was disappointed when she recognized them as the Falling Water siide. They wouldn't have come from the direction Tuuli had to travel. A young man from their group came and sat by her.

"Bures," he said, looking at his feet. "I'm Kyllo. I remember you from last gathering and the one before that."

Siru warmed as blood rushed to her face. She remembered Kyllo, too. He was always polite, full of fun when games were played. He was shy, seldom speaking, but helpful to anyone no matter which siide needed an extra hand.

"I'm Siru," she said, looking down, but before she could say anything else, her mother called her to help stir a pot of stew. Her lame arm flopped to her side as she rose to do as her mother wished.

Her father and others invited Kyllo's siide to settle on logs around the fire. They passed around a basket of smoked fish and talked with old friends. Each recalled stories of gatherings during their younger years—when their faces didn't wrinkle so and when they had more teeth in their mouths. During the day, old and young netted salmon, graylings, and other fish in the cold river. Dogs chased with the children. Big brothers and sisters hoisted little ones onto pet reindeer for rides. Everyone collected wood to build big bonfires that crackled with licking flames.

The rich aroma of roasting venison ribs and fish filled the chilly air; the herders' mouths watered as they tended the grazing reindeer. After stirring the stew, Siru mixed a dough and set it on flat stones to bake. Siru's mother sat with her own mother. Everyone gossiped, glad to see the families from whom they'd moved away after they were caught during the courtship races. New babies cooed as they were admired and passed from lap to lap. Names were suggested to women who would soon give birth. "How about Ággí? Or Gájtu? I like Mokci. Ulmmá if it's a girl. Darbmu is a good name."

When Siru's mother and father found they were camped close to the clan to which Hánas had been born, they told of his coming with the strangers and translating for them. They told how Tuuli had called him *Broken Branch*. Hánas's people were glad to hear he was well but sad that his mother, who they'd always liked for her cheerful voice and good humor, had died. "How," they asked each other, "could Hánas so easily give up the ways and beliefs of his people and betray them by leading cruel strangers?"

Word traveled fast among the clans that Tuuli had taken the ashes of Poppi and her mother to the Mount of Four Winds. Traveling with her were Kulta and her pet deer. Many whispered and wondered, "Did she hide the Drum of the Four Winds to save it from the fires?"

After the full-moon day of celebration, there would be only a day or two of rest and of packing and saying good-bye to their friends and relatives gathered there. They would then all go in their separate directions to winter encampments. They would not see each other through the dark season, the melting season, and the long daylight time. Only when the leaves turned colors and began to fall would they meet again. Siru shivered when she heard her father say it was already cold enough at night that the snows might come at any time and that the deer would start their migration to winter grounds within a few days. She hoped Tuuli would be back by then.

Noaidis from every siide huddled together to talk. They worried about the dwindling reindeer herds and the hunger all clans had suffered during the past cold, dark time. They compared what chants and joiks they had sung to turn back the hunger and to strengthen their herds. They worried that too many of their people no longer believed their noaidis could save them and found the strangers' promises to be comforting. Not one had an old drum, but some had secretly made new ones to replace those burned.

Then they talked about the youngsters they'd been training. Four had reached the age of testing. They were sorry Jabemeahkka had taken Poppi to the next world. He had been the oldest among them for many gatherings. They raised their voices as one, chanting an ancient song of grieving, asking the spirit of Poppi to be with them.

Tax collectors from the south had already intruded upon the gathering to demand payments. They claimed the land belonged to their king. The clans argued the land belonged to the deer. The tax collectors just laughed and took the best skins, furs, and meat. Then traders came from all directions to swap their goods for what was left of the furs from ermine, fox, and wolves. They brought goods with them from the big cities to the south. Cities with strange names like Stockholm. And Turku. They brought stories of faraway life. They told of kings with castles, churches with spires that reached to the skies. And of universities where students read books and listened to learned men talk of mathematics, the stars and skies, and travels across a big water to the other side of the world. Their voices boomed in the star-studded nights, disturbing the sleep of the Saami who spoke softly so as to be one with the quiet trees, stars, and moon around them.

The traders spread their pots and pans on the ground. "Better than birchbark baskets," they said. And they showed lengths of cloth woven of fine threads, threads finer than the finest sinew of the tiniest deer. Woven, the threads made a thin, flexible cloth that could be sewn into any kind of clothing. Hats, gloves, coats, tunics, dresses, skirts, shirts. Siru touched the clothing that dazzled with many colors. The Saami used juices from berries, red and blue; of roots and leaves for yellows and greens, and of the earth itself for rich browns to make soft colors to dye the skins they wore for clothing. These contrasted with the clothing the traders brought—woven wools and cottons, bright and vivid. The traders scoffed at the skin and fur clothing the clans wore. "Just feel how nice this cloth is," they offered when trading.

Some Saami, attracted by the bright colors, traded beautiful ermine and fox furs for a woven shirt, hat or scarf, but many others questioned, "How could the thin materials keep one as warm as our clothing?" The skins and furs were from their deer, the fox, otter, and wolf—all brothers of the earth. They draped and hugged the body of the wearer. The woven clothes of the strangers let the wind blow right through and would wear thin and ragged quickly.

The women, as well as the men, fingered metal pots and pans. Their smooth, hard bottom and sides made them a tempting trade. The sewing needles were finer than those they themselves made of bone, so some women traded smoked fish or a fur robe for a needle.

And the traders brought exotic foods. Finely ground flours made of rye and barley. Many traded their best skins for them, but few traded for molasses because it was too strong and not as sweet as the honey they found in wild beehives.

After the first flurry of trading was done, the traders brought out clay crocks of fermented grains. Rye brew and barley brew. They'd laugh as they traded with the men. "Ground rye for your woman to make bread. Brewed rye for you. It will make you laugh and sing. Warm you up. Forget your worries."

The traders didn't bother to learn the names of the people, but they pretended friendship and made up names for the Saami—Long Chin, Four Fingers, Broken Tooth, Droopy Eye, Ragged Coat. They called them by those names, clapped them on the back, and poured full cups of brew around the campfire in the evenings. When the men were reeling with strong drink, the traders started more dealings. Some, eager to have the throat-warming drink for the long, cold winter ahead, accepted the trade without thinking they gave too many skins for so little liquor. The traders winked at one another. Siru's mother whispered for her to notice how the traders poured an even larger portion for a man who was reluctant to trade, hoping to get his thinking so crooked they'd be able to get many furs for just a little mind-blurring drink.

They also told of their king. His fancy clothes and crowns. His castle. His silver chair. How he traveled with matching horses pulling his carriage of gold. The people listened, not believing, thinking these were just good stories. "You don't believe your ears?" the strangers asked. They directed their words to girls budding into womanhood. "Then come with us," they invited. "Come, see with your own eyes."

"And you," they'd point to the young men. "Come and be a soldier. There are big wars for you to test your strength and become a hero. Girls like soldiers and heroes."

Though the strangers caused much disruption among the clans, the people put away their differences to enjoy dancing, singing, and stirring of great stews of roast rabbits, grouse, and fish. Food was the center of the gatherings. When there was plenty, everyone felt good and happy. It was easy to ignore the dark shadows when their stomachs were full. Still, as much food as was eaten, much more was smoked, dried, and put into baskets for the winter, the same as they had done all summer.

While others sang and told stories, Utsí chewed his nails and drummed his fingers on his knee. He got up often, taking one trail or another out of the encampment. Sometimes he returned a short time later; sometimes he was gone for a long time. When Utsí left on his jaunts, Siru waited a short distance up the trail he'd taken. If he saw her, he'd say, "Go back. Do not wait for me." Siru felt confused and wondered why he left so often.

Some others noticed Utsí's behavior, too. "What are you looking for? Or is it *who* are you looking for?" a herder ribbed him.

Another took up the joshing. "Are you finally going to run this year and catch a wife? Or are you afraid they'll all get away from you?"

Even his father joined in. "You're old enough. You should have run last year already. Look at all the beautiful women here to choose from. Or do you want me to choose for you?"

Utsí looked at Siru, then stood and walked away from the camp. She followed. "This is the year we're going to run, aren't we?" she asked.

He looked down and then straightened up. "I'm leaving with the strangers when the gathering is over. They've promised to make me an important man. More important than any noaidi."

"That's good. I'm glad for you," said Siru. "Let's run the race first. Then I can go with you as your wife."

"No, Siru. That's not possible. The strangers don't want you. It's your arm. Your worthless arm. They say that it's a sign of wickedness living within you. Your arm is a bad omen."

Siru's throat filled with a lump that pushed upward, threatening to take her breath away. She couldn't talk. She couldn't even cry. Utsí's words stung. Never had anyone said anything bad about her arm. Utsí couldn't mean what he said. She held her good arm out to him. He shook his head and spun away, leaving her alone, aching for the cruel words to be gone from her ears. Her tears flowed. They flooded her cheeks and fell to the ground. They sprinkled onto the green mosses. Beavi shone upon them, making sparkles of light. Siru moaned at the beauty of her tears. Finally finding her voice, she sang, hoping to mend the deep rip in her soul.

Even now at midday,
Even with Beavi's rays
Shining warmly,
I am cold and torn.
Gloomy specters dance
As purple shadows follow.
I am cold and torn
Even now with Beavi's rays
Shining warmly.
Even now at midday.
I am cold and torn.

When the gathering was near end, many openly worried about Tuuli. If she didn't return, the Many Rowan siide would be without a noaidi and protection of the drum. If there wasn't one in their siide, and another clan had two or three, they could agree to invite one to come with them. But they wouldn't want to do that. It was the pride of each clan that they were able to have one of their own.

Tuuli was the right age and was born marked to be a noaidi. Many had watched as she bent an ear to the wind, even though she seemed reluctant to tell what she heard. She had sat by Poppi's knees as he talked to the drum, listening, watching, and learning. Everyone hoped she would return soon.

Many whispered from ear to ear, "I hope Tuuli has the Drum of the Four Winds. The strangers searched all bundles looking to see if they could find any still hidden. They didn't find any. We told them all had been burned."

As at every gathering, a story was told, as a warning to all who listened, the story of a young man from the clan of Deep River. His skills were great even before he reached full height. His noaidi teacher had pushed him and taught him at a rapid pace, but the young man misused his knowledge and powers. He played tricks. He sought to gain furs and food he didn't work for. He danced and laughed when he should have been comforting and healing others. Finally, he had been stripped of the name *noaidi* and expelled as an outcast, a trickster. News still reached his people from time to time that some traveler or small clan had seen him and had traveled with him or had sheltered him briefly during a bad spell.

Some said he traveled without companion of any kind, human or animal, and that he carried little on his back. Still others were sure he led a pack of wolves wherever he went. Some said he survived on food a pet raven brought him. Another said they'd seen an eagle drop a fish for him. Some even said they heard music whirling in the air around him when they crossed paths with him in the wilds of their land.

"Tuuli will be as powerful as he would have been, and she doesn't misuse her skills," one of the noaidis said, careful not to say the outcast's name. Everyone nodded and then sang a joik that would bring Tuuli safely back from her journey.

Always on the mind of the people were the strangers. There were several at the gathering already. Some people enjoyed the stories the strangers told about a new god, but many turned away from all such meetings. Some plotted to chase them out of the encampment. Others wanted to hear more of their promises for a better life.

The day the moon shone its fullest would be the day the noaidis tested each who hoped to become one of them. And it would be the day of the courtship races. Of reindeer races. And a day of singing and dancing. Siru had always liked the big bonfire that was set to burn until late into the night. And, of course, she, like everyone, looked forward to a feast of fish, venison, grouse, rye breads, stews, and cranberries.

➤➤➤❮❮❮

That night, the men who were still awake drinking the traders' liquor were interrupted by a strange group entering the encampment. In the light of the perfectly round moon, they saw an elongated shadow outlined by the dying flames of the evening campfire. As the group approached, the shadow divided to show two men carrying something between them. When they got closer, it could be seen that one was a man with a beard and hair hanging long from beneath his hat. The other man wore the woven clothes of a stranger and carried a large pack on his back. The two carried a third person on a sling made of saplings, birchbark, and deerskin. That person was wrapped tightly in a fur robe from head to toe.

"Help! Help!" one called out.

The men drinking around the campfire stood. Many others roused themselves from their sleep to see what was happening.

"We need a healer," said the one who wore the clothing of a stranger. "We have Tuuli. Is this her siide? Are you her people?"

"Our Tuuli? Poppi's Tuuli?"

"Yes, that Tuuli. She needs a healer right away. She sleeps the sleep of one lingering between the worlds. She has welted bruises everywhere."

"Come, come," said Siru's mother. "Bring her here."

As Siru and her mother made a pallet for Tuuli by the fire, Siru's father went to waken the noaidi from the Lake of Many Grasses clan, who was the best healer. Everyone was up now, their sleep disturbed. Some fed the campfire again and stoked its flames to new life. Many recognized Hánas. His clan welcomed him. They eagerly asked many questions, but he was busy dabbing honey on Tuuli's lips, so he didn't answer.

"Where is Kulta?" asked Siru.

"Kulta died, as well as her deer. Tuuli is alone," offered the narrow-shouldered man. His floppy hat made it impossible to see his face in the sputtering fire. Deep shadows of the night hid him even though the moon shone brightly. No one asked his name, and he did not offer it.

Some people looked questioningly at Hánas and nodded to the man, but he pretended not to understand and didn't speak any name for him, either.

"When I first came upon her at Bear Rock, her clothes were soaking wet," explained Hánas. "Strange words spun into the air from her breath. I couldn't understand or rouse her. She was cold as death. I was wrapping my coat around her when this kind traveler arrived. He had found her belongings on the riverbank and was looking for her to return them. He made potions to warm her inside and wrapped her in a fur robe to warm her outside. Then we carried her here. That's all I know. She still sleeps too deeply, and her breaths are too shallow. I'm afraid her spirit is wandering far from her body."

x

29

A BREEZE SWIRLED ABOUT TUULI'S HEAD, sweeping across her brow. Soothing her cheeks.

Awaken, Daughter of the Wind.
Awaken, Sister of the Bear.
Awaken, Child of the Sun.

Tuuli floated in the thin air above the ground. Through beams of moonlight, she saw a noaidi bending over a sleeping person who lay on a birch frame built above stones heated in a fire. The noaidi threw his head back. His lips parted in silent chants. He brought his mouth close to the person's nose and blew nine breaths. Then he clapped two stones nine times. He passed a rowan branch over her nine times. From a woven birch basket, the healer scooped his hands full of water and sprinkled the rocks hot from fire. Steam rose and enveloped the deathly still person. Wondering why she didn't hear the familiar spitting and sizzling of water splashing on hot rocks, Tuuli floated closer to watch. It was then she saw it was herself that the noaidi attended. How could she be there—wrapped in warm furs—and here—watching?

Her fragile being trembled above her earthly body. She looked to the dark skies around the moon. There she saw the hazy outlines of her mother and of Poppi waft and change into cloudy shapes that gradually disappeared among the stars. She looked down again upon herself. Then she looked to where she'd seen her mother and Poppi, hoping they would call to her so she could follow them, but they were gone. She felt an earthly tug. Softly, she floated downward and let her life spirit slip into her own body.

Then Tuuli felt a soft quivering at her side. With one hand, she searched for what it was. Her drum, still tucked into its deerskin pouch, beat steadily at her touch. The healer nodded, but continued his chanting.

The Drum of the Four Winds. It is here, by me, but where am I? Am I back at the winter camp, or am I at the autumn gathering? Tuuli pulled the drum to her chest and listened. It beat stronger and stronger, encouraging her heart. Little by little, she roused herself and remembered being very cold and then very warm. She remembered wild dreams and great frights. And Hánas holding her hand, touching her forehead, wrapping her in his coat, and singing for her to live. After that, she remembered nothing.

Warm and safe with the healer at her side, Tuuli snuggled deeply into her robes, and she fell asleep again. When she awoke, the wind blew on her face, stirring her eyelashes. It gently whooshed across her face and swirled into her ears.

"What is it, Wind?" she asked.

Rest now.
Your journey is not over.
You will go away from your people.

You will never be alone.
Where you go, I will go.
The Northern Star will follow you;

As will the Great Bear in the night,
and the sun, the moon,
and your family to the eighteenth generation.
In your flesh, your bones, and your blood.
All will be with you.

"Why is my journey not yet over? Where must I go?"

Swoosh. The wind softened and swirled but spoke no more. Tuuli sat up. She shook her head. Her tousled hair fell into her eyes. She did not want to journey more. She was home now, with her people. With the drum, she could call upon the spirits of the other world to help her, and the wind would whisper warnings. She needed both to strengthen the will in her people to fight the strangers and to follow the ancient way. Though weak and tired, she fought to stay awake, but as if webs sealed her eyes, they closed, and she fell asleep again.

Never could she have imagined the dream that sleep brought her. She was tethered to a tall animal the strangers with white hair and silver beards called a horse. It was as tall as if one reindeer stood on the back of another. She held on tightly, frightened to be astride, riding along with nine men on nine horses. The men wore woven clothes and carried strange sticks. Their voices were loud; their words sharp. "We're taking you to see the king," they said. "He wants to test the magical powers you are said to possess."

Tuuli awoke shaking and sweating. Test? What king and what kind of test would he give her? She only wanted the test from the noaidis to prove she was prepared to lead her people. She would tell them of how she'd flown with the eagles, of how she changed into a bear and a salmon, and of listening to the wind. And she had the Drum of the Four Winds. Her life was with her people. Poppi and Aiko had taught her many secret words of healing, but she would have to learn more.

Little by little, Beavi's thin rays chased away the dark. People stirred. It was the day all the Saami had waited for, the best day of the gathering.

Siru and her parents got up but told Tuuli to rest more. She sank into her furs, resisting sleep, not wanting the dreams to return. But she did fall asleep, and more dreams floated to her.

This time, Tuuli was on a great boat that swayed in a big lake of never-ending waters. The boat was many times larger than the skin boats her people made. The traders had bragged about huge boats that sailed on salty waters many times bigger than any of their lakes. They bragged the waters were wider than any Saami river was long. Tuuli couldn't even imagine that much water. In her dream, the boat was so big, if she counted the people on it, she would have to count her toes and fingers at least five times.

They were on a journey, she was told, which would last two cycles of the full moon. "And where," she asked, "are you taking me?"

"To the other side of the world," they answered.

"Am I dead that I'm going to the other side of the world?" Tuuli asked.

They laughed. "No, you're not dead. Just on a voyage."

"Time to eat." Siru shook Tuuli awake. She stroked Tuuli's hair. "Every day, I worried about you alone out there in the far lands. Here. Eat." With her good hand, she held a wooden bowl of salmon stew.

Tuuli roused herself and took the bowl. The steamy aroma filled the air; she hungrily scooped a bite.

"You don't look well, and you've been muttering strange words," Siru said. "Are you badly hurt?"

"I had many dreams last night," Tuuli said.

"What were they?"

"Kah! Nothing but a lot of mixed-up things." She didn't know what to think about her dreams and didn't want to tell them. Even though Siru had always been clever about figuring out what dreams meant, Tuuli didn't want any help now. Besides her dreams, Aiko and the wind had both told her of a journey, but she was not going to leave. She would stay to fight the strangers' message.

Siru took a bite of her own stew. "When you listen to the wind, what does it tell you? When you tap the drum, what does it say? Can you foretell what will be?" she asked.

"Not so many questions at a time." Tuuli sucked on a fish bone. It was soft, so she chewed and swallowed it. "Your mother knows what happened on the day I was born. She will remember how I was marked to be a noaidi."

Siru put her bowl down. "Utsí has always wanted to be a noaidi, but the wind never told him anything. He thought you might not return from your journey, and if you didn't, he would try to be what he's always wanted—noaidi of our siide. Secretly, he spent a lot of time steeping potions of roots and herbs. He left often. Sometimes for many days. When he came back, he was hollow-eyed and weary. I asked, but he wouldn't tell where he'd been or what he'd been doing. I watched as he tried to make a drum, but the skin tore as he stretched it over the frame. He tried another, and that tore, too. On his third try, the frame splintered and fell to many pieces. That's a bad omen, and it frightened him, so he started sitting at the circle meetings with the strangers again.

"Remember when he, you, and I used to sit with Poppi while he taught us about our people and our ways? Utsí couldn't remember any of the sacred chants and songs. He still doesn't remember more than small bits of our people's story. He's angry because he wouldn't ever be able to pass the noaidi test. That's why he wants to go with the strangers. They told him he could be a powerful man if he followed their ways. He wouldn't have to listen to the wind. He would not have to remember anything, because it would all be in the book they have."

"Are you leaving with the strangers, too?" asked Tuuli, even though she was afraid to hear the answer.

"No. Utsí said they don't want me. They won't take me—because of my arm."

Tuuli saw Siru's eyes tear up. She put an arm around her friend and said, "I'm sorry Utsí has chosen the strangers over you. If he leaves, he will be a broken branch just like Hánas. But I'm glad you're staying. If Utsí thinks being a noaidi makes one better than any other, he's wrong. Everyone is important to our siide, but no one is as important as the deer. Even though I didn't choose to be born this way, I know it's what I have to be."

"Aren't you glad you were born to be a noaidi?" asked Siru through her tears.

"I wasn't, and I tried to block the wind out for a long time. I didn't want this because the wind did not warn me that my mother was going to die. The drum could not tell Poppi how to heal her. But the wind does talk to me. I knew the strangers were coming. I know now that I have to do everything I can to turn them back."

"Do you have Poppi's drum?"

Tuuli hesitated. She remembered how her friend had turned away from her that day so long ago, but now she needed to tell the truth. When she was tested by the noaidis, she would bring the drum with her and everyone would know she had it, so she said, "Yes, I have it."

Siru clasped her good arm to her chest. "I'm glad, and many others will give thanks, too. It's a good omen that you were able to save it. Now things will get better for us. This has been a hard summer while you've been away. Not only were there many tax collectors, but the grazing has been poor for the deer. More than one group of strangers visited our camp, and one group is still here. Many have mistreated us. They've beaten some people and have threatened others with death. They say they are going to follow us back to our winter camps, too." Siru became quiet. She put her good arm to her heart and said, "I'm so sorry that I ever doubted our ways and that I was willing to lose our friendship for the strangers. Can you ever forgive me?"

"Yes, of course I can, and I do. The strangers bring a strong message. I have even thought how much easier it would be to go their way instead of fighting their words. Tell me, has Hánas been with them?"

"No. No one had seen him until he helped bring you here."

"I wonder where he's been if not here. Please don't tell anyone about the drum just yet. There might be some who would give it up to the strangers," Tuuli said.

Siru nodded. "I'll hide it for you until then, just in case the strangers search your bundle."

"Thank you, my friend," she said, hugging her.

"Sister," Siru whispered.

"Sister," Tuuli repeated. And the wind took their words and swirled them to the sky.

30

HOLDING THE DRUM OF THE FOUR WINDS, Tuuli entered the leaf-covered bower where the noaidis waited. Seeing Poppi's ancient drum, the noaidis almost forgot to greet Tuuli. Then, remembering their ways, they each stood and nodded briefly to her and pointed to a fur-covered stump for her to sit on. After Tuuli sat, they quietly chanted a joik of thanks that she had kept the drum from burning.

"This drum was saved," said the noaidi of the Falling Water clan. Then, nodding to Tuuli, he said, "It gives me hope that more have been hidden from those who would desecrate them."

"It does give hope to us all, but I don't think it's safe to leave it in the hands of one so young. The strangers have been asking about her. They will search her for the drum," said another.

"No," Tuuli said. "This is the drum of Poppi and of a long line in my family. I kept it hidden when challenged many times to hand it over. Yes, I am young, but it stays with me."

Then she held the drum to the oldest noaidi. "Take it. Does it quiver and hum for you? Does it beat with your heart?"

He tapped on it. No sounds, no low vibrations rose from the drum. He passed it to the next. From person to person, it was handed around the circle. The drum thunked and plunked but did not send beautiful sounds to the ears of anyone.

"Maybe it's gotten wet," one suggested.

"Maybe it's been ruined on your travels," said another.

"No, I have kept it dry and safe. Pass it to me," Tuuli said. As soon as she held the drum in her hands, it throbbed and hummed even before Tuuli tapped lightly.

"It *is* Tuuli's drum," admitted the noaidi who had sung songs of healing for her the night before. "Not only has been it been in her family through many lives, but now it is choosing her over all of us."

"We are astonished. It's a long time since we have had one among us who could drum talk with the spirits of the dead *and* wind listen. Welcome. Now it is time for you to mark the drum as your own. What will you draw on it?"

"Poppi was born when the moon covered the sun, so he drew that. My mother was born when the butterflies left their chrysalis, so that is her mark," Tuuli said, pointing. "Guovza circled our goahti three times when I entered this world; my sign shall be a bear and three rings."

As Tuuli drew her mark, the oldest stood and passed Poppi's rowan walking stick over her nine times, saying, "Your noaidi name will be Guovza to honor Brother Bear. You will gain your earthly strength from him. We lift your name to the spirits great and small so they celebrate with us. Look, even Beavi has broken through the clouds for this moment. You are now and always will be noaidi of your siide, Many Rowans. You become one in a line of many. Now sit. Drink some of this broth, and tell us more of your journey."

Tuuli did. She told of the arrival of the strangers, hiding the drum, Poppi's death, Bieg's storm, Stallu's chase, and the death of her dog, Kulta. She told of everything except her dreams and her meeting with Aiko. They all nodded and then invited her to stay awhile to work the drum.

After they'd sung some sacred songs, the noaidi of the Hawk Hill clan said, "You are young and beautiful. We will call upon the salmon of the rivers, the eagle of the sky, the swans of the lake, and the rowan of this earth to be by your side. They will bring you many births. Each child of your body will be a joy to our people. We want you to run at the courtship races today."

"Yes," all agreed. "You should have a husband and start a family right away. We will all bring potions and chant the ancient words to bring you great fertility so you will have many children. Hopefully, they will be marked as you were. Our people will then be truly favored by good spirits, and we will become strong again. All our people, not just your clan, will depend on you. Our fate is tied to yours."

Tuuli thought of her dreams and answered, "But I am so tired and weak. I would not be able to get away from anyone, and I want to choose who catches me."

"Say if you have a favorite. We can make sure he catches you."

"I used to favor Hánas, but he is no longer one of us. Even though he saved me and I owe him my life, I fear he would take the life that I want with my people and that he would bring me to live among strangers. It would be as if he strangled the very life in me that he saved. He no longer believes the way we do. Let me wait until the next gathering. Then I will be strong and will have had a chance to consider who is most likely to help me provide many children."

Each noaidi nodded, agreeing with Tuuli's wisdom. Then they all raised their voices in a joik of celebration to Beavi above, to the trees around them, to life-giving waters, and to the earth below.

Holding her drum under her cloak, Tuuli left the circle and stepped outside. Many had gathered around the leaf-covered bower, waiting. When they heard the joiking, they knew she was now noaidi.

"Vuoi, vuoi, vuoi! We are so happy for you." They voiced their gladness. Siru hugged her. Utsí came up and told her that he wished her well, but as he turned to walk away, he whispered, "Run in the race. I will catch you for my bride. We will go with the strangers—to a new life."

Standing back, outside the crush of the well-wishers, but away from the strangers, was Hánas. Holding her drum close, Tuuli went to thank him for saving her life. She felt her face redden as she neared, and her breath came quickly. She held her head down so he wouldn't notice.

"You've been accepted," he said before she could thank him.

"Yes."

"I knew you would. You were born into this, and your pleasure shines from within you."

"They want me to run the courtship race, but I told them I was too weak." Saying these words, Tuuli realized there was another reason she didn't want to run. And it was Hánas.

"I am not traveling with the strangers anymore," he said. "I didn't know how cruel they would be or that they would destroy lives. Too many of your people have been hurt or killed. I need to return to my adoptive family for a while, and then I will decide if I stay with them or return here. I don't know if my siide will take me back or if I will be accepted by any of the families. I hope I will not be banished with no name. I know that I am like a broken branch." He smiled at Tuuli. "Do you remember when you first called me that? It hurt, but I was still glad to see you."

"I think I know how you feel," she said. "On my journey, I was very alone. I had hidden the drum and the lame deer. I blamed myself for bringing troubles to my people. Sometimes I doubted I would make it back to the warmth of the campfires. I was alone and so far from everyone."

"But you are back and have proven yourself. After bringing the strangers among you, I feel responsible for the evil they have done. I have searched my heart. Even though I will no longer travel with them, I can no longer believe in the power of the drum or dreams. If I can't do that, I'm afraid my siide will not accept me."

"Everyone looks kindly on you because you found me and brought me back."

"Well, yes, some have thanked me, but none have invited me to their meals. I am not welcome. If I stay, I may have to be like the one who wanders alone."

"I don't think that is your fate."

"Do you know my fate?"

Tuuli hesitated. She thought of her dreams with the two wolves. Was one Hánas? She didn't know, so she answered, "No. The wind and the drum have not told me."

"Tuuli, I no longer believe they have that power."

"When I was cold, almost to death, I heard a voice singing our ancient words of healing. Those words brought me back to this earth. The voice I heard was yours. You sang a healing joik. Doesn't that show you are still one with us?"

"Yes, I sang for your life, but I sang because you believe, not because I do," Hánas said.

"The wind told me—oh, it seems so long ago—that the strangers were coming and you would lead them. And some of my dreams have already boded the future for me."

"Those are just dreams. You had heard at the autumn gatherings about the strangers going to the clans. The wind and dreams cannot foretell what is yet to happen."

"I was hoping you had changed," Tuuli said, pressing the drum to her heart. "I know I will never change. I will never give up what all my grandmothers and grandfathers before me believed. I will never give up the wind and the drum!"

"Even though we don't agree, if there is ever danger for you, Tuuli, I will always try to help you."

"All I know is that I have more journeys. You have already traveled far. What is it like to go to other lands? To learn other tongues? To dress like another person? To eat other foods? Are you still yourself, or do you become someone else?"

"A little of both, Tuuli, a little of both. But I have seen enough of the world to the south to know more troubles are coming for all the siides. Bigger changes will threaten your lives."

Tuuli remembered her flight into the future but wondered what changes Hánas meant. Before she could ask, new strangers entered the camp, leading horses. Hánas turned her from them so they couldn't see as he took the drum from her and hid it under his coat. "It won't do to run," he said. "I wish I could have, but I didn't foresee the great trouble I brought when I led them to your camp."

"What do they want?" she asked, her eyes fixed on his.

Tears welled in his eyes. "This new group of strangers has been waiting for you to return. Traders and tax collectors have spread a rumor that you are a powerful noaidi. They're afraid that you can use magic. They call you names, like *witch*. Their king is very powerful, and he wants you. Remember this, Tuuli: I will always do what I can to help you."

The strangers circled them. "Go away," they said to Hánas.

"No, I stay with her," Hánas answered, pointing at Tuuli.

Then one of the men brought a horse forward and told Tuuli to get on its back.

"Never," she said. "My place is here with my people."

"The king has commanded you to come with us."

"I have no king. No one commands me but the spirits of my ancestors."

"He is your king. He can command you because you live on his lands."

"I live here, on the lands of the deer. They have grazed here longer than your king or any of us have walked this earth. We Saami are the people of the deer," said Tuuli. "This is where I belong."

The stranger stepped toward Tuuli and spoke again. "We come in peace and goodness, but we will do what we are commanded by our king. Come, do what's best for your people, and we will leave them and the deer alone."

Tuuli crossed her arms and remained still.

"Come now, or we'll slaughter all the deer. Then you'll see if you can survive the long winter."

Her heart thumped, and she could hear the drum thumping under Hánas's coat. It beat not with her heart but with his. It was talking to him! Not daring to look, she instead fixed her eyes on her people. Their faces were frozen, but their eyes spoke. They stood still, but they waited for a signal from Tuuli for them to surround the strangers. There were many more Saami. They could easily overpower the nine men.

"You don't believe we can do this? You think you can overpower us?" All the strangers moved far back from the cooking fire. When they were well away, one of them threw a pouch into it. A roar like thunder! Streaks of flame shot up everywhere. Wood, ashes, a whole side of venison that had been roasting, and debris exploded into the air.

The people screamed and ran. A blasting wave shocked them. They fell to the ground. Everyone, even the strangers, beat at the sparks and flames that fell onto their heads and clothes. Burns stung their faces and hands. Burned skin peeled back, exposing flesh and bone.

Tuuli placed her hands over her ears. All sounds were muffled as if she had many scarves wrapped around them. Everyone else held theirs, too, and shook their heads to clear the ringing. Their faces burned with blackened flesh. They grimaced in pain. The noaidis ignored their own wounds to tend to others. Some jumped at the strangers, snarling like wild animals. Fights and scuffles took place. The tallest stranger held up another handful of the powder and said to Tuuli, "Stop them, or it will be worse."

"Now you know," said another. "We can sprinkle this powder throughout your herds. The blast will kill many deer and scatter the rest. Your witch has no choice but to come with us, or you are all doomed."

How could they fight the black powder? It had a power stronger than any noaidi ever had. Tuuli called for her people to stop fighting.

When all settled, the strangers searched the bundles and clothing of the noaidis, then tied them all to trees. "No tricks," they told the people. "Two of us will stay behind. If any of these witches cause trouble, they will use more magic powder."

Her people surrounded Tuuli. While dabbing balms on her burns, they begged of her, "Do not go. We will find a way to stop them."

"They will destroy all we have and all we are unless I go," she answered. "Perhaps I'll be able to convince that king of theirs to leave us alone." Tuuli hoped that she sounded braver than she felt. The tallest stranger came toward her. She stepped forward, separating herself from her people. Her heart wrenched. Her knees felt weak, but it was what she had to do to save the deer. Never would she have thought the first thing she would do as noaidi would be to leave those who meant so much to her. Never would she have thought that going with the strangers would be preferable to staying.

Hánas came forward. "I'll go, too."

Siru rushed to Tuuli and said, "I, too, am going."

One of the men held up a long stick to bar their way. "No. We take only this evil one."

Two men boosted Tuuli onto the back of a tall horse. They warned her not to try to escape. With much kicking of the horses and loud commands, they started to ride away, a cloud-covered Beavi bringing a chill to everyone. Her people joined their voices in the joik of mourning sung for one that is lost to them.

Mai, Aay Aay
Mai, Nay, Nay
Mai, Laam, Laam

The strangers who stayed behind struck two of the singers and threatened more, commanding them to be silent. From everyone, tears—bitter tears—fell to the red and gold leaves of the birch already on the ground.

Fearful of falling, Tuuli held on to the mane of the horse. Looking back one final time, even through the blur of tears, she saw her drum vibrate under Hánas's coat. He waved to her with one hand as he cradled the drum in place with the other. *The drum talks to Hánas.* Silently, and with a look to the skies, she wished with all her might that he would listen to it.

From the corner of her eye, she saw Aiko creep from tree to tree in the surrounding woods. Brother Bear was there, too. As she watched, man and animal blended their bodies into one. At the same moment, Beavi broke through the clouds. Warm rays caressed her back. In the woods, Aiko, as a bear, followed. The wind whispered through the branches of a willow, and the stranger's horse carried Tuuli away.

**THE
SECOND
JOURNEY**

Wounded Wolf

A wolf caught in a trap gnaws off her leg.
To live. To be free, she leaves something of herself behind.
I, too, gave up a part of myself to be free.
I am wounded wolf.
I am Tuuli.

31

TEARS ROLLED FROM TUULI'S CHEEKS AND FELL onto her hands tightly holding the mane of the horse she straddled with fear. The thought of seeing Hánas holding her drum, and the drum beating next to his heart, hidden beneath his coat, ripped at her heart. *Could it be that Hánas is marked as I am?* He had been torn from his people and forced to live with the strangers when he was very young. She could understand now how terrifying that must have been for him, as she, at that very moment, was being forced from her people to go with the strangers. Maybe Hánas would now choose to follow the drum and his ancestors' ways. Maybe Hánas could lead her siide through the long, cold, dark periods, and knowing the ways of the strangers, he could find a way to bring her back to her people.

These thoughts tumbled through Tuuli's mind as she struggled to stay on the great beast whose back rocked with each stride. When she finally felt she could relax in the steady swaying of the horse, she peered into the woods surrounding them. She listened for branches snapping not caused by the horses. She lifted her nose, but the stench of the horses was so strong she could not smell if Brother Bear followed.

And she worried about the reindeer. Had the strangers tossed the black powder and lit it in the midst of the herds after she left? If so, many would have died from the blast. Others would be wounded. And those that survived would be scattered.

The first day, the band of ten horses, nine strangers, and Tuuli traveled long and hard. They stopped only to let the horses drink at a creek or for the men to relieve themselves. At one such stop, the stranger with a long scar across his forehead stood by Tuuli's horse. Facing her, laughing and exposing his penis, he let his water out right there. Tuuli turned her face away, but another did the same on her other side. Finally, she closed her eyes and silently suffered the harsh words and laughter. Saami men would never have done that.

When night fell, the strangers tied her to a tree as they set a fire to roast the rabbits they'd hunted during the day. Tuuli's stomach rumbled with hunger as she smelled the roasting meat, but when the time came to eat, they handed her only hard bread. As she chewed through its toughness, she thought of all the berries her people had picked. All the salmon and graylings they had fished and dried during the days of long light and warmth. She longed for even a small sip of the springwater that gurgled from the earth at the gathering. The strangers didn't bring her anything to drink, so her mouth was dry and the bread hard to swallow.

The men laid furs to sleep on. They snored deeply through the night. Tuuli lay on the cold ground. She slept for only short snatches and wished for the warmth of Poppi's robe.

She had nothing. Not even Poppi's rowan walking stick. The strangers had hoisted her onto the tall horse before she could gather the bundle that Aiko and Hánas had brought back to her.

In the morning, frost coated the grasses and trees. The sun wavered thinly in the gray sky and gave off very little warmth. Tuuli shivered, cold to the bone and very hungry. The strangers stirred porridge over a little flame. Still tied to the tree, she tried to signal to the men that she wanted to warm herself by the morning fire, but the scarred one just laughed and spit on the ground at her feet. When the men were done eating, she was given what remained of the thin porridge but nothing to drink.

When they were riding again, the stranger with the scar across his forehead rode close to her. First, he reached over and stroked her buttocks. She tried to move her horse away, but he always kept his horse right next to hers. Then he stoked her breast and said soft words. She hit his hand away. Her cheeks reddened. She wanted to cry but forced herself not to. A stranger with hair the color of rowanberries shouted at the scarred man, so he jerked his horse's head away and left her with more worries to pile upon those she already had for her people and the deer.

That night, after a thin porridge made with a sharp-tasting root and some flour, the man who'd fondled her during the day laid a blanket on the ground, pushed her onto it, tied her hands to a tree, threw another blanket over her, and then lay down next to her.

The rowanberry-haired stranger came over, gave him a kick with his boot, and said sharp words to him. The man lying next to her just laughed and rolled closer. He slid his hand up her leg to her thigh. His calloused hand rasped the softness of her leg. Then he loosened the strap that laced her leggings. Tuuli screamed and squirmed to get away. Her struggles only drove him to get rougher. He stuffed a handful of moss into her mouth. He yanked at her clothing until he had her bare from the waist down.

She kicked and rolled as he pawed at her body. He roared rough words as he held her down and forced himself upon her. She cried out, but the mosses muffled her sounds. Her pain drowned in her tears. He thrust mercilessly. Tuuli's head banged against the tree each time he shoved himself within her. The pain inside and the thudding ache of her head joined together until her spirit flew and she felt herself fly high, winging like a white bird on the black clouds of a coming storm. And then it was over. The beast stood. He spat out the word, "*Håxa,*" and wiped his mouth on his sleeve. When he returned to sit at the campfire, none of the strangers spoke a word, but one came and loosened the bonds that tied her to the tree.

Tuuli turned to her side, pulled the moss out of her mouth. To her people, moss was a gift. It was used to pack wounds to stop bleeding. Some mosses were steeped with warm water for a drink to heal someone who had painful stomachaches. And some were cooked into their soups and stews. And now it had been used to gag her—to prevent her from crying out in pain or to call for help. It was a cruel use for the moss of her land.

Despite the ache and shame she felt, Tuuli crept to the dying campfire. She would warm herself even if the men objected. But none did. Where, she asked herself, was Brother Bear? Was Aiko still following? Were the nine strangers with weapons too many for him to fight off, to save her? Beavi was down for the night. The wind was quiet as though it could not whisper a single comfort to her. As though what had happened could never be blown away from Tuuli's memory.

The next day, snow fell, making travel more difficult. Tuuli tilted her head back and caught icy flakes by sticking out her tongue. The men never offered her anything to drink, so she silently said her thanks for the tiny melted droplets. The food she was given was barely edible; the men took the best of everything and gave her mere scraps.

The next day, they arrived at a wide expanse of water—larger than any lake Tuuli had ever seen. A boat, huge, like Tuuli had heard traders brag about, swayed among the rocks of the shore. They walked a narrow board to get on the boat, horses and all. A short man who had red flaky patches of skin on his face forced her down a rope ladder and pushed her into a small room. He slammed the door tightly behind her.

She couldn't see out, but she felt the boat move on the waters. She tried the door, but it would not budge even when she shouldered it with all her strength. She shivered in the cold and dark. When the small crack above the door no longer showed any light, she knew night had fallen. There was nothing to lie on, so she curled up in the corner farthest from the door. The pungent odor of rotted fish stung her nose. She cried out to the wind, wanting sweet breezes to cleanse the air, but it could not reach her through the wooden boards of the boat. When she put her hand to the floor to change positions, fish scales stuck to her. With a finger, she flicked each one away. Tears gathered in her eyes, and she wished each flick would send one more stranger overboard and into the icy waters.

That night and every night, the stranger with the scarred forehead came to her. When he was done with her, he'd spit at her feet and mutter, "*Håxa.*" Then two other strangers entered and took turns with her. Tuuli no longer cried out for help. Even though there was no moss in the little room to muffle her cries, she knew there was no help for her in her shame.

Tuuli suffered alone in the small room between the brutal visits of the men. One brought her crusts of dried bread, and once a watery soup to sop the bread in. He set it on the floor near the door. He never looked at her while he held her down beneath him, but when he was done, he moved the food closer to where she crouched and quickly bent to go out the door.

To stay as warm as possible, she pulled her knees to her chest and held them tightly. She hated her own stench. She used her own spit to rub on her face and hands. She unwound her hair and straightened it as best she could before braiding it and wrapping it around her head. She sang joiks softly to herself as she imagined herself becoming a white bird and flying high above her beautiful land. She comforted herself remembering how she had played with Kulta or had gone sliding across an icy pond with Siru. They had strapped reindeer antlers to their feet and glided through the dark days of the cold time. She hummed the soft melodies that her people blew on willow whistles.

The small room with hard walls did not let the wind blow whispers to her or let Beavi's warm rays shine upon her, warming her shoulders, her back, and her face. And she had no drum. She let her mind flow to her siide's campfires where Poppi tapped the drum while everyone dreamed their own dreams and the crackle of the burning wood joined with the sound of leaves spinning from trees in the breeze as they did during the falling-leaf time.

She had no idea how long she was to endure this journey. She listened for the wind, but there wasn't even a comforting whisper coming through the walls. She had not known she would suffer so sorely. She told herself to be strong, to endure, and when she finally was able to face the king of the strangers, she must be able to convince him to stop sending his people to all the siides of the far north and to leave their reindeer alone. With the cold season setting in, Beavi would shine less and less each day. Tuuli shivered. Dark days were ahead.

32

Hánas held the Drum of Four Winds to his chest as he watched Tuuli ride off with the strangers. He felt the drum quiver and beat with his heart. He heard it thump softly.

No! No! This cannot be. I have never wanted the drums to speak to me, even though, as a child, I felt they did. My new father tells me that they evoke demons and separate one from the true God.

He saw Tuuli glance back at him. High on a horse, she looked terrified. She still had black ashes and burns on her face from the explosion. How easy it had been for the strangers to use the black powder, thrown into the fire, to frighten the Saami and to convince Tuuli that they possessed a power greater than that of any noaidi.

He held the drum tighter, hoping it would stop. Hoping it was reaching out to Tuuli and not to him. *What am I thinking? I don't believe in the drums.* Even in the chill air, he felt sweat trickle down the sides of his body, from under his arms. Then the wind whispered to him.

Follow. Follow Tuuli.
Be with her.
Follow. Follow Tuuli.

175

The drum would not stop, no matter how tightly he held it. He hoped no one noticed, especially not the strangers who would take it, burn it, and then punish him.

Hánas felt his head lighten, his heartbeat quicken, his breath come more rapidly. He must be imagining this. The wind and the drum were choosing him! It must not be. It was against everything he'd learned from the father who'd raised him after his own father and mother died.

Still confused as to what was happening to him with the wind and the drum, something moved in the woods. He looked but couldn't believe what he saw. It was Aiko, walking alongside a bear and then blending, becoming one with the bear, following the men who were taking Tuuli away.

It was what the noaidis said could happen, yet Hánas had never seen it, had never believed it. No matter how much in harmony one was with the brother and sister animals, one could not become one with them. It was what he'd learned in the schools of Stockholm. In the churches of Stockholm. It was not possible—no matter how much the Saami believed it and how many stories they told of shifting their human selves into that of an animal brother or sister.

Perhaps he was hungry. Perhaps he'd taken too severe a blow to his head during the black powder blast. Maybe the stew he'd had the night before had some of the mushrooms that could bring you to another world for a short time. There had to be an explanation for what was causing his visions and for the wind voices he heard.

Then a loud voice shook him out of his reverie. The reindeer were starting their migration back to the winter grounds. Despite the need to pack all their belongings and food they'd dried for the cold time, the Saami sang joiks while they worked and took time to say farewell to their friends and family from other siides.

Several older grandmas gathered in a circle and sang a joik for Tuuli's safety and for her return. Youngsters who'd planned to run the courtship races lingered with one another, planning for the next leaf-falling time when they'd gather again. Others went to each of their families and asked for permission to marry so they wouldn't have to wait.

Utsí was still there. When the last of the strangers left, they had signaled for him to stay. Disappointed, he'd hung his head and wouldn't look at Siru, her family, or even his own. He finally gathered his pack and set out to follow the migration.

Siru felt her heart grow still and icy when she thought of how he'd been willing to follow the strangers even though they refused to let her go along because of her lame arm. She was resolved not to thaw toward Utsí. Someday, maybe there would be another who would want to run the races with her. Maybe the nice man from the Falling Water siide who'd spoken to her when she'd been waiting for Tuuli's return. Maybe. But Siru had another worry. No blood had ever flowed from her body as they did for Tuuli and others her age. How could she assure anyone that she could birth babies? If Poppi were still living, she would ask him for roots or leaves she could steep into a potion. Or if Tuuli were there, could she tap the drum, talk to the wind, do anything to help?

Hánas went to the people of his parents' siide. "I ask for your forgiveness. I did not know the strangers would be so cruel to you."

The noaidi took out his drum, and everyone gathered around to watch as he placed several tokens on the skin and then softly tapped it. The drum vibrated. The tokens danced.

When the noaidi stopped, everyone waited quietly until he spoke. "You have Tuuli's drum?" he asked.

Hánas nodded.

"Keep it with you until you can give it to her," the noaidi said. "And don't be afraid to raise it to the skies as so many before you have."

Hánas paused. The drum was part of everything he had been taught was evil. Then it hummed against his chest. "I will do that," he finally promised. The people of his siide broke their silence. Many clapped him on the arm and said he would be welcome at their campfires anytime he wanted to return.

Then he went to Tuuli's siide. He asked forgiveness for bringing the strangers. "I will run with your deer to winter camp and help you in any way I can, but I cannot stay through the cold season. I need to travel back to Stockholm. There I hope to find Tuuli and help her return to you."

The drum beat more strongly under his coat. "I have the Drum of Four Winds," he said. "I'll leave it so you can give it to Tuuli when she returns." He started to take it from under his coat.

Three grandmas came forward and put their hands on Hánas's chest where the drum lay close to his heart. "We see the drum beat with you." They smiled. "Keep it. It will be safe with you until you find Tuuli."

After the migration, the Siide of Many Rowans settled back in their winter camp. When Hánas took leave of the people, Siru's father gave him Tuuli's bundle that held the bedding robe that had been Poppi's. "Take this to keep you warm on your travels." Another handed him the white pelt from Gabba. "Take this, and may all that is good follow you." A third gave him the rowan walking stick. Others presented a basket with generous amounts of dried fish, venison, and berries. Then they moved as one in a circle and sang a joik. The wind swirled and sang with them.

> *May the forest beautiful protect you.*
> *May winds hum and be gentle.*
> *May you surely find your way.*

Hánas pulled the drum from under his coat and tapped it gently as they all sang together. He fell to his knees. It felt natural and comforting, so he stayed and lifted his arms to the stars, to the moon, to the Great Bear in the sky.

Then they bade him safe journey and said, "Come back to us. Bring Tuuli."

A strong wind blew, chilling him to the bone. He held his coat closer to his body as he thanked them and turned to his long journey toward Stockholm. He would be traveling in the dark most of the time. It would be cold and snowy until he turned toward the coast. There, the weather would be milder, and the farther south he got, the sun would rise and light his way for a few hours each day.

At times, the wind gusts burst so suddenly that they sucked his breath away as he hurried through the woodlands. When he was tired, he cut some brush and stacked it under the shelter of a leafless birch and sat with his back to the tree. He wrapped himself in Tuuli's fur robe and draped Gabba's pelt over his head and shoulders. The violent blasts persisted. Snow fell more heavily.

Hánas looked up and watched the trees swaying fiercely in the wind. Leaves were plucked from the trees and the ground and swirled madly in the air. This storm was not gentle and kind. Hánas had always liked when breezes swayed the trees and sang tender melodies, but now the trees creaked mournfully in the brutal winds. Even though surrounded by such turmoil, Hánas closed his eyes and finally slept. His dreams tangled from one scene to another. In one, he was traveling with the deer. In another, he swayed in a boat that crossed wide waters. It seemed he was on a journey that never ended.

When he awoke to a new day, the wind had calmed, and flurries of snow fell quietly, covering leaves, mosses, and rocks. Hánas stood and stretched. He took the drum out. Tapping it softly, he welcomed the day and asked for Tuuli's safe journey—and his own. He ate dried berries and fish and then headed south. Toward home. Toward Tuuli.

33

A SUDDEN JOLT AND LOUD SCRAPING OF WOOD ON WOOD shook Tuuli from her dream. Shouting accompanied the noises of docking the boat, noises she had never heard before and couldn't match up to what could possibly be happening. After some time, the door was unbarred. The rowanberry-haired stranger stood aside and beckoned her to leave.

Outside, the wind blew stiffly. Tuuli shivered, but Beavi shone so brightly that she, who had been in the dark so long, had to close her eyes. Little by little, she opened them to take in the view. Many big boats lined the shore. They creaked as they bobbed and rocked in the wind. More people than she'd ever seen lined the shore; others rode horses, many walked on foot. The clamor was unlike anything she'd ever known. Frightened, she tried to find out what made the strange noises, but there were too many to separate. Her ears hurt. She had covered her ears with her hands when the stranger took her arm and pointed down a plank that led to shore.

Tuuli was painfully aware of how she must look. People stared—they didn't even hide their smirks and laughter as they pointed to her clothing of deerskins, her dirty and tangled hair, her feet covered in hide boots.

Once again, she was hoisted onto a horse. Now high above the throng, she looked at those who were looking at her. They wore the clothing of the traders and tax collectors who'd come onto the lands of the Saami. Their hair and eyes were lighter than those of her people. Some yelled, "Håxa!" as she passed by. The word was harsh—almost like someone spitting. It reminded her of the man who'd torn her insides and made her bleed.

Angry and hurt, she wanted them to know that she was not *håxa*, so she called back to them, "Tuuli. I am Tuuli." The soft gentle sounds of her name comforted her a little as the wind picked them up and carried her name in this new land.

Then to her surprise, she heard, "Tuuli!" called back from the crowd. Not once, but twice. "Tuuli! Tuuli!" The voice was familiar, like a Saami voice. A song to her ears. She turned toward the sound and saw a man being pushed away by the crowd. "*Ag'gja! Ag'gja*, Beto!" she called to him.

And once more, a faint "Tuuli!" reached her ears as the horses clopped and took her farther away. Could it really have been her father? Her father who'd abandoned their people after her mother had died? Throngs of pushing and shoving people gathered as far as her eye could see. She could no longer see the man who'd called out. Maybe she'd just wished to hear her name. Maybe the wind whispered it back to her. Maybe someone had just repeated what she'd called out.

Not only did she think it impossible that her father had seen her from the crowd, but as the strangers led her farther and farther away from the boat, she saw how many paths there were, how many buildings, and how many people. She began to wonder how Aiko or Hánas would ever find her. Where would they even begin? Hánas had lived in places like this with strangers. Was this where he had lived? Would he know where to find her?

The sun was low in the sky when the group slowed. Ahead stood a building so massive that Tuuli could imagine all her siide, with all their goahtis, and even the pens for the tame deer fitted inside with a lot of room to spare. They stopped as the sun slipped below the tops of the trees and darkness settled in.

The men got off their horses and walked them to an enclosure. The scarred man signaled for Tuuli to slide off. Her legs gave way when she hit the ground, and she sprawled at his feet. He prodded her with his foot. Despite her weariness, she sprang up. The rowan-haired stranger pushed the cruel man away. Taking Tuuli's arm, he pointed to the large building and said, "*Stockholm Slott. Konung Karl.*" The strange words meant nothing to Tuuli, but she repeated them. He nodded and said, "Slott. Konung Karl."

She wished Hánas were there with her to change those harsh-sounding words into gentle Saami. Hánas. Her thoughts turned to him. Was he following? Was her drum still with him? Beating with his heart?

The arrival of more strangers interrupted her thoughts. The newly arrived men seemed to be in charge of those who'd led her there. Their discussion lasted a long time. Tuuli was sure they talked about her as they nodded, shrugged, and pointed in her direction. She shivered in the chill of the early evening air. Finally, one who wore clothing with intricate red and yellow designs took her by the arm. Holding a lit torch, he led her through a gate where several more strangers stood holding sticks that looked to have knives attached to the ends.

They walked inside a high wall, away from the large building, along a pathway. In the dim light, Tuuli saw pens that held big birds. Others held fat, short-legged animals that made odd grunting sounds. Dried grasses poked out of another building. Arriving at a shed that was roofed with a straw thatch, the stranger lifted a heavy bar, opened the door, and signaled for her to enter. Inside, he pointed with the torch to a straw bed covered by a bearskin, an empty bucket, and a jug with water. Then he left. She heard *clunk* as he set the heavy bar back into place.

It was completely dark inside. She felt along the walls but didn't find any openings. She checked the door. It didn't budge. Once again, she was captive. When the man had held the light, she'd seen piles of dried straw and grains she could not name. Feeling her way, she found the bearskin, the bucket, and the jug. As she was lifting the jug to her lips to drink, she heard the door being unbarred again.

Two women stepped inside. One carried a torch. The other set a large bowl of steaming stew on a wooden plank. Then she opened a cloth pouch and took out a round of bread, a chunk of white cheese, and an apple. Tuuli's mouth watered at the sight of so much good food. She thanked the women again and again, but they just backed out and barred the door.

She turned the empty bucket upside down for a stool. In the dark, Tuuli drank the stew broth. She picked chunks of meat and other delicious morsels from the bowl with her fingers. She savored them in her mouth before swallowing. She tasted the cheese. It was mild, like the cheese her people made from reindeer milk. She tore a chunk of the bread and ate that, too. She saved half of the bread, cheese, and apple even though she was still hungry. She didn't know when she'd be given food again. Then she drank more water.

She yawned. Her legs wobbled from sitting cramped on the boat and riding on the horse, so she lay on the bearskin. "Brother Bear," she murmured to herself. "Comfort me, cradle me, keep me safe, as I now sleep." But comfort and sleep did not come. Tears did. And the walls swallowed her sobs so they were not heard by the curious who crept close outside.

When the women returned the next morning, they carried fresh steaming bread wrapped in cloths, a berry sauce, a jug of milk, and a bowl of hot black liquid. They waited for her to eat. When she sipped the black drink, it curled her tongue with bitterness and smelled a little like moldering duff. The women laughed gently to see the expression on her face. One poured some milk into the bitter liquid and gestured for Tuuli to try again, saying, "*Kaffe. Drick Kaffe.*"

Tuuli repeated the words and sipped again. The milk had cooled the drink and gave it a mellower taste. It was still sharp and bitter to Tuuli, but the women looked so eager for her to like it that she held the bowl in both hands and sipped until it was gone.

Later, the women came again. They carried two buckets sloshing with water. They spoke their strange words to Tuuli. She shrugged. They made motions with their hands and arms to show washing hands, face, hair, arms, and whole body. Even though bathing seemed like a good idea, Tuuli had no idea how she was going to wash with the buckets of water. Then the women began to undress her. She didn't try to stop them until they reached her very last garments. She tried to hold them tightly to herself, but the women persisted, saying in soft voices, "*Tvätta. Gott. Tvätta.*"

They had undressed her so gently that Tuuli untied her own leggings and helped take off her last covering. The women took down her hair and unwound her braid. Then they dipped cloths into warm water and washed her back. They handed her a cloth and motioned for her to wash the rest of her body. They poured some of the water on her hair and nodded for her to wash that, too. Tuuli felt the layers of sweat and dirt and the filth of the scarred stranger wash away, so she scrubbed at her skin. When all the water was gone, the women handed her a woven dress and coat to put on, along with a strange pair of shoes. Tuuli shook her head and pointed to her own clothes.

"*Nej*," they said and started to pull the new clothing over Tuuli's head.

When she was dressed, they wrapped her in a bearskin, opened the door, and led her out into the bright sunshine. No wind blew, so the chill of the day didn't penetrate her clothes. She shielded her eyes in the sudden brightness of Beavi shining upon her. They led her to a bench, and one sat down with her. She ran her fingers through Tuuli's hair and held it to the warm sunrays to dry. All the while, she tried to talk to Tuuli, pointing to things and saying the name for them. *Gris* is the word she repeated for the little fat animal that grunted. *Kyckling* was a big bird, bigger than the grouse she had hunted at home. *Häst* was the beast she'd ridden on. Tuuli liked the woman. She was tall with white hair that glowed in the sun. She was calm and smiled as Tuuli struggled to repeat a word until it sounded right.

Tuuli wanted to ask where she was and if she would get to see the king who, according to what the strangers told Hánas, had wanted her. She realized that even if she got to see him, there was no way for her to express what she wanted to say. Hánas would have been able to help, but he wasn't there. Again she wondered, where was he? Was he still with her people? Did he still have her drum? Would he be able to find her? Would she ever be free to go back to her people? She raised her head to listen to the wind, but none blew within the thick walls.

And what about Aiko? And was it really her father that had answered her as she rode through the throngs of strangers? So many questions, and there was no way to get them answered.

She needed to learn the words of these people. Words like *gris* and *kyckling* were not going to be enough.

Tuuli turned to the woman who was drying her hair. "Tuuli," she said, pointing to herself.

"Tuuli," the woman repeated and, pointing to herself, said, "Frida."

"Frida," Tuuli stumbled over the name. It seemed hard to say, but she tried it over and over again until the woman clapped her hands and said, "*Ja! Ja!*"

Day followed day. Locked in the dark storeroom for long stretches of time, her first thoughts were of escape. She was tired of waiting to see the king. She still didn't know enough of the language to ask the women any of her questions. Then she thought of her siide. How were they faring without a noaidi? Were they thinking about her? Would they have enough dried berries to last the winter? Would they be able to fish the wild rivers, or would the cold freeze them over?

When the women came to bring food, drink, water to wash, and to empty the bucket of her waste, Tuuli learned all their names. Besides Frida, who was the tallest, there was Greta, who never smiled but willingly taught her words after braiding her hair and pinning it high on her head. Marit was the youngest. Tuuli thought they might be about the same age. She chattered and sang little songs even when Tuuli tried to turn her attention to teaching new words. Whenever a young man walked through the courtyard where they sat, Marit blushed, touched her cheek, and followed him with her eyes.

Tuuli was amazed at Marit's open interest in men. She herself was ever fearful that the stranger with the scarred forehead would come to her at night even though she had never caught sight of him since she arrived there. Once she saw the stranger with rowanberry-colored hair. He glanced in her direction but gave no other sign of recognizing her. Every day, she was allowed in the courtyard for longer periods of time, but never alone. She looked forward to her time in the brisk air. High walls prevented her from seeing into the town, but she could see the castle just past the gardens. She looked to the skies. Few birds flew overhead. Frida taught her the names of all that did.

Each day when the women had to leave, they slowly walked her back to the storehouse. "*Ledsen,*" they'd say, lowering their heads. "Sorry," Greta repeated as she backed out and closed the door. And then Tuuli would think of escape, but even if she could get away from the women, there were men with the fire sticks always pacing along the walls. And the thought of the scarred man frightened her.

34

AT THE TOP OF A HIGH HILL, AIKO STOPPED and shrugged. The bear stopped, too. Aiko shrugged again. He closed his eyes and willed himself to step away from the bear. When he felt the warmth of the great animal leave him, he opened his eyes. A sprawling town lay before him. And beyond it, he saw the jagged coastline of a huge water.

Aiko would be on his own in his search for Tuuli. Already, he and the bear had run and hid from a hunting party that had shot at the bear. Aiko combed his fingers through the bear's fur. He found a spot of dried blood. The wound was already healing. No seeping. No swelling. The bear would be all right. "Many thanks, my brother," Aiko told him. "Now go far from here. Be safe."

After watching the bear disappear among the trees, he surveyed the town from the hilltop. He saw the huge enclosed courtyards with a big building within. It must be the king's castle. That must be where Tuuli was. He walked into the town. At first, he stayed in the shadows, noticing everything and hoping not to be noticed. He looked for food. It had been three days since he'd eaten anything other than some roots the bear had dug from the frozen earth.

The whole journey had taken a long time. On the first day, as he had hurried to keep up with the horses that had carried Tuuli, he'd slid on wet leaves and twisted his knee. Even though he packed it with frosty moss, it had swelled. Walking had been painful, and soon he was well behind the group. He'd followed their trail to the coast and had seen the boat well on its way. He carried nothing except some roots, his knife, and the flint in the pouch he kept tied to his waist. But he had no dried berries. No meat. He'd hunted, but because of his injury, he had not been successful very often. Then he'd walked many days, sticking close to the coast, before reaching this place.

Now he listened to the words of the people as he approached an area where many boats were moored. They were of the same tongue as the tax collectors and traders he'd met on his wanderings through the years. He knew how to ask for food and drink using their words but hadn't learned much more. Now the little he did know would at least help him get something to eat.

Approaching a group of men, he asked for food. They looked him up and down, then just turned their backs and ignored him. Aiko touched his hair, his beard, and looked down at his deerskin clothing. He must look very strange to these people. If he were to find Tuuli, he needed to dress differently to blend in. He considered becoming one with a bird, but when he saw a woman crouched near an open fire pulling the feathers from a small bird, he decided against it. He thought of Tuuli and how he had taught her to become a hare. He hoped she hadn't done that as he watched the woman poke a stick through the bird and hold it over the fire. A hare would not last long here either.

He wondered about Hánas. Was he still in the cold, dark north, or had he traveled to this town, too? If so, he needed to find him. He would then have someone to teach him more of the language. Together, they could find Tuuli. Some Saamis had listened to the trad- ers' stories and become curious what life was like outside their siides. They had headed south, so he looked at everyone he passed. Would he be able to find others of his own people who would help?

His stomach ached and growled. He felt light-headed. Feeling faint, he followed good smells into a shop showing meats and fish hanging from hooks. The butcher shook his head and pointed to the door. A woman gave him a sharp look and hurried out with her package. Aiko walked farther in. The thought of something to eat made him brave. The butcher gave him a gentle shove toward the door. Aiko lifted a knife from a table. The butcher put his hands up and stood back. Instead of threatening him, Aiko began to slice a hindquarter of venison into chunks the size of other meat on display. The butcher watched as he then skillfully sliced the flesh from a large salmon, leaving the slabs of meat boneless. Still feeling faint, Aiko asked for something to eat. The butcher pointed to some scraps of smoked fish. Aiko nodded his thanks. He tried to eat slowly even though he wanted to wolf down the pieces. When he finished, he continued cutting meat until it was time for the shop to close.

The next day, Aiko returned. He watched as the butcher sliced the skin from a pig. When he realized that it was much like skinning a deer, Aiko took the knife from the butcher and continued the task. The butcher sat and wiped his eyes. They were red and crusted. He blinked often as thick tears seeped from the corners. Aiko also noticed that hunters and fishermen who came to sell their meat and fish took advantage of the butcher's poor vision. They switched the good meat they let him smell and touch with meats of poorest quality when the butcher turned to wipe his eyes.

Aiko held a piece of meat under the butcher's nose. Then he picked up another piece and pointed out the layers of fat turning green. "The meat traders . . . no good to you," Aiko told the butcher. He pointed to himself, saying, "I buy fish and game. I get fresh. The best." Aiko hoped the butcher understood the words that sounded broken to his own ears.

The owner nodded, so Aiko spent the day near the shore, buying fish as the fishermen came to shore. At the shop, he cut it into clean fillets. The butcher sat in the corner watching and wiping his eyes. That night, he pointed to a corner of the shop and gestured sleeping. Aiko gladly settled down for the night.

The next day, Aiko sorted through the dried plants he and Tuuli had picked so long ago. He crushed the leaves of two and the root of another. He boiled them in water. After the potion cooled, he picked out the leaves and root. He brought the liquid to the butcher.

"For your eyes," he said and then showed how to bathe each eye in turn. "Every day—twice." He held up two fingers. "Morning and night."

The next morning, the butcher gave Aiko a pair of shoes, a jacket, and trousers. When Aiko thanked him, he said, "It is nothing. I cannot wear the jacket and trousers anymore." He patted his protruding girth and laughed. "My eyes feel better already. I have heard that you Saami can make magic. Now I know you can. Thank you for the medicine." From then on, the butcher taught Aiko more words in Swedish every chance they had when no customers were in the shop. Aiko learned the new words quickly and asked for more.

Aiko was eager to look for Tuuli. He remembered that the men who took Tuuli from the autumn gathering had said the king wanted to see her. He asked the butcher if there was more than one town, more than one king, more than one castle.

"Many towns, many castles, just one King Karl," said the butcher.

That's all Aiko needed to hear. Each day after the shop closed, he headed right to the area close to the king's castle. On moonless nights, he dared to creep close to the walls surrounding the castle. He cooed like a dove, hooted like an owl, kronked like a raven, and even snorted like a reindeer, always hoping that if Tuuli was there, she would hear and signal him back. More than once he was chased away by a guard who had been sleeping on duty but was roused by the cooing, hooting, and kronking.

Late one afternoon, the butcher said to Aiko, "My good wife is having trouble walking. A sore on her leg seeps with pus." Aiko didn't understand some of the words, so the butcher used many gestures. Finally, he brought Aiko to his wife.

"Do you have a medicine as good as the one you used for my eyes to help her?"

Aiko nodded. He examined the sores carefully before taking a kettle from the fire. He poured warm water into a bowl to bathe the woman's leg. He crushed some roots into a paste. He dabbed the poultice onto the sores. After spreading more of the paste onto a cloth, he wrapped it around the leg with inflamed sores. He returned day after day until pus no longer oozed and the sores healed. Only a few small scars remained.

The butcher's wife took Aiko's face into her hands. "Thank you. Thank you. My husband said you were a good man even though you are Saami. Whatever you need, just ask." Then she took her first steps for a long time without pain. The butcher celebrated by bringing home a plump roast. The next day, he invited Aiko to sit at the table with them for his evening meal.

No matter if he was working with the butcher or buying fish at the shore, Aiko's thoughts always returned to figuring out how to get inside the castle. In the thin layer of snow that had fallen the day before, he drew a map of the walls surrounding the castle, the walkways, and the trees. He talked to the butcher about Tuuli. He could say everyday things easily in the new language, but to ask if she might be a captive in the castle was more difficult. He was sure he said many things wrong, so when the butcher shrugged, he thought he didn't understand. When he asked the butcher if he could deliver some fish to the castle as an excuse to get inside, the butcher shook his head and said, "*För farlig.*" Too dangerous.

Every day as he gutted fish and tossed the entrails into a wooden barrel, Aiko made up words to a joik that he sang to himself so the butcher and customers wouldn't hear. A joik with magic words asking for help from the spirit world. If ever he had needed help from beyond, it was now.

35

Winter was at its fullest when Hánas recognized the land he was traveling through. It would be just a few days before he would again enter the home of his adoptive father in Stockholm. Leaving the siides, he had headed toward the coast in hopes of finding a ship on the Bay of Bothnia that he could signal. It would be much faster to sail than to cover the distance step by step in the cold and snow of winter. But no ships, not even any small fishing boats, had been close enough for him to catch their attention.

His muscles ached. He was weary and almost out of food when he came upon a hunting party. They took him into their group. Over the campfire at night, they drank heartily of ale and ate roasted rabbit. They told Hánas they had been part of a group that was bear hunting with King Karl.

"Good thing the king left early," cheered one of the men as he hoisted a jug of ale. "We never have as much fun when he's along. He is such a serious bear hunter!"

"It's the only thing he has to do. He has so many servants he can be idle and twiddle his thumbs all day if he wants. I wish I had the life of a king," complained one of the hunters.

"Oh, he hasn't had it so easy. He was only five when his father died. That can't be more than ten years ago. He's king, but he's not king. He has to deal with all those advisors who try to convince him to do things their way. What does a young man know?"

"I hope I survive enough of these bear hunts he insists on so I can celebrate when they crown him king. I'd like to see him kick all those advisors out of the castle. That is what I'd really celebrate."

Hánas only half listened to the hunters' gossip about the king. His own father complained about the regents who advised the king, too. When Karl became king, he would be formally crowned and would be in charge of Sweden and all her lands. But that was still two years away. For now, Karl could still be a young man of leisure and bear hunt all he wanted.

"We usually don't hunt this late because most bears are hibernating already, but there have been reports of one that roams in the woods close to the town. That's all the king needed to hear, so he demanded this hunt."

Another said, "The strangest thing happened just a few days ago. I saw a bear, and when it stood on its hind legs and shook itself, I saw a man separate himself from the beast."

"You must have had too much to drink." The hunter next to him poked him in the ribs.

"I hadn't had anything to drink. The bear ambled in a circle, looking muddled. That might be the bear the king shot at."

A sharp pang felt like a stab in Hánas's chest as he heard of the bear. "Did he kill it?"

One of the hunters answered, "Just wounded it. We tried to track it but never found it. It was as if it just disappeared." Then they all kept teasing the one who'd told of the bear's strange behavior.

Hánas thought about Guovza, the bear that had followed Tuuli when she was taken away. At the time, he'd been dazed by the blast of the black powder, so he didn't believe his eyes. He thought he'd seen Aiko and a bear become one and slip through the woods, following Tuuli. Was it possible that the king had wounded, and maybe killed, that same bear? If so, was Aiko dead? Hánas shook himself. *What am I thinking?* Of course, Aiko could not shapeshift into a bear, and the bear had not come to protect Tuuli.

To calm himself, Hánas asked for news of the town. The men passed small bits of gossip. Hánas pretended to be interested in every story of great fish caught, or the babies born, or ships going back and forth across the Atlantic to the New World, carrying passengers and trade goods. Next, he asked, "Tell me the bear story again. Tell me about the man that looked like he was with the bear." Then he prodded them for gossip from the castle. "Was there a young woman who was brought there a full moon or two ago?"

"Ja, there is a håxa from the far north who came back with some of the king's men. I don't know if she is in the castle walls or if the men are keeping her as a servant."

All the hunters laughed. "Servant. Hah!"

So Tuuli was in Stockholm! The stories disturbed Hánas. She wasn't safe.

A full moon rose over the town when Hánas and the hunting party arrived. Hánas thanked the men and departed for his father's house.

"You're home!" his mother cried while she hugged him and kissed both sides of his face. At the same time, she ordered the servants to fix a meal and heat water for a bath. She seemed to have aged since he left six months earlier. Her face was more lined. Gray hair showed along her scalp.

"You have been gone too long," she said. "Your father has been in bed for seven days. He is weak with ague and is too feverish and shaky to go to his warehouse. His ship is returning from Amsterdam soon; he will need your help when it comes into port."

His father was asleep, so Hánas bathed. Then he relished the fresh bread, cheese, smoked fish, and coffee his mother set before him. "Tell me about your travels," his mother begged when he'd finished eating. "Did you convert any of those dirty heathens?"

"Mother, don't say that. Remember they are my people. They live good lives and don't bother anyone."

His mother pursed her lips and reached for her sewing bag. "You are tired. Maybe you should go to bed now," she said.

Before going to bed, Hánas unwrapped Tuuli's drum, felt its soft vibrations, rewrapped it, and hid it far back on a shelf. The next morning, he entered his father's bedroom. The fever that racked his body still hadn't broken. Hánas thought of Tuuli and all the people of the siides who knew which leaves and roots to boil in order to break fevers. "Has the doctor given Father any medicine?" he asked his mother.

"Yes, but nothing has helped," she answered as she bathed her husband's forehead with a cool cloth. Hánas wiped his father's sweating chest with a dry towel. Then he asked a servant to bring more cool water, and he sent another to the butcher shop to get a chicken and fresh fish.

When the servant returned, he said to Hánas, "When I told the butcher of your father's malady, he said maybe the Saami man who comes to help him could brew a potion to ease the fever. He told me how the man had made compresses that cured the running sores on his wife's leg and had healed the infection in his own eyes."

"I'll talk to him later. Now, I need to be with my father and listen to his instructions."

Hánas worried. His father's breath came in ragged bursts, and he had trouble forming full thoughts. It took a long time for him to tell all Hánas needed to do when their ship came into port. There was the inspection of the cargo, the unloading of the goods, making sure that the right goods were delivered to the right merchants who'd ordered them, and that the rest was taken to their warehouse for delivery to the New World that coming spring. There were fees to collect, the crew to be paid, repairs made to the ship, and new orders taken for another trip.

When Hánas went to the butcher shop to ask about the man who possibly could make a potion for his father, the butcher pointed to the docks. "He went to bid for fresh fish." Hánas went to look for him. He was astonished when he recognized Aiko. The two greeted each other as brothers. Others looked at them. Some sneered, "Saami heathens!"

Hánas took Aiko by the elbow, and together they walked behind some pillars where they could talk. They each wanted to know what the other knew about Tuuli. Aiko told the gossip he'd been hearing.

Hánas warned, "When you come to give a fever-breaking potion to my father, let's pretend not to know each other. My father and mother are against me having anything to do with the Saami who live in the town."

36

THE TREES MOANED AS THE WIND ENDLESSLY BLEW, heaping snow in courtyards and around the little hut where Tuuli had learned to feel at home. The women had done much to help her be comfortable. They'd brought her a lamp that gave off a yellow glow. They'd also carried her a pile of furs she could wrap herself in at night and during the cold days.

One morning, they'd found Tuuli bent over her bucket vomiting the food she'd just eaten. They gently lifted her cloak and ran their hands over her stomach. There was just a small rise, but it was enough.

"*Baby, Unge,*" Greta said.

Tuuli nodded and repeated, "*Baby, Unge.*"

The women whispered among themselves. Marit turned away, but Frida and Greta shook their head. Tuuli didn't understand their words, but she could tell from their gestures and tone that they were troubled.

Even before she'd become aware that she was carrying a baby, dreams—bad dreams—had come to her at night. In them, she was back at her siide. Monstrous beings tore their way into her goahti and forced themselves upon her, men half-human and half-creature. Sometimes the creature-half was a frog, sometimes a serpent. And sometimes it was Stallu. Stallu with antlers like a reindeer. Squat and ugly Stallu. Each time, during the violence of the assault, she'd waken with cold sweat running from every pore in her body and her heart pounding. Her head ached. She would not be able to sleep anymore that night, so she'd rise and light the little lamp. Squatting and holding her knees, she rocked on her heels and keened joiks until her heart calmed.

When Tuuli first noticed that her flow of blood had not happened with the moon's cycle, she wished for the leaves and roots that she could chew or make into a drink. They would wash the growing child away like the spring floods that swelled the rivers.

Now that the women knew she carried a baby and didn't seem pleased about it, she tried to make them understand that she needed to drink a potion to empty herself of the life within her. She gestured leaves and roots, a drink, and swept her hands from her belly to the earth. The women seemed to understand. Marit lifted her own cloak and pointed to her own swollen belly. Then she pointed to the snow that was collecting outside. She bent to the earth and with her fist, hit the ground to show how hard it was. She raised her face. Anguish filled her eyes. Tuuli understood. Marit was pregnant and didn't want to deliver a baby, either. Unfortunately, the plants and roots that they needed did not grow during the cold season.

Winter held steady, but mild. Tuuli felt her belly grow little by little. As she grew, so did her fears. Fears of birthing a child without the women of the siide to surround her with care. Fears of who had fathered the child and what her baby would be like.

And with the growing of her belly, new dreams wove into her nights. At times, she dreamed that the baby was born. It would be a beautiful boy with dark eyes and dark hair, looking not at all like the strangers who had broken into her and laid their seed to join with hers. Other times the baby would be monstrous with two heads—one with light hair and eyes the color of the lakes. The other looked like the babies of the Saami women she'd helped in their time of birth. And once, Tuuli awakened screaming.

The birth child of her dreams had sneered with sharp wolf teeth as she brought it to her breast. The little boy had suckled vigorously and painfully. He'd sung joiks in the strangers' tongue on the second day. He'd walked on the third; run after reindeer on the fourth. On the fifth, he'd rejected her breast and, with his sharp fangs, he'd ripped into the fleshy rump of a living deer.

Alone in the dark of the night, she feared the dreams that came with sleep. The first dream was what she wished for her child. The two-headed baby showed that the child came to be from two different people. The third dream disturbed her. How unnatural that child was! If it showed the future of her baby, there would be no gentle life for him or her.

It was after the third dream that Tuuli made a decision. She would have to get away from here. And if she could not free herself, she would find a way to send her child back to the siide, far from these strangers. She did not want the baby she held within her to grow among these people. She was more determined now to learn the strangers' words so she could make her plans to save the child.

When Greta came to bring food or to help her with bathing, Tuuli held on to her arm to get her to stay. She repeated every word Greta said. She pointed to objects. She learned the words for *walk, climb, eat, run, drink, laugh, smile,* and *talk* by doing these things. She also learned the words for the many foods the women brought her. She finally learned enough so she could ask simple questions like, "What place is this?" and most importantly, "How do I leave here?"

Frida and Greta encouraged her. Tuuli learned they were on the grounds of a large castle where King Karl lived. Frida lived on the grounds, but Greta only came during the day to work. Marit often came, too, but left soon after bringing food and taking Tuuli's soiled clothing to be washed.

One day, Tuuli managed to convey other thoughts. Were there many people like her living in the big town surrounding the castle?

Could they find the man who'd called out her name when she arrived? Could they bring him to her? Or her to him? "His name is Beto," she said in the strangers' words. "He is my father."

The women looked from one to the other. Frida wrung her hands. Greta sat next to Tuuli and put her arm around her. Tuuli didn't understand all the words they used to answer her, but she kept a spark of hope within because they didn't say, "Nej."

The day came when the women brought armloads of soft white clothes. They bathed Tuuli even more carefully than usual. They scented her hair with the buds from cedar trees. They rubbed soot from the remains of a fire on the lids of her eyes. They wrapped a cloth around her belly and pulled it so taut that Tuuli groaned and stopped them from giving it yet another tug. Then they had her step into a dress that had layers and layers of cloth. It was then that Tuuli realized they were trying to flatten her stomach and cover it with many gatherings so that her swollen belly didn't show.

"*Varför?*" (Why?) she asked.

Marit smoothed the dress around her shoulders, but Greta explained, "*Karl Kungen.*" The king wanted to see Tuuli.

Finally. She hoped she knew enough of the strangers' words to ask the king to let her return to her people and to beg for them to be left to live their lives without disturbances.

As she planned what to say, Tuuli traced fine blue threads of embroidery on the dress that created a tangle of flowers with many petals such as she had never seen. The long sleeves felt tight on her arms, but the neckline scooped so low that Tuuli felt uncomfortably exposed. She looked down to see her chest half-uncovered. She asked for more clothes to cover herself. "*Mer kläder?*"

She brought her hands up to cover her neck and chest. Greta gently took her hands down and signaled for her to sit. Frida pulled fine stockings onto her feet. They were long, reaching above her knees.

Greta tied bows at Tuuli's thighs to keep the stockings from falling. Then Frida slipped soft leather slippers onto her feet.

When Tuuli put her hands to her breasts, Greta took them down again and softly said, "Nej." Then she began to plait Tuuli's hair. She made many braids and pinned them in a crisscross design. She wove ribbons and cedar greens in and around the braids. Finished, the women stood back and looked at Tuuli.

Greta clasped her hands together and said, "*Du är ganska.*" Frida ran a hand over Tuuli's cheeks and agreed. "Yes, she is pretty. The king will think so, too."

"*Kom, nu.*" Marit reached for Tuuli's arm and opened the door. A stiff wind blew in, chilling Tuuli. She drew back, covering her chest with her hands. Greta picked a bearskin from Tuuli's bed and wrapped it around her. Then both women led her from the storage hut.

A bright winter sun's slanted rays shone into Tuuli's eyes. She blinked and raised a hand to shield them from the sharp brightness. Ice-frosted branches swayed in the wind. A stem of cedar blew from Tuuli's hair. The women hustled her faster toward the huge castle looming in the near distance. Just as they entered a cobbled walk that led to a wooden doorway flanked by four men holding the king's banners, a cloud moved in front of the sun and darkened the day. A chill took hold of Tuuli that even the bear-fur wrap couldn't keep out.

37

Four men stepped forward, blocking the entrance to the castle. They carried long weapons. Tuuli shrunk back. One tore the bearskin from Tuuli, handed it to Frida, and told the women to leave. Then two guards led her down a long passage. Many people lined the way. As she passed, they stopped talking. Some stared rudely. She brought her hands up to cover her chest. Blood rushed to her cheeks. She looked straight ahead and willed herself to be brave. She was finally getting a chance to plead for her people and her own freedom.

"Wind. Wind," she implored, but no wind could come to her within the thick walls.

Her guides stopped at a tall closed door, the likes of which Tuuli never could have imagined in her wildest dreams. Carvings decorated it. Carvings of animals with fierce eyes and long teeth, like a bear's, but longer. Curious, Tuuli reached out to feel the carvings. Her guide scowled and slapped her hand away.

They waited. The people along the long hallway murmured to each other. Some laughed aloud. Tuuli perspired even though her dress was too flimsy to keep her warm. She tried to keep her knees from quivering, but they would not stay steady. She hoped her shaking wasn't visible to those behind her. She wished for Greta, Frida, or Marit to be with her. To take her elbow. To keep her calm. To tell her that everything would be all right. She tried to recall the words Greta had taught her to use with the king, but she couldn't remember a single one.

When the door opened, four men wearing white ermine furs on their shoulders beckoned her to follow. Tuuli breathed deeply and took her first unsteady steps into the king's chamber. Bears! Bearskins lay on the floor all around the room. The heads of bears hung from the walls.

Their teeth were bared. Tuuli's stomach squeezed, shooting bitter bile into her throat. So many dead bears. *Why were their heads cut off?* Bears were sacred to her people. *Why would anyone kill so many?*

She wanted to raise her arms into the air to ask the bear spirits to be with her, but just then her guides parted, and she saw a young man sitting on a silver chair. He didn't look much older than she was, but it must be King Karl. He nodded and sat straighter when he saw her.

The two of them looked back and forth at each other for a long time. Tuuli calmed because he looked so young and unsure of himself. Not knowing what was expected of her, she waited for the king to say something, but more time passed without him saying anything. Finally, she decided if she was to ask for freedom for herself, her people, and her deer, she must do it now. Not remembering the Swedish words, she sang in her own language, hoping there was someone in the room who could change her words into the ones the king would understand.

I am Tuuli,
Daughter of the wind.
Spirit sister of the bear.
Return me to my people,
To the deer.
We need so little.

You have so much.
You take our land, our furs,
Leaving us barely enough to live our days.
Your ways threaten our deer.
Our ways are those of many grandmothers and fathers
Who taught us to honor the deer, the land.
I beg of you. Leave us alone in the cold far north
With our fragile lives.

The king stayed silent for what seemed a changing of the moon. When he did speak, his weak chin trembled. Tuuli strained to hear what he was saying. Too many words she didn't understand, so she just stood, looking at him, trying not to see the bears all around, trying to keep her knees from quaking.

"*Vänd dig om.*" Tuuli didn't know those words. The king gestured a spinning motion, and the men behind her took her by the shoulders and turned her round and round.

"*Komma.*" That Tuuli did know. Slowly she stepped closer to the king. "*Komma,*" he repeated, gesturing her to come even closer. "*Vänd dig on.*" Tuuli turned around again.

Then the king said something to the men behind her. They pulled the folds of her dress tightly to her, showing the roundness of her belly.

"*Med barn!*" shouted the king. He slammed his fist on the arm of his chair. "*Smutsig! Smutsig!*"

Tuuli felt his heated anger. His face tuned red as he shouted. A couple of his men scrambled out of the room and returned carrying a cauldron. Six women followed carrying pitchers of water. They filled the tub.

"*Jaga djävulen ur. Dotter ar mörker, rena din själ!*" yelled the king, standing from his silver chair.

Two men grabbed Tuuli from behind. They pushed hard and dunked her head into the tub. Under the water, she could still hear the king bellowing, "Chase the devil out. Daughter of darkness, cleanse your soul."

When they pulled her up, Tuuli gasped. Water streamed from her hair, her face. She held her stomach as she coughed. Her ribbons dripped onto her dress. She watched the cedar boughs from her hair as they floated on the water and then sank.

38

AIKO BROUGHT A TONIC BREW FOR HÁNAS'S FATHER each day. By the third day, the patient felt much better. His fever had broken. He gathered enough strength to sit up in bed for short periods. His appetite improved. He asked for bread to dip into warm broth.

When he was strong enough to sit for longer times, he gave Hánas orders on how to look after his trading business. So Hánas went to the warehouse every day. First, he had to list the trading goods that would be loaded onto the ship that would sail to the New World as soon as milder weather came. Furs from the ship that had arrived in the fall from across the Atlantic were heaped on shelves. Hánas counted the bales and checked the number against the manifest. He sorted other goods and set them out to be sold: molasses, rum, whale oil. Tobacco. Rye. And grains. Then Hánas began the task of hiring men to pack goods that would be sent from Sweden to the settlers of the Massachusetts Colony: glass, linens, hardware, machinery, and household goods. Hánas checked orders and oversaw the packing.

After Aiko closed the butcher shop each day, he made his way to the warehouse to meet Hánas. They shared any news they might have heard about Tuuli and planned how one or the other would get inside the castle walls.

"The king is very young. Not a bit older than I am," Hánas told Aiko.

"Then maybe he'll be easy to convince that he should free Tuuli."

"Maybe not so easy. His advisors surround him all the time, so it would be difficult to meet with him alone. Worse yet, he is very religious. He has no regard for the Saami. To him, we are dirty pagans. He would sooner burn Tuuli at the stake than be concerned about her welfare."

"Then why did the king send some of his men to bring Tuuli to him in the first place? What does he want her for?"

Hánas answered, "Probably because he'd heard stories about her. About how beautiful she is. About how she is rumored to be the most magical of all the Saami." Then he shook his head. "Exaggerations. Rumors. Gossip. All except the part of her beauty."

The two men walked outside the walls of the castle again and again. They drew plans. Hánas prayed, and Aiko sang joiks.

It was almost spring before Hánas's father gained enough health so that he could go about his business again. Many merchants of the town had been leery about working with Hánas. Even though they respected his father, they didn't like that the boy was a Saami. Regardless, they found him to be honest and easy to do business with, so a few closed deals with him. Others, who wanted to buy trade goods from across the ocean or were looking to ship their wares, snubbed him, saying they would wait until his father was well enough to do business.

When his father checked the work Hánas had done, he clasped a hand on his shoulder. "You have taken care of my business well," he said, but he said nothing about the men who had refused to complete transactions with Hánas. Even though several had refused to work with his son, he needed their partnerships, so he invited them for a drink and shook their hands when they finished their deals.

Spring came, but Aiko and Hánas still had not been able to figure out how to free Tuuli. The gossip they heard lately brought new fears. Most news pointed to Tuuli being kept on the castle grounds but never seen outside the walls. One of guards spat when he told bystanders that the Saami dog-woman was fat with child. Another guard described her as a great beauty who had lured King Karl to her chamber to impregnate her so she could have power over him.

A fisherman's wife said, "That håxa chanted pagan songs even when he brought her to a holy church. He ordered her whipped, but that didn't stop her evil songs."

"I heard the king found her to be so impossible and unwilling to accept God that he banished her from his sight and gave her to his courtmen to do as they wished."

"Everyone says she changed a washerwoman into a shrieking blackbird just by waving her hand and chanting her strange words."

"It is even rumored that the king hired a food taster in case she put a poison spell on him."

"The hunters who were with the king when he killed a bear said that the carcass changed into a flock of ravens that attacked the hunting party and tried pecking their eyes out. They had to fight them off until the next morning."

Hánas and Aiko laughed at some of the gossip, discounting it as pure imaginings, but other parts worried them. What if some of it were true? Was Tuuli safe? Was she suffering, and might worse yet come for her?

When Hánas brought up the subject of Tuuli to his father, he listened and seemed interested. He asked many questions, wanting to know all about her. Hánas told how she had been taken against her will because the king sent for her. Hánas asked his father to talk to the king's kinsmen he knew and ask for an audience. He could then plead for her to be released to him.

"Too dangerous," replied his father. "I have to be careful if I want to keep my trade profitable. You have never been fully accepted by the people here because you are Saami yourself. Many still ask why I ever brought you into my house. Even though you've learned our language and accept our God, you would be suspected of being disloyal if you go ask for that girl's release from the king, and it would be bad for my business."

When Hánas persisted, he said, "Forget about her. She is just a pagan girl of the northern wilds. I should not have let you go with the missionaries." He turned back to his accounting books to let Hánas know the subject was closed.

That night, Hánas overheard his mother and father talking. "I can't have him ruining my business here. I'll send him on one of my trading ships that cross the Atlantic. He'll be far from the castle, far from that girl, far from any temptation to make another trip to the Saami in the north," his father decided.

The next day, his father called him to his office. "The weather is warming, and it will soon be time for another journey to Massachusetts Bay Colony." He added, "I want you to go. You need to learn the business on that end, too. There is great wealth to be made trading there. The colonists are eager to buy our goods."

When Hánas met with Aiko, he said, "My father is sending me across the ocean to the New World. I will be away at least four months, if not five. Depending on the seas, maybe a full year. We need to free Tuuli before the ship leaves. I can stow her aboard. In Massachusetts, she can be free, and after a time, she can come back to her siide."

Early the next morning, his father woke Hánas with an even more surprising order for him. "Get up. A boat is waiting for you. It will carry you to Gothenburg. Here is the list of goods for you to buy. Have them stored until you pick them up later this month on your way to the colonies."

Hánas resisted. "The waterways are still dangerous. It would be better if we stopped there on our way across the Atlantic. That would save us a trip."

"The shipping lanes are open now. No more arguing. Go." His father waved him away. The next day, Hánas sailed.

Aiko didn't know what to think when Hánas was not there to meet him the next day. He spent some time at the docks asking about ships headed for the New World. He was relieved to know that none had left to cross the Atlantic yet.

Not knowing when Hánas would be back, Aiko decided upon a plan that he could carry out himself. Relying on the gossip to bolster his story, he filled a vial with a harmless potion he stirred together. Acting as boldly as he could, he went to the entrance of the courtyards and asked to see Tuuli.

"I'm here to protect the king—and all those who live and work on the castle grounds—from one who would harm them," he explained to the guards. "She's an ungodly person who will use spells and curses any chance she gets." Then Aiko said that she should not be killed on the castle lands because her heathen spirit would forever haunt the castle and all the inhabitants. "My potion will make her comatose. I will then carry her out of the castle lands and far away before giving her a lethal dose."

The guards listened to Aiko, but when he was finished, they roared with laughter. One asked, "Are you the father of the bastard she carries? What a story you tell, you Saami heathen! Go! Get out of here, before we split your gut and feed your entrails to the pigs. The only way your håxa witch will leave is when the king says it is time to bring her to the fires!"

With that, the guards pulled out their swords and ran at Aiko.

39

FRIDA AND GRETA STAYED BY TUULI'S SIDE during her labor that lasted a whole day and night. They spooned broth into her mouth and wiped the sweat from her brow. They'd urged her to push while taking turns cradling her in their arms. In the dim of morning, a baby boy was born. They carefully washed and swaddled him in clean wraps. Then they bathed Tuuli and dressed her in clean clothes.

Spring was flowing into summer already on the birth day. Birds had returned in great flocks, so the air was filled with song. Frida padded a bench for Tuuli out of doors so she could sit in the sunshine amid the budding flower gardens while nursing her baby. Greta busied herself showing Tuuli how to hold him while nursing. Tuuli was amused with the attention and advice. She had helped many of her own siide women during and after birth, so knew how to nurse, but she patiently listened and let Greta fuss with the baby, placing him just so in her arms.

"What will you name him?" asked Frida.

Tuuli had thought about this for a long time. "Lásse," she said. "I know not what tree he will be a branch of, so I will not name him for anyone I know."

Alone the first night with her baby, Tuuli unwrapped his blankets and examined his whole body. She kissed each tiny finger and toe. She traced his brow and nose with her little finger. Fine dark hair covered his head except at the very top. Tuuli gently moved her lips over the hair as she quietly sang a joik to him. When she looked into his dark eyes, he held the look with his own eyes for a long time. Then he moved his mouth as if asking the same questions that Tuuli held in her own heart. Who was this boy with the mixed blood of herself and an odious stranger? How could she free herself to raise this perfect little one among her own people? Would he be a wind listener? Would the drums speak to him? Or would he grow up always wanting to return to the land of the strangers? She whispered into his tiny ear, "Who will you be, Lásse? Who will you be?"

When Frida and Greta discovered that Marit was with child, they had questioned her about the father, but Marit had just shrugged and wrapped her shawl tighter around herself.

Days after Tuuli delivered, Marit lay down in the laundry where she was supposed to be washing linens. She writhed as sharp pains shot through her belly. Greta found her there and with the help of Frida brought her to Tuuli's place. Greta stayed while Frida rushed off to get Marit's mother. The four women took turns tending to Marit. The day turned into night and into day again. Tuuli made soothing teas for Marit to sip. She rubbed rich cooling cream onto Marit's back and tummy while singing soft joiks. The pains still viciously racked Marit's body. The women gave her a twisted cloth to put between her teeth so she would not bite her tongue while in pain.

When night came again but no baby, Tuuli pressed on Marit's stomach, round and round, until she felt that the baby was feet-first. She took Marit's mother's hand and had her feel, too. Then she motioned that the baby needed to be turned before it could enter the world. By this time, Marit was exhausted from the pain. "Yes, turn it," she begged.

None of the women had ever tried such a thing, but Tuuli had seen it done once before. She pressed again, feeling the shape of the baby, trying to find its bum, so she could try to push it upward. At that moment, Marit had a strong contraction.

"Don't push yet," Tuuli said.

"I have to." And with that, Marit screamed and pushed again. The baby's feet started to show in the birth canal. Blood gushed. Marit pushed again, and the baby moved farther along the canal. It was too late to turn it. Tuuli took hold of the feet and gently pulled. She encouraged Marit to push more, but Marit just screamed with pain. Finally, the whole baby emerged.

It was a girl. Tuuli handed her to Greta while Marit's mother knotted and cut the cord. The baby entered the world without a cry, so Greta held her upside down, causing the baby to wail so loudly that all the women sighed with relief. Greta had heated a bucket of water, so she dipped a cloth to wash the blood and tissue from the little girl's face.

"Is she beautiful?" Marit asked from where she lay.

Greta didn't answer. Soon all could see that the washing did not remove a large red stain on the baby's cheek. More washing revealed the bright red continued down the little girl's neck and onto her shoulder. It was a bad omen. Marit cried when she saw her baby. Her mother pointed to Tuuli and said the dreaded word, "Håxa!"

"Nej, nej. Nej," Tuuli said. "I didn't do anything to hurt the baby."

Nothing she said calmed Marit and her mother. Frida told them over and over that Tuuli had saved the little one and had helped all she could, but they insisted that Tuuli be sent away before she could cause any more harm. Greta signaled for Tuuli to follow her outside. They sat on a bench, holding Lásse in the thin spring sunshine. Suddenly, Frida shouted for them to come. "Marit is bleeding! We don't know how to stop it."

Tuuli ran to help, but Marit's mother blocked the doorway so she couldn't enter. "Nej. Nej! Not you!"

Greta shrugged to Tuuli. "I've never been able to stop bleeding." Then she went inside anyway. Holding Lásse tightly to her, Tuuli stood facing the sun. She tried to remember the powerful words Aiko taught her to stop blood from flowing. Soon Greta came out. "It's bad," she said. "Do you know of a tea or potion that will staunch the bleeding?"

Tuuli didn't have any roots or leaves, so she shook her head. She raised one hand to the sun and sang the words she remembered. A brisk breeze began to whirl around the courtyard. In the flurry, flocks of warblers and siskins circled above. A white bird spread its wings and floated on the wind currents high in the blue sky. In the spinning of the winds, Tuuli's hair loosened from the twisted knot high on her head. The winds picked it up and swirled it about as she held her own son tightly and sang louder and louder.

All this happened in the same moment that there was a changing of the guards at the castle, and many of the sentries saw Tuuli twirling with the sudden burst of wind. The strangeness of her song fell upon their ears. They were dumfounded amid the flurry. And then it stopped as quickly as it had started.

Tuuli was brushing her hair from her face in the calm when Frida came out announcing that the bleeding had stopped. "We didn't need you at all," Marit's mother said as she left to make arrangements for a horse and cart to bring her daughter and grandchild to her home.

In the days that followed, Greta brought news that Marit refused to bring the red-stained little girl to her breast, so the baby had been given over to a wet nurse. Tuuli looked at her own baby nursing contentedly. She listened to his soft suckling sounds and watched as he kneaded her breast with his little hand. She could never have left her little boy with someone else to cuddle and nurse, even though he was planted in her with pain and shame.

40

EVERY DAY, AIKO LISTENED TO THE GOSSIP brought to the butcher shop by the fishermen and the customers. He did not hear any direct news of Tuuli until one day the wife of a palace guard excitedly told of a sudden flurry of winds and birds and a strange woman with a baby, who was kept hidden inside the walls of the castle grounds.

Her friend whispered, "She is a real håxa, a witch. She stirred the winds and invoked the birds by her songs. At the exact moment that she was calling upon the dark spirits, a daughter was born to a serving woman who had been kind to her. The baby was stained with a huge raspberry-red mark on her cheek, neck, and shoulder."

Another joined in, "I heard that, too. The mother blamed the håxa for her child being born with a blood sign of impending doom. The poor mother had nothing to do but send her baby away. Now she hides herself and her shame in a dark room, thinking gloomy thoughts, worrying when and what disaster will happen next. She eats little and weakens more each day."

Days later, news arrived that one of the king's merchant ships had sailed into a sudden storm on its way to Stockholm from Denmark.

The ship foundered and sank. The men on a nearby ship witnessed the whole ordeal. They gathered on the wharf. One spoke louder than the rest. "Winds spun that doomed ship and rocked it with violent waves, but our own vessel, even though close by, was hardly distressed by the winds."

Their story stirred the people of the town to a frenzy. *It must be the håxa.* Many clamored for her to be brought to trial. She had such great power that she brought death and disaster on the seas as well as in their town. Burning at the stake would be the best punishment for her and a warning to all other Saami håxas.

In the butcher shop and throughout the whole town, everyone buzzed with stories about the witch. Women flocked to churches. They burned candles. They beat their chests and appealed to all the saints to save them. They called for Tuuli's trial and burning at the stake to happen. The demands of the people swelled each day. Groups gathered in the streets. They passed gossip and incited more and more anger.

Aiko feared for Tuuli. He walked along the walls of the castle once again, looking for a breach through which he could squeeze himself. He went deep into the forest. Along the way, he picked mushrooms, roots, and leaves. He crushed the leaves. He peeled the roots. He stirred memories of his forebears with chants and potions. He raised his hands to Beavi. He throated a simple joik. He called to the raven. He called to the bear. He called to the fox. He called to the hare.

Raven, fly high.
Look over the wall.
Bear, lend me your strength.
Fox, teach me to be so sly.
Hare, lead me to succeed in all.

He heated the mixture over a small fire. When it was ready, he snuffed the flames and hid in dense brush so no one would see him while he was in a trance evoking the ancient ways. As night fell, he sipped the mixture. As juices slid down his throat, he willed himself to ride high in the air with the night birds. He asked for their sharp eyes to help him see the way over the castle walls and to find Tuuli.

When he opened his eyes, rays of Beavi shone directly upon him, almost blinding him with their brilliance. He lingered on his bedding of leaves and branches, bringing back the visions he'd had of himself climbing the castle wall where many vines grew. Dropping from the steep inner side of the wall to the ground could be dangerous and difficult to scale on the way out. He wished Hánas were there to help make a rope ladder so Tuuli could climb her way out, but that was not to be, and he dared not wait. He would have to get her out that night.

During the day, just about everyone who entered the butcher shop brought more and more gossip of the trial and burning of the håxa. It was set for the morrow. One woman beamed with joy as she laughed and talked about how happy she would be to see the witch burned. Aiko looked for the oldest fish, one that should have been thrown for fertilizer into a garden, and wrapped that for her order. The butcher kept Aiko busy cutting meat for customers, so he didn't have time even for a noonday meal. It was almost dark when the shop closed. He hurried to the forest to find tough vines to twist into a rope, but couldn't find what he needed in the dim evening light. He needed to act.

He sat on the soft ground and sank deep into his thoughts. In a low, solemn chant, he droned a joik that joined him to the spirits of the earth and of the sky. He peered through the blackness of night with Owl. He flew over the walls on the wings of Raven. Brother Hare led him to Tuuli. Then Fox guided them all safely past the guards.

41

THE BUTCHER WAKENED FROM A FRIGHTENING DREAM. His heart raced, and his nightshirt stuck to his chest, soaked with perspiration. He looked at his wife lying next to him. She snored in bursts. That must have been what stirred him. A full night's sleep had escaped him for several months now. His age was showing, and with it, his bladder urged him to get up and go to the outhouse or to use the bucket under the bed more than once each night.

He was not a particularly religious man, but feeling agitated, he prayed to the saints an exhortation that he could fall back asleep. Weary, he closed his eyes, but repeated sounds roused him again and again. What were they? A storm blew heavily. Was it the wind or a branch hitting the house during the gusty night? He turned over, but more worries disturbed him. Even though the butcher shop had been busy every day, Aiko often begged for time off. "I must find a way to free my friend. I feel she is in danger," he'd repeat often, tugging at his hair.

The butcher's customers called Aiko's friend *håxa*. The stories grew more and more incredible each day. He heard that she had put a spell on a baby so it had weakened and died. Then she had cursed a ship so that it foundered and sank. The king was enraged because he was unable to find any bears on his hunts. She was suspected of having cast a spell every time something went wrong. Yesterday, she'd even been blamed when a nobleman's wife had fallen and broken her arm. And in the day to come, she was going to be judged and burned at the stake.

The tapping sound broke into his thoughts again. It was definitely a tapping. A tapping on his window. Neither the wind nor a branch would make that sound. With a sigh, he heaved himself from bed and went to the window. There huddled in the rain were two people—Aiko and someone wrapped from head to toe in a blanket.

Stumbling in the dark, the butcher lit a lamp and unbarred the door. "Come in out of the storm," he whispered.

"Quiet. Quiet." Aiko pressed a finger to his lips. "And no light."

"What's happening?" asked the butcher as he turned the lamp's wick down.

Whispering as he slid a blanket off the person with him, Aiko said, "I've got Tuuli here. And her baby boy. We need a place to stay until the storm blows over."

42

HÁNAS STOOD ON THE FORWARD DECK of the trading ship as it navigated among the many islands that laced the waters outside the port of Stockholm. He drummed his fingers on the rail, impatient with the slowness of the journey through the sandbars and dangerous waters. He leaned forward as if he could hurry the ship along.

His thoughts ran to Tuuli. Was she safe? Was it true that she carried a baby, and if so, whose was it? He could think of no one that she would have given herself to. And he was eager to meet up with Aiko to find out if he'd made a plan to free Tuuli. The ship he was on carried household furnishings, linens, lamps, farming implements, and many other goods that his father intended to ship to the Massachusetts Bay Colony. When the boat came into port, his father would speedily unload the ship and reload everything onto a larger and stronger boat that would make the journey across the Atlantic. He, Hánas, would have only three or four days before he left again.

The first thing he did after leaving the ship and its goods entrusted to his father's manager was to go to the butcher shop. The owner was busy with a long line of customers. His business had doubled since

Aiko had taken over the task of buying from the fishermen and farmers. He owed it all to Aiko, who selected the best fish and meats that were offered, and he was skillful at slicing cuts of meat to perfection. The butcher nodded to Hánas as he entered. Sweat ran off the butcher's brow. Summer's heat was at its fullest. Hánas wondered where Aiko was. The butcher could have used help in the warmth of the day with so many customers remaining. As he waited for the line to dwindle, snatches of gossip caught his ears.

"Did you hear that the håxa got away?"

"*Ja*, and her trial was supposed to be today."

"When they went to get her, she was gone."

"The night guards were questioned, but none saw or heard anything."

Could it be they are talking about Tuuli? Hánas caught the butcher's eye, who kept wrapping a leg of mutton but pressed his lips together tightly and slowly nodded. Hánas's heart pounded in his chest. Now sweat gathered under his arms and on his forehead. He hoped Aiko and Tuuli were together. Then there would be hope that they'd get away.

A woman who held a baby in her arms said, "The king has sent a hundred searchers into the forests, on all the trails and roads, everywhere. He has spies at the docks, too. She won't get away."

Another added, "The searchers have been told not to return until they find her."

"And here we were hoping to see her burn this very night."

Hánas felt light-headed. He leaned against a barrel of salted fish. Finally, the shop emptied and the butcher signaled him into the small back room. Sides of venison, pork, and mutton hung from hooks ready to be cut into roasts and chops. A clay pot of intestines soaked in brine, ready to be stuffed with spicy sausage meats. A pile of hooves from pigs lay on a sheet of bark ready to be salted. Heat, fear, and the cloying odor wafting from the meat and fish made Hánas's stomach give a sudden heave. He managed to swallow the surge, but he had to lean against the wall to steady himself.

The butcher asked, "Are you all right?"

"I'm overcome. Tired from the voyage. The waters were rough. High waves. The boat pitched and rolled." Then Hánas whispered, "I know whom everyone is talking about. I feel helpless. I should be thankful she is free, outside the castle walls, but I fear for her safety. So many would have her burned."

A customer entered the shop. The butcher pushed Hánas into a corner and told him to stay out of sight. When the butcher returned, Hánas asked why Aiko was no longer helping him in the shop.

"He was yesterday, but he has other things to tend to today and maybe for many days."

Hánas almost dared not ask. He whispered, "Tuuli?"

Again, the butcher slowly nodded. A deluge of relief flowed through Hánas. More customers entered the shop, so the butcher pointed Hánas to the corner again and went to help them. The customers were slow to give their orders. They talked of how the moon clouded over when the håxa was escaping.

One said, "I saw the shadow of a flock of night-flying birds carry the witch away!"

Another said, "I saw the stars form a stairway for her to escape up to the sky before the birds flew her away."

When they finally left, the butcher said to Hánas, "Leave now. See your father and mother. Then come after dark to my house."

Hánas wanted to ask more, but the butcher held a finger to his lips, shook his head, and then handed him a roast and a slew of small herrings to bring to his mother. At home, his father read over the manifest of goods bought, the prices, and then figured out what each item would be sold for in the New World. Hánas tried not to fidget. For supper, his mother spread a feast of herring, fresh breads, cheeses, cakes, and pastries she'd baked in anticipation of his return. He'd only been gone a short time, but she already worried because he would be on a ship again within a very few days.

"Eat," his mother said. "I made all your favorite foods." She patted his hands, his shoulders, and his head. He felt like a little boy again.

"Do you remember your first day coming to this house? You were only about ten years old. Oh, so frightened! You tried to hide your tears at night. I couldn't calm you. I didn't know your words, and you didn't know mine. You didn't want to give up your old clothes. Not even when we made you take a bath."

"Yes, I remember it all so well. I could tell by your voice that you were kind. You cooked foods you thought I'd like, but they were so new to me and I was so lonesome for my dead mother that I couldn't eat much."

"I led you by the hand to show the house, the foods, the town. I had you repeat each word until you could say it perfectly. Most people thought we were crazy bringing a Saami boy into our house. I'd wanted a son for so long, I didn't care you were one of those. And now you are my son."

Hánas held her in his arms. She had always been so good to him, and now he must leave. And he must betray her trust.

Weeping, she said, "If your father weren't so old, you wouldn't need to do a man's work yet. You know I miss you every day you are away. So many ships are lost in Atlantic storms. I will pray on my knees every evening for your safe return."

After the huge supper, his father invited him back to his desk to go over orders again. Hánas cleared his throat constantly. He felt impatient. He wanted to go to the butcher's before it was late—before they went to bed for the night. He was anxious to know what the butcher knew about Aiko and Tuuli.

43

Sails caught the wind and billowed, thrusting the ship forward. Crewmen hurried on deck, pulling ropes and adjusting sails when the gusts were strong. The boards of the hull squeaked as the sailing ship Hánas had secreted Tuuli on rocked back and forth with the Atlantic waves.

"Tell me again why we come on this big boat so far away and not return to my siide with Aiko and my Lásse?" Tuuli asked.

"It would not be safe. Not for you. Not for Lásse. Not for me. Not for your people and your deer. The king commanded hundreds to scour the land for you. My adopted father even walks on eggshells because some suspect that he helped you escape. And Nils, the butcher who hid you, if anyone saw you and Aiko at his house, he, too, would be in danger. There are so many angry people. If they knew, the fires set for witches by the so-called nobles of King Karl's court could be used to burn the life from my father and the butcher. For now, it is better to be far away, out of their reach."

"Who knows that I am with you on this ship?"

"The butcher and my father might suspect, even though I told them that you had gone with Aiko to the far north."

"What is this witchcraft that they burn people for? All I did was sing joiks to stop Marit's bleeding. It was the same that Poppi and any noaidi would have done for a new mother. The woman lives. The baby, too."

"Yes, but the baby was born with a red stain on her face, neck, and shoulder."

"Nothing I did caused the bloodred stain," said Tuuli, beating her fist on her chest. "I tried to tell them, but I didn't know enough of their strange words, so they didn't understand."

"I know. I wish I'd been there so I could have helped and turned your words into their words. Then you would be free."

"Free? Ever since I arrived at that castle they call Stockholm, I have had no freedom. No chance to walk outside the walls of the castle. No chance to pick berries or fish for graylings. Most of the time, I was trapped in a dark storehouse."

Tuuli had told this part of her story to Hánas many times on the ocean journey, but she needed to say it again and again. Each time, she wanted to tell him the worst part, the vile men, and what they'd done to her. He must wonder who'd fathered her son, but the memories were raw wounds to her, and the words would cut him, too, so the words remained unspoken, curling like twisted roots gripping her heart.

"Even you—on this ship, on this rocking water—keep me hidden in the dark. When will I ever be free?"

Hánas bent his head low. His voice cracked as he said, "Maybe I am wrong to bring you so far from your people. I hide you from others on board who might report to the king that you were on this ship. I only want you to be safe."

Tuuli turned from him to hide her tears. She no longer knew what was right and what was wrong. She missed her son. Her breasts ached with an emptiness, missing him, his sweet smell, his gentle eyes, his lovely mouth.

"Aiko has told me how he gained entrance over the castle walls and found you there," Hánas said, breaking the silence that grew between them.

"Did he say he flew in with a flock of ravens?" Tuuli asked, glad to have something else to talk about.

"Yes." They both laughed picturing Aiko, high in the dark sky, flapping his arms, surrounded with ravens.

"It wasn't quite like that," Tuuli said. "Greta wanted to help me escape the fires set for me, so late that night, she came with a sling for Lásse to be tied to my back. She also boosted me as high as she could at a place in the wall that was out of sight of the guards. I had just scrambled high enough to grasp the top of the wall. I wasn't sure I could raise myself higher to get my feet up, when Aiko grabbed hold of my hand. He had come to save me at that exact time!"

After two full changes of the moon, the day finally came when Hánas opened the door to Tuuli's cabin and said, "Come. See. The shores of the new land are in sight." He handed her a hat and coat of his own. "Tuck your hair up. We'll disguise you like a man. Not that it'll do any good. Some of the deckhands already suspect that you're aboard."

The sun shone warmly on Tuuli's shoulders as she stood on deck. The ship rocked and rolled with the waves of never-ending waters, and she swayed with it. The sky was the same beautiful blue as in the land of the Saami. The white clouds were the same, too. The waters below rippled with silver tips. Like the lakes at home, but so much bigger. She spun around and saw how vast the ocean was. Her legs felt wobbly, so she held on to the rail watching the waves splash; she rocked back and forth with the rise and fall of the ship.

Beautiful earth lay ahead. She looked forward to hearing birds sing and wondered if the wind would whisper to her here, so far from her home.

The *Kristina* nosed closer toward a port near an old wooden fort that overlooked the wide expanse of waters that separated Europe from the New World. Hánas held Tuuli close as the waters calmed and the ship slowed. A scurry of men pulled the canvas of sails and tied them tightly to the masts. Eager to be on dry land, those on board gathered on deck and talked excitedly among themselves. "A new life.

A new start. Riches can be made here." Tuuli was not excited. She wanted to be home. With Lásse. But she kept her head down and became part of the crowd.

Onshore, Hánas tied a bundle to Tuuli's back and handed her Poppi's rowan walking stick. Tuuli held the stick to her cheek, to her heart, and ran her hands up and down its length.

"Where? When? How?" she asked.

Hánas gave a little laugh and answered, "Do you think I would have left your bundle behind when I journeyed from the cold north to return to my adopted home?"

At that moment, Tuuli felt a gentle rhythm thumping on her back. "My drum? I never heard it inside the ship."

"Yes, your drum. The white fawn's pelt. And your sleeping robe." Hánas heard the drum beat, too, as he had many times when he had hidden it under his coat. He was glad the drum was now with Tuuli. He wouldn't have to struggle, wondering if he were meant to be a noaidi. He wouldn't have to wonder if the god of his adopted people was the one and only true god while the drum called to him.

"How could you have kept all this secret from me for the whole journey?" She playfully tapped him on the arm with the walking stick.

Hánas didn't answer. He just stood by her side. Then he murmured softly in Saami words. "You will be fine. You are safe now. A new world awaits us. Even though I will have to return to my father with this ship full of trade goods, I will come back. And someday, when it is safe, I'll take you back to your Lásse."

He was strong and assuring, but her heart yearned for her home, her goahti, her people, the reindeer, the land where the sun didn't shine for two passes of the moon each cold season, yet shone almost every moment of every day during the warm time. And most of all—Lásse.

Hánas hefted a larger pack and tied it to his own back and said, "We need to find housing. The butcher gave me the name of a gun-smith and his wife. They are relatives of his wife. It will be good for you to be with a family." A cloud passed over the sun, giving Tuuli a chill.

THE THIRD JOURNEY

Báiki

I am Tuuli.
Far from my people.
Far from the home that is always in my heart
Wherever I go.

44

A GIRL WITH HAIR AND SKIN DARKER THAN TUULI'S served the meal, carefully placing pewter platters of potatoes, onions, quahogs, and hot bread before them. She did her work quickly without saying a word. The gunsmith's wife, Good Woman Kron, called her Waban.

Aboard the ship, during the crossing, Hánas told Tuuli about slaves from Africa that had been brought to the Massachusetts Bay Colony.

"What is Africa?" she had asked.

Hánas unrolled a sheepskin onto the dark floor. "Here," he pointed, "Saami lands. Here—King Karl. Here is Africa. Here—wide ocean we are crossing. And here is the New World to which we sail. The slaves aren't free," he continued. "They have been bought by their owners."

"Owners?" Tuuli had trouble understanding what that meant. She herself had not felt free when she was on the castle grounds of King Karl, but she hadn't been forced to do any work. Now she wondered if Waban was a slave even though she was not black as night as Hánas had described the Africans.

239

After the meal, Hánas gave Good Man Kron a pouch full of coins, and to his wife, a set of fine tableware. Good Woman Kron exclaimed over the beauty and delicacy of the plates and cups.

"Thank you for the wonderful gift," she said as she spread the plates on the table. "And, of course, we'll keep this girl as if she is our own daughter." The wife said this without looking at Tuuli once. Even during the meal, she looked right past her, as she had the serving girl. Tuuli felt a small shudder.

That night, after Hánas left, the wife lit a lamp and signaled for Tuuli to follow. They climbed many stairs until they reached a small room at the very top of the house. Good Woman Kron took a comb and a bar of soap from her pocket and laid them on a small cot. Then she turned and went back down the stairs without a word to Tuuli. Soon Waban struggled up the stairs carrying a tin tub. Later, she brought buckets of warm water. After pouring them into the tub, she signaled for Tuuli to bathe and said, "*Tvätta.*"

Tuuli said, "Ja." A shiver passed through her. *Tvätta* was one of the first words she'd learned from Frida. Why was washing herself the first thing strangers always wanted her to do? Tuuli tried a few more of the Swedish words she knew, but Waban just said, "*Sømn*," and went down the stairs.

Days passed as Hánas kept busy unloading the trade goods he'd brought across the ocean. Then he spent more days buying whale oil, dried fish, ground corn, even cattle. He came to the Kron house each evening when his work was done. They all sat in a small room while they visited. "I'm loading as much as I can for the trip to the islands of the West Indies," he said.

"What will you trade for?" Tuuli was amazed when Hánas unrolled the vellum map again and drew his finger across the ocean, down and then up again, to show the route he'd take.

"There, I'll take on sugar, molasses, and tobacco, but I won't trade the whale oil. That all goes back to Sweden. My father said those things bring a good price at home."

Home. Tuuli drew her finger across the wide ocean that separated her from Lásse. So far away. Tuuli felt tears gather. The wife Kron noticed, pursed her lips, and stabbed her needle into the embroidery she worked on.

The days passed slowly for Tuuli. She tried to help Waban in the kitchen, but the Good Woman turned her away. She tried to talk a bit with the wife, but she turned away again. When she opened the door to go for a walk, the wife closed it and said, "*Nej, nej,*" and pointed for her to go up to her room.

The gunsmith dominated Hánas's visits. He asked about Sweden—his homeland. He worried aloud about the Indians, the Wampanoags. He had heard rumors that their *sachems* were complaining about settlers who stretched their farms into native hunting lands.

The gunsmith spat into his spittoon. "Bah," he said. "The English call that Indian chief *King Philip* because he's the head of many other sachems. He's no king. A savage doesn't deserve to be called so."

Tuuli noticed Waban stayed in the kitchen working during these conversations but that she often stopped to listen. She herself only understood some of the words being said. Her knowledge of Swedish wasn't enough. She wanted to ask Hánas questions. To tell him how things were for her. That for days on end, she had nothing to do. Once when she tried to talk to him in Saami, the smith had interrupted and then spoken right over her. The smith always stayed with them until it was time for Hánas to retire to his boat.

On the day that Hánas's ship was loaded, he came to take his leave. He brought Tuuli two dresses and a shawl like the ones women in the colony wore. She felt the cloth—smooth and thin. The one blue like the skies. The other red like the berries of the rowan tree. She held the dresses to herself. The skirts were full and reached the floor. He also brought her a small book.

"Thank you for the dresses. I'd rather wear clothes made from deerskin, but I know I'll have to wait until I return." She then handed the book back to him, saying, "I will have nothing to do with strangers' books."

She wouldn't touch it again until Hánas explained, "It's called a dictionary. In it are words that will help you learn the language of the colony." He continued, "I also found a tutor who will come and help you learn to speak and read English."

"Thank you, but I want to go back with you. I miss my Lásse. I need to be with him."

"Stay here with the smith and his wife. I've left them money for your keep and for anything you might need. Just ask. They'll get it for you. They assured me that they will care for you like the child they never had. In just twelve or thirteen full moons, I will be back."

Tuuli begged again, "Don't leave me here. I don't think they'll be good to me. The woman Kron doesn't let me do anything. She won't even allow me to leave this house."

"I think she's just concerned about your safety until you learn the language. The tutor will start coming tomorrow. When you know English, it will be easier for you to go out among the people of the town."

"I want to go back with you. To my people. My heart hurts to be so far from Lásse. Take me with you!"

"It is too dangerous," he answered, but his voice quavered. "When I return, perhaps I will have news that it is safe for you to go back or that I can find a way to bring Lásse to you. Remember, the king and townspeople were clamoring for your death by fire. It is better that you are here, out of their reach. You are safe now. No tongues of fire can reach you here."

45

THE DAY AFTER HÁNAS LEFT, GOOD WOMAN KRON scooped Tuuli's new dresses and comb into her arms. "*Inte i mitt hus,*" (Not in my house) she muttered over and over as she carried them to the tiny hut in the backyard where Waban slept on a bag filled with cornhusks. Tuuli gathered her own bundle with the drum and fur pelts. She gripped Poppi's walking stick as she followed.

From then on, Tuuli helped Waban scrub floors on her knees until they stung and ached. Her hands chapped and cracked. The two stirred chowders over a hot fire, kneaded brown bread, and sliced onions for stews. They picked corn and squash from the backyard garden. Every evening, they carried reeking slop pails to empty in the ditch behind their hut. Tuuli and Waban did not have their own slop pail, so they squatted over the open ditch to relieve themselves. In hot weather, the stench from the ditch stung their noses when they finally finished their day's work and retired to the hut.

Before bed each night when the weather was mild, they went to a small cove to swim and wash themselves. It was there that they rinsed their dresses and then spread them on bushes near the house to dry.

When the young man came to teach Tuuli English, the Good Woman told him not to come. "But I've been paid. I will come and do my job," he insisted.

"*Inte i mitt hus*," the smith's wife said. "Go to the back hut, if you must, but only after she has finished her work. It is best if you forget about teaching her English and spend your time purging the heathen from her."

From then on, the tutor came as dark settled. Tuuli and Waban sat cross-legged on Poppi's fur robe while the young man sat on the corn-husk bag. After a day or two, he brought a three-legged stool with him.

They each pointed to his or her chest and said their names, repeating the sounds until the others were able to say it perfectly. Alden Cooper. Al-den-coo-per. He told them that his father made and fixed barrels that were used for storing whale oil, apples, grains, and so much else just as his father and grandfather before him. "My father earns us a good living because everyone needs barrels. He wants me to follow him in business, but I don't want to be a cooper. I don't care about having a big house and fancy clothes. I want to study at Harvard, so I'm preparing to go there."

"What is Harvard?" asked Waban.

"It's where I'll go to learn more Latin and Greek. I'll be able to read the Bible in those languages. I want to be a minister of God the Almighty, who made heaven and earth."

"Oh, like Nanabozho," Waban said.

"No. Not at all. You shouldn't even think they're the same." Alden Cooper frowned. "I will serve the one true god, not some heathen demon."

Tuuli asked what a minister was. Alden took out a black book. "This is my Bible. When I'm a minister, I'll use it to bring the word to many people. I want everyone to follow the true ways. Already," he said, nodding to Waban, "some of your savages have converted and come to the college to learn so they can go out to your people and tell them stories of my Lord, too."

Tuuli shuddered when she saw the black book. She'd traveled so far, yet here it was again. Master Alden was just like the strangers who came to their siide wanting to make the Saami turn against all they believed. Tuuli scowled. She looked to where her drum was hidden inside the pouch Poppi had made for it so long ago.

Although she was not happy about Master Alden's intents, Tuuli was glad that she and Waban were learning a language together so they could talk more to each other. Tuuli learned new words quickly and soon was able to put her ideas together without thinking too long. At night, she asked Waban to teach her words in her language, too.

Saami, Swedish, English, and Wampanoag words sometimes mixed and tumbled in her head until she hardly knew which was which at times. It seemed as though each had a different flavor on her tongue. She liked the softness of Waban's language. The words flowed like the waters of a gentle stream, just like Saami. She taught Waban *guovza* for *bear*, and Waban taught her *maske*. Tuuli learned that *cone* was Waban's word for *sun*. It was so different from her word *Beavi*. They giggled with each other when they had trouble saying each other's words right.

Waban told stories of her people. "We live by the forest where there is good hunting. We fish the waters, too. And dig for clams. We plant gardens of corn, beans, and squash. We use skins from the deer for our clothing."

"Yes, yes, yes," said Tuuli. So much was the same as her own Saami.

Then Waban told how she'd gotten her name. "On the day that I was born, my mother wrapped me in the fur of a pure white deer. The sky had been filled with gray stormy clouds, but soon a strong wind whirled and whooshed, blowing them high across the big waters. My grandmother named me Waban for the wind that gusted and swooped when I took my first breaths."

"My name honors the wind, too," said Tuuli, "but it is for the wind that blew breath into me when I was born with none of my own."

Then Tuuli pulled Gabba's white pelt from her bundle. "Look," she said. "We have white deer, too." And then she tried to explain how the little fawn had been born with a lame foot.

"What do you mean?" asked Waban.

245

Tuuli curled her own foot and pretended to be limping.

Waban laughed. And Tuuli joined her. The two lay on their bedding laughing until their sides ached. They and their people were so much alike. Tuuli's heart softened for the first time since she'd been separated from Lásse. She'd found a sister far from home. *Numisses* is what Waban called her. *Sister.*

The next time Master Alden came, he asked Waban, "Why do your people resist the word that I and others bring to them? We only want to save your souls."

Waban replied, "We already have our spirit brothers. We do not need words from—"

He raised a hand and hushed her. "Because your people resist the word and won't sell their land, I have heard word the town council has voted that the Wampanoag will have to give up all their muskets. They're afraid the natives will rise up against the townspeople."

"Why?" asked Tuuli after the tutor had gone.

"It's been a long time since I have been free to go to my people. The English wanted the land, but our sachem wouldn't sell to them. They burned our village. My mother and father died in the fire. I was captured. Then I was put up for sale as a slave. The smith Kron bought me to serve his wife. And the Coat People took our land anyway."

"When will you go back to your people?" Tuuli asked.

"I think never. I am not free to go. If the Krons aren't pleased with my work, I'll be sold again to someone else. Maybe to someone who will treat me even worse."

Tuuli thought of how the strangers had used fires to destroy the drums and to threaten to scatter the deer. Strangers had taken her against her will. Two sides of the ocean. So far apart. And yet the same things happened.

"My people suffered hunger many times when the cows of the newcomers trampled our corn and squash. They took our land, built their houses, and pushed us farther and farther into the woods. Coat People are never satisfied. And the big boats bring many more who take even more of our land. It is time to fight back," Waban said, "and that is why they fear us."

Then Tuuli told of the strangers who came to her siide; they also wore dark coats. They were Coat People, too. Their language was different—not English but Swedish, the language the Krons used at home. No matter the language, they were cruel. They took what they wanted and destroyed the rest.

One afternoon, Good Woman Kron left the house carrying her black book as she did in the middle of every week. Before she left, she rapped her umbrella against the table and said, "Don't be lazy. Bake fresh bread and have the evening meal ready when I get back." She needn't have said that. Waban and Tuuli always had the evening meal ready when the pointers on the tall clock in the hallway aimed straight up and down. As they mixed the ingredients for the bread, the gunsmith Kron came home. They heard him stomping from room to room even up to the third floor.

"Oh, no. Not again," Waban whispered, wiping her hands on her apron.

When he came into the kitchen, the smithy leaned against the cupboard and watched the two as they covered the dough and set it to rise. Then, as Waban turned to get another chunk of wood for the fire, the gunsmith grabbed her by the arm and pulled her out of the kitchen and toward the stairs to his room.

Tuuli ran up the steps two at a time following the pleas of Waban crying, "No! No!" The smith pushed Tuuli back. He slammed the door in her face. She pushed against the door with her shoulder. She banged with her fist. Red-faced, the smith burst out of the room, hit Tuuli in the chest, and forced her to the stairs. There he kicked her feet from under her and would have propelled her down the steps if she had not held fast to the railing.

"Stay out of this, dirty pagan! Or you'll be next!" He stomped back to his room, loosening his trousers as he went.

Clunk. Tuuli heard him bar the door from the inside. She heard a slap. She heard, "Shut your mouth!" Then Waban no longer struggled or cried out.

Shaken and hurting, Tuuli went down to the kitchen. She tried to block out the sounds from up the stairs while she stirred the beans. With each creak. With each thump. With each bang, Tuuli relived her own awful assault on frozen ground so long ago.

The bread had almost completely risen when Waban came back down. Tuuli rushed to hold her. Together, they cried. Together, they shucked oysters. Together, they added wood to the stove. Together, they shaped loaves of bread and put them into the oven. They set the dining room table with dishes that Hánas had carefully packed and brought across the ocean. Two silver spoons, two forks, and two knives. Glasses and mugs. Waban reached to the high shelf for a pewter platter and bowl for serving the meal. Tuuli pulled the bread from the oven. She tapped the crust. It made the hollow sound of a loaf well baked. She tapped her own chest. Her heart beat with anger. Hollow. Tuuli cut the bread. Waban looked at her. Tuuli held the knife and pretended to stab. Once. Twice. Three times. Waban almost smiled. She filled a kettle at the pump and put it over the fire to warm.

The Good Woman came home. Delicate aromas swelled in the kitchen as the meal cooked. The Good Man sat at the dining room table. Tuuli and Waban listened to him saying the words of thanks. When they heard, "Amen," they carried the platters of food and set them on the table. Back in the kitchen, Waban and Tuuli passed a tin mug back and forth between them, dunking bread crust into a tea they'd steeped with leaves from the woods.

46

THAT NIGHT, THE WIND BLEW HARD. Rain throbbed on the tin roof of the little hut. "He troubled me many times before you came," Waban whispered in the dark. Her sobs mingled with the wind and hung like a chill in the little room. "I thought he was done with me when you came, but it was not to be."

Tuuli arose from her bedding and lay close to her friend, holding her softly. Her own dreams that night clawed and dug deep into her memory of the violence on her own body by strangers.

The cold time came and went.

The sun and warmth followed.

On the afternoons when the Good Woman faithfully tucked her black book under her shawl and left the house, the Good Man faithfully left his work at the gunsmith shop and came home to bed Waban.

Tuuli hated those afternoons as much as Waban did. Each time, Tuuli remembered her own helplessness—her hands tied to the tree.

Moss stuffed in her mouth. Her cries unheeded. All the while she heard the creaking of the bed and the banging on the headboard, sour bile rushed into her own throat. Tears flooded her eyes. Some fell into the mutton stew she stirred. On to slices of sausage sizzling on the cooktop. And into the cornmeal she mixed for cakes.

The two were shaking the eiderdown pillows from the smith's bed in the fresh air when Waban asked, "Why you cry so much for me?"

"A bad man took me against my will, too. Others followed him. And then I had a baby." Tuuli rocked her arms as though she held a baby and cooed a soft joik. "Lásse," she said, "my Lásse."

Waban dropped a pillow to the ground and hugged Tuuli. "Where is your Lásse now?"

Tuuli stretched her arms and pointed to where the sun rose. "Far away. Many days across the big water."

They both looked to the ocean. A whaling ship drifted toward land. Dockworkers already stood onshore waiting to help tie the boat to pilings along the pier. Women rushed to the shore, waving, hoping to see their husbands, sons, or brothers on deck waving back.

"I fear every cycle of the moon that my blood will not flow. If I get with child, I'm sure I will be put on the sales block as once before. Except this time, if no one buys me, I will be put on a ship and sent far across the ocean." Waban held her hand to block the sun's reflections on still waters of the bay.

A breeze kicked up. Tuuli held her head high, listening. No whispers had come to her on the wind since she'd come to this strange land. Her only comfort was that Hánas would be returning soon.

The full bloom of summer came and with it a sweltering heat. Tuuli and Waban often carried their bedding outside and slept under the moon and stars, welcoming ocean breeze to dry sweat from their bodies. Waban pointed out groupings of stars and told Tuuli what her people called them, and Tuuli told the stories her people repeated around campfires. They took turns visiting the landings of each ship. Tuuli drew a picture of what banner the Swedish ships flew for Waban. Blue with a yellow cross. Days came and went, but no Hánas. Often, Waban nudged Tuuli to keep stirring a porridge or to keep her mind on measuring salt into soup. She whispered, "He'll come."

The second leaf-falling time came. More than twelve full moons had come and gone since Hánas had left her with the gunsmith and his wife. She shivered as she listened to gossip from the dockworkers. On the pier, a wooden board listed which ships were feared to be lost in the vast ocean. *Had one been Hánas's?* The autumnal storms were coming on, making it even more dangerous for any ship to make the crossing. Whaling ships even tied up for the winter.

One night, Tuuli showed Waban how to hold her close while she swallowed a mushroom and tapped her drum hoping for a vision, for help. But it was not to be. Just as the wind brought her no whispers, the drum brought her no help.

The next day while they peeled apples for a pie, Waban had run out of the kitchen to bend over the ditch to vomit. That night, Waban ran to the ditch and emptied her stomach again. Out of the corner of her eye, Tuuli saw the Good Woman stand at the back door watching as Waban bent over with vomit streaming from her mouth.

"Have your bloods stopped?" Tuuli asked as she wiped Waban's mouth.

"It's been too long since they flowed," her friend answered.

The next day as Tuuli was dusting on the second floor, she overheard the smith and his wife talking. "That girl! Slattern! We must get rid of her. She is throwing up. Most likely is pregnant. I'll not have her or that other heathen in my house any longer."

"Ja, ja," the Good Man replied. "When spring comes and there are slave ships in dock, we'll sell them both if Hánas has not returned by then."

"No, not later. Now! I grant you Hánas doesn't even want that girl. She should have been gone by now. Just like the money he left for her. Long gone!"

47

"WE MUST GO, BUT WHERE?" TUULI ASKED after telling Waban what she had heard. After the evening meal, the two scaled a slew of fish. They layered and salted them in a new barrel. When they were finished, they rubbed mint leaves on their hands to take away the fishy smell. A chill crept into the air as the sun lowered in the sky.

"We must go—soon. Before the weather turns. We'll look for my people. Maybe some have returned to the burned-out village." Worry lines creased Waban's forehead. "What if they hunt us down and bring us back?"

Just then, Alden Cooper arrived. He walked with a limp and plopped heavily onto his stool. "I won't be coming anymore. No more lessons. I was only paid for a year. That is long over. And smithy Kron has told me not to come out of charity." He winced as he stood to leave.

"What happened?" Tuuli asked.

"I was digging for clams along the shore. I know better, but it was such a beautiful day, I took my shoes off. A broken shell cut deeply into my foot. Now it is red and swollen."

"Let me look at it," Tuuli said. When she saw the foot, she told Waban to heat some water. Then she searched through her bundle until she found leaves she could pound into a mash to make a mixture for drawing out infection. She soaked his foot in warm water, packed the wound with the poultice, and wrapped it in a clean cloth. "Don't get it wet," she told him. "Come again tomorrow so I can put on a fresh compress and clean cloth. In a few days, your foot should be much better."

The next day, the Good Woman went to her prayer group, and the smith came home to force Waban upstairs. Tuuli put a pork hock with sliced onions into the oven and slipped out of the kitchen. She headed for the woods. When she returned, Waban was crying as she churned butter.

"What did he do?" Tuuli asked.

"It was worse than ever. He made me crawl back and forth on the floor after he'd stripped me of my dress." She showed that one sleeve was almost torn off. "Then he pulled my hair until my head snapped back. Crack it went! I cried out, but he just slapped me. He shouted harsh words I couldn't understand. But I did understand when he called upon his god to cleanse me—*Dirty Indian* is what he said. Then he demanded his god to wash away the demon child growing in my belly. At last when he was done with me, he yelled *Amen. Amen.* His spittle flew into my face with each word. Then he hauled his fist back and hit me in the stomach."

"Never again will that happen to you. We go tonight," Tuuli whispered to Waban. Then she showed Waban the roots she had gathered.

Opening her hand and showing a key, Waban whispered back, "Look what I took from his pocket." Together, they peeled squash to roast with the pork.

Before the evening meal, Waban ground the roots Tuuli had dug during her foray into the woods. Then she steeped the mash in lukewarm water to make a golden liquid that would induce sound sleep. At supper, the smith took a second tankard of beer. Waban stirred the potion into it. Tuuli did the same with the Good Woman's tea. When the kitchen was scrubbed, the dishes put away, the squash peels thrown into the ditch, and slop buckets emptied, Tuuli slid a knife from the shelf and hid it under her apron.

That night when moonlight streaked through the widely spaced boards of their hut, Waban shook Tuuli gently. "Now," she said.

Waban bundled her few things, folded a blanket over her arm, and lifted the bar from the hut's door. Tuuli wrapped her sleeping robe around the drum and stuffed them into a bundle. She reached for Poppi's walking stick. She looked around. There was nothing else she wanted. Not the shells she'd found on the coast. Not the comb Good Woman Kron had given her. Not the extra dress. She ducked through the low doorway, followed close behind her friend. They crept away, leaving the stench of the slop ditch behind.

When they got to the smith's shop, Waban fitted the key into the lock. They pushed open the heavy door. Inside, they found what they wanted. "Only one," Tuuli said. "Maybe the smith won't notice if just one is missing."

Waban nodded and wrapped a musket in her blanket. They locked the door and headed for the river. A *mishoon*, or dug-out canoe, rafts, and small boats were all tied along the docks. Only a skinny dog, nose to the ground, moved along the banks.

Tuuli dipped her paddle into the waters of the swiftly flowing river. Behind her, Waban bent, matching her every stroke. They paddled against the current, never resting. The falling-leaf moon floated above them. Tuuli watched brittle leaves spin past the mishoon. The beauty of the night, the soft *hoo-hoo* of owls did nothing to lessen the terror of who might be following.

Far from town, Waban began to sing softly. Tuuli matched her paddling rhythm to the melody. The solemn tune brought a song to her own throat. At first she rasped. It had been so long since she had sung to the night.

Gii Dah Gaaki
Aye Yon Wei
Aye Yon Wei

She sang to tie her heart to the moon above. The very moon that shone for her people at this very moment. She sang, wishing her words to reach Lásse's ears. She tried to imagine what he would look like now. He'd have been walking for many full moons, stumbling on tree roots, smelling wet mosses after a rain, and running his fingers through the thick fur of the reindeer. Would Siru be cuddling him on her lap? Would he be calling *her* Mother? Would Siru tell him about his real mother who was so far away? This same moon could be shining on his head at this very moment.

Also, this moon would be shining and welcoming the last day of the gathering of the Saami siides. It would bring a day of feasting and song, and courtship races. She thought of Hánas, too. Where was he? And Aiko? A moan escaped her lips, born deep within her and traveling to the stars. What would this same moon bring for her and Waban? She paddled in a land she didn't know. She wanted to unwrap her drum and raise it to the dark skies—to the golden moon—but paddling is what she must do now. So she paddled though tears blurring her eyes.

Much had happened since that gathering—the last day Tuuli had been with her people. The strangers had flaunted their power over the Saami by throwing black powder into the fire. But it was a false power. Not given by their god but living in the powder itself. Since then, Tuuli had learned that anyone could create a flash, a boom, an explosion if they had that powder. She'd seen it here in the colony. It was packed into the long barrel of muskets. Like what Waban had taken from the smith. When put to fire, they roared loudly, and could kill a deer, a bear—or a man.

Tuuli glanced back at Waban, who tilted her face to the moon, still paddling and singing soft words. Her long black braid hung over her shoulder and lay across her rounded breast. So, Tuuli also turned her head to the moon and let the cool rays flood her own face. But just for a moment. At the front of the mishoon, she needed to peer into the waters ahead, looking for stumps, fallen trees, or rocks, anything that could block their canoe—perhaps even tip it on its side, dumping them into the rushing waters.

As the night went on, frost glazed the reeds along the banks. Hard paddling warmed Tuuli inside, but her dripping perspiration and the river's cold mists dampened her dress so it clung to her body, chilling her skin. Finally, when they were nearly exhausted, the morning sun edged above the horizon behind them, casting red streaks across river waters. Waban drew her paddle with force and turned the mishoon toward shore. Tuuli matched her stroke and set the mishoon for landing near a low bank. The canoe scratched along gravel and empty clamshells. They hopped out and hauled it away from the river and hid it behind a copse of thornbushes.

Both flopped onto the mossy ground. Their arm and back muscles trembled from the exertion of the night. They stretched their legs that quivered from hours of kneeling and squatting. Were they far enough from the town? Were they being followed? Questions and fears—unspoken—creased their brows.

Despite hollow grumbling stomachs, they lay together to sleep on Poppi's fur robe. When Tuuli awoke, fragments of a nightmare still ruffled her. She dreamed she'd been alone paddling a mishoon on the never-ending waters looking and calling out for Lásse. Chasing her were many boats filled with men and women calling, "Burn, Hâxa! Burn!" She wished for more sleep, but anxieties and fears tangled in her head, stealing any chance of serenity.

When Waban awakened, she opened a pouch she had hidden in the folds of her dress. She broke a piece of brown bread in two and handed the larger to Tuuli. Then she brought out dried blueberries and a slab of smoked cod she'd taken from the Good Woman's larder. Hungry, they ate with both hands.

Tuuli kicked off her shoes and waded in the cold waters. Clay oozed through her toes. A minnow brushed her leg. She bent to pick crayfish and throw them onto the shore.

"Come in," she invited, but Waban shook her head, held her stomach, and gagged. Her whole body quaked. Tuuli ran to her and held her just as vomit gushed forth. Tuuli pulled her down. Together they rocked until all spasms subsided and Waban's face no longer twisted with anguish.

"How did you do this? How did you carry a baby made by someone you hate?" Waban kneaded her belly while her tears flowed.

"At first, I didn't want the baby. I wanted to grind roots and leaves that would loosen the baby's grip on me and then would flow from my body. I dreamed he would be born a monster. I was frightened. But then he was born. So perfect. So beautiful. So soft. He cooed and filled himself at my breast. How could I not love him? You will love your perfect baby, too."

It was still full daylight. They would not drag their canoe back to the river until evening, so they gathered dried wood and kindling. Tuuli waded in the waters again, looking for anyone who might be following them. She could see no one coming along the river, so she looked for a flint. "It's all right," Waban said, "I can start a fire without one." She rubbed one stick against another vigorously. For a long time, nothing happened. Then a slight line of smoke arose. She rubbed harder and finally they saw a faint glow on the sticks. Tuuli held a dried leaf to it, and then some dried moss. A small fire took. They added bits of tinder little by little until a fire crackled and flames licked the air.

They wrapped crayfish in large wet leaves and steamed them in hot embers. Waban pulled her crayfish apart and ate carefully. This time, the food stayed down. Tuuli found a few nuts still hanging on a hazel bush.

"*Shennucke*," Waban said and then mimicked a squirrel.

"Shennucke," Tuuli repeated. The squirrels already had gathered most of the nuts for the winter. The sun sank lower in the sky. Tuuli carried sand from the shore to cover their fire. They spread dead branches and leaves over the sand to erase all signs that they'd been there.

When Tuuli bent to put her shoes back on, she found a large tear in one. They were the shoes Frida and Greta had brought for her visit with the king. They were not made for warmth or for walking in the forest. She sat to stuff the tear with some leaves. Waban sat next to her. Her shoes were those the Woman Kron no longer wanted—flimsy town shoes.

"How are we going to make good foot coverings for the cold season?" Tuuli asked.

"Moccasin," Waban said. She pulled Ruusu's skin from Tuuli's pack. She pretended she was cutting it to fit her foot and then sewing.

"That's how we make our winter boots, too," said Tuuli, and then she repeated *moccasin* until she could say it without Waban laughing and telling her to try again. The sun fell behind the trees. Tuuli sang a song to end the day while Waban raised her arms and sang, too. Their melodies blended even though their words were different. Dark shadows stretched from the trees. The moon floated overhead. They lowered the mishoon, loaded their small bundles, and knelt to paddle toward the people of Wampanoag—Waban's people.

48

LIGHTS OF GREEN AND GOLD STREAKED AND DANCED in the night sky as Tuuli and Waban paddled onto a smaller river that joined with the big one they had been on. Waban pointed to the curtains of light and said, "When our great Nanabozho finished creating this land, he traveled far north to rest. In the cold, he builds huge fires to warm himself. These beautiful lights are his fires reflecting in the sky. They remind us that he is still with us."

"I like your story," Tuuli said, "but we have a different one."

"Tell me."

"Stallu is an ugly monster that lives in our far north. He steals young girls to be brides for himself. One day, when he was about to capture another, she ran from him across fields, around lake shores, and finally up a mountain. He caught up to her when she reached the top with nowhere to go. Just as he grabbed for her, she jumped. Instead of falling to her death, the wind picked up and flew her high in the skies. The lights are her colorful scarves floating as she dances in the winds." As Tuuli told the story, she thought of her own encounter with Stallu. It seemed a long time ago, and so much had happened since then that she wasn't sure if it had really happened or if she dreamed it.

"My people would say our story is the true one, but I like yours, too," Waban said. "The Coat People want us to forget about Nanabozho and to listen to what their book says. I will never do that. And I would never expect you to change your ways." As she spoke, a ray of sunshine pierced the black of night. "We're almost there, just past another bend in the river."

The people were just rising from their warm bedding. Waban greeted them, telling the names of her mother and father. Those who remembered Waban's family surrounded her, greeting her kindly. They wanted to know where she'd gone after her parents were killed. After hearing how she'd been sold as a slave, they asked her to tell of her escape many times over.

A wrinkled woman with few teeth waved everyone away, saying, "Let them eat. Let them rest. There will be plenty of time to talk later." She scooped corn porridge into gourd bowls for everyone. She sprinkled wild mint and ginger onto the fires. Gentle aromas filled the air. Tuuli breathed it in deeply. The hot porridge steamed onto her face as she ate until her bowl was empty. She felt light-headed, and her muscles ached from heavy paddling, but she was so glad to be away from the town and the Krons. After eating, she and Waban lay down to rest.

When Tuuli awoke, shimmering clouds covered the sky. A light breeze kissed her cheek.

Awaken, Sister.
Open your eyes.
The home you carry in your heart is far away.
A new home awaits you.

The wind was speaking to her as it had not since those dark days in Stockholm. Tuuli smiled to herself. These people were much like her people, but home was where Lásse lived with her siide. Where he was would always be the home she carried in her heart. That was *báiki*.

For now, she was glad to live with Waban and her people until the middle of the next warm season. When she returned to the town, she'd have to stay in hiding. She'd go to the docks only when big boats came in carrying the banner of blue and yellow. She hoped one carried Hánas.

Rousing herself, she unrolled from her fur bedding that she had spread under a tree even though the old woman insisted that she sleep in a *wetu*. Waban was already wading in a finger of the river, bending to wash herself in the fresh waters. "Come in," she called to Tuuli. "The water's cold, but it's refreshing." Tuuli didn't need a second invitation. She shed her clothing on the bank and stepped into the river to do the same.

They played in the waters, feeling freedom for the first time in many passings of the moon. Little children who heard their laughter and splashing came to the banks to watch. Soon many of them tossed their clothes on the shore and jumped into the chilly waters, too. One had a dried gourd. They played catch with it. Another boy tossed a stick for his dog to fetch. Tuuli and Waban lifted little girls onto their shoulders. They bobbed up and down while the girls hung on to their hair and giggled.

When they left the waters, Tuuli and Waban shivered along with the children. Tuuli didn't know when she'd felt so happy. The wrinkled old woman was there, holding deerskin skirts, leggings, and shawls for them. "Thank you. Thank you. Thank you." Tuuli couldn't stop saying the words. She pulled on the skirt and shawl, feeling soft skins against her own. They were so much better than the dresses she'd worn at the smith's house.

"Nootimis." The woman said her name.

Waban pointed to a big tree and told Tuuli that the woman was named after the oak because she was so strong and had lasted through many sicknesses and wars, just like the tree. She was also the *sachem* for the village. As sachem, she was the chief for her people. Tuuli pointed to herself and gave her name. Then Waban explained that she, like Waban, was named for the wind.

Nootimis put her hand on Waban's belly and spoke some gentle words. Waban held the sachem's hands to her belly and told how the gunsmith had forced her many times. Nootimis offered to make her a potion of leaves and roots to wash the baby away.

Waban looked at Tuuli and said, "You love and miss your Lásse. I cannot wash my unborn away knowing how you feel about your baby."

All the people of the village were getting ready to move to their winter lands. Before they left, they were preparing a celebration to honor the passing of the warm season and to ask for a mild winter. Men were digging a wide and shallow pit. Boys and girls gathered rocks to line the pit and wood for the fire. A party of young men and women took mishoons and paddled to an inlet of the big waters. There they dug for clams and checked their lobster baskets. When they came back, they had baskets full of the gifts of the sea for their celebration. They also had armloads of rockweed they'd gathered from the waters.

Before the fire was lit, Nootimis raised her arms to the sky and murmured words that Tuuli did not understand. Waban explained, "The fires will burn until the rocks lining the pit are scorching hot."

The children spread rockweed on the hot stones, the clams and lobsters on top of that, and more seaweed on top. While all this was happening, Waban helped make a huge chowder, and Tuuli helped wrap corn, squash, and onions in corn leaves. These were put on the seaweed to cook also. One of the children, a boy with big brown eyes and long eyelashes, said to Tuuli, "We are going to have a delicious feast."

When their work was done and they waited for the feast to be ready, Waban helped Tuuli cut a deer hide to make the moccasins they would both need for traveling to the winter grounds. Before long, Tuuli's mouth was watering with the aroma of cooking food. Children ran around playing with the dogs. The youngsters stood in groups talking and singing. Older folks told stories and laughed at the children. Pipes filled with tobacco were passed from hand to hand. At first, Tuuli was unsure about taking the smoke into her mouth, but at

Waban's urging, she lifted the pipe and inhaled. It stung a little—deep into her chest—and made her cough. Her eyes watered. She passed the pipe along quickly.

"That happens to everyone at first," Waban assured her. All this, except for the tobacco, was so much like the falling-leaf gatherings of her own people that tears clouded Tuuli's eyes.

When everyone had eaten more than his fill, they circled around a drummer. When he beat a slow rhythm, young and old danced round and round in the same direction. "When we go in the direction of this hand," Waban said, lifting her left hand, "it is to thank the good spirits. When we go in the direction of my other hand, it is to show respect to the evil spirits and to keep them away." The dance steps were easy for Tuuli to follow, and she felt at one with all the people, moving first to thank good spirits and then, changing directions, to keep evil away. At a break in the dancing and drumming, Tuuli sat beneath a tree. She heard her own drum throbbing in her bundle. She wanted to take it out; she had kept it hidden for so long, but she was tired, so she leaned back and closed her eyes. One by one, her ancestors appeared before her, each holding a drum. *Thum. Thum. Thum.* Tuuli silently thanked each and every one. From Hupi to Iiri and Poppi. Would there ever be a time again when she could freely take out the Drum of Four Winds and join herself with the spirit world of the ancient Saami?

49

THE FIRST NIGHT AFTER WABAN'S PEOPLE SET UP their winter village away from the sea bays and in a forest where they could hunt and find plenty of wood, Nootimis gathered everyone to tell a story. Families sat around the night fires to listen as venison, squash, and corn roasted on hot coals.

Many flocks of geese arriving when the ice and snow melt.
Many birthings and dyings of grandfathers and grandmothers.
Many bloomings of the yellow-flowered tree.
Many.
Many of these have passed since Nanabozho, our great creator, told of the
Seven Fires. And we do as he did.
We tell of the Seven Fires.
Father tells son.
Mother tells daughter.

Nootimis's voice filled Tuuli's ears and sank to her heart. A deep loneliness for her own grandfather, mother, and son brought tears to her eyes. Would she ever be able to tell Lásse the stories of his people?

The Fourth Fire warned that a strange new people
with light skins would come to our shores,
from across the big water,
from far-off lands.
Fifty harvests have passed since this prophecy came to be.

Waban's people moaned softly as they swayed together. Tuuli swayed with them.

The coming of the pale skins who wear coats has been a plague for us.
They brought disease.
More than half our people, the Wampanoags, died.
With so many deaths, we are no longer a strong nation.
When other tribes come to fight for land, we cannot repel them.
We have lost much.
Every warm season, more big boats bring more Coat People.
They cut trees to build houses and towns.
We are squeezed onto smaller and smaller pieces of land.
Even if we move farther away,
the pale people come and burn our villages.
They capture us.
And take us for slaves.

Everyone listened quietly. No dogs barked. No child cried. Even the mosquitoes dared not bite. After telling her story, Nootimis passed the talking shell to Tuuli. Holding it with both hands, she told of how the strangers with pale skin and long coats had come to her people, too. She told of how they burned the sacred drums. How they demanded everyone follow the black book or their herds of reindeer would be destroyed. How they even burned noaidis, who were like sachems, at the stake while they were still alive. She told of her journey alone to the far northlands to the Mount of Four Winds and how she had seen the future for her people. She told of Lásse and how she had to flee or be burned at the stake in the land of King Karl.

※⟫⟩⟨⟨※

It was not a peaceful winter for Tuuli and the Wampanoags. On the coldest of days, when the wind blew its strongest, the grand sachem, Metacomet, came to their village. As grand sachem, it was up to him to meet with each of the other sachems to make important decisions.

The people crowded into a long wigwam to keep out of the gusty winds. Nootimis whispered to Tuuli and Waban, "Before Metacomet became grand sachem, his brother Wamsutta was. One day, the colony's leaders invited Wamsutta to a meeting. He went but was kept captive for three days. Soon after he was allowed to return to our people, he fell ill and died. Metacomet is sure his brother had been poisoned. He is still very angry and mourns deeply. When the Coat People learned Metacomet was very important, they named him *King Philip*."

Metacomet began, "I have heard that the leaders of the colony have decided that we must give up all our muskets, knives, and clubs."

Waban spoke up. "Yes, when Tuuli and I lived in the town, we heard talk of this, so it must be true. They fear that we will fight to take our lands back." Then she went to her wetu and brought the musket she had taken from the smith's shop. She handed it to Metacomet.

"We must hide this and all others. Let us wrap them in skins and bury them. They must not be found during the raids." Many spoke the same words—they would not give up their weapons.

"But they know we have muskets and bows to hunt with. Knives to skin the deer and cut our venison. Axes to fall trees. Clubs to pound with. They will snatch some of our women and keep them until we give up our weapons."

Many spoke those words, too. Arguments flew back and forth.

"Maybe we hide some. Give some up and make new ones secretly." Other voices agreed.

Metacomet raised a hand to silence everyone. "I will talk to Sachem Nootimis this very day. And if she and all the other sachems agree, we will resist. It is time to fight back against these people who take our lands, threaten our way of life, and destroy us. Too many have already died or been enslaved."

"Yes," agreed a young man. Nodding toward Waban, he said, "Think of her story and how she was mistreated. We can't let that happen to anyone else."

Metacomet continued, "The few muskets, clubs, and knives we hide will not be enough against their many firearms. There are small, isolated farms and villages in the countryside. When the time comes, we will attack those first. That's how we'll get more muskets."

The listeners were silent as Metacomet told of his plan. When he finished, they buzzed with questions. A war against the white man? Were there enough of them to fight so many? Each one offered the name of a nearby tribe that might help because they, too, suffered at the hands of the Coat People.

So the winter passed. Plans and more plans. Maps were drawn. Weapons made and hidden. Spies made note of how many people lived in each farm and village and guessed how many muskets they had.

⟫⟪

Just as fervor for the fight grew, so did Waban's belly. Her baby became more and more active. While Waban rested, Tuuli worked with the other women. She shook out bedding, scraped hides, ground corn, and smoked venison over small fires. She liked being part of the tribe's life. "Drink this broth," she told Waban. "I made it from mint and dried cranberries." She braided her friend's hair while she sipped the liquid.

"It is good to be back with my people even though my parents are gone," Waban said. "I have you to thank for so much. I wouldn't have dared escape if you hadn't been with me."

The sun shone longer each day. There had never been a day without light throughout the cold season. Tuuli had wondered why it was so different where she lived when the sun didn't rise for many days. Waban and Nootimis told her stories of how the great Nanabozho had provided the sun and moon for them, and all else that they needed on this earth.

"It's like our reindeer," Tuuli told her. "Their meat provides us with food. Their skins provide us with shelter and clothing."

When green shoots pushed up from a thin crust of snow and dainty flowers opened their buds and flocks of birds returned, the deer retreated farther into the forest. It was time for the Wampanoag to travel back to the coast. There they would put up their yellow poplar bark homes for the summer.

Then Tuuli would make her way back into the town, but not before Waban gave birth. "My baby will be born when the mosquitoes hatch and pester our people. I hope they don't suck too much blood from my newborn," she said.

"I'll chase them away from your baby," Tuuli said as she remembered her dream of the hordes of mosquitoes that she likened to the strangers who'd come into the lands of the Saami. "And I wish I could squash the smith and his wife as easily as mosquitoes," she added.

Waban held her belly and nodded.

Nootimis came into their wetu to see Waban and to offer a porridge she'd just made. When they finished eating, she rocked Waban in her arms and sang a gentle song. Together, the three made plans for the birth. Nootimis told of a woman weaving a cradleboard for the baby.

Others made moccasins. Many came bringing smoked fish or dried berries and to give their advice.

Waban and the sachem also suggested the best ways for Tuuli to stay near the town while she waited for ships to come again from across the ocean and yet not be discovered by anyone who'd tell the gunsmith. Tuuli told them about Aiko and Hánas and how they'd both saved her from freezing and then again from captivity on King Karl's castle grounds.

Nootimis nodded. "We are so alike. Strangers come to both our peoples, take our lands, stomp on our beliefs, destroy our lives. We wait, but we are getting ready to fight back."

Tuuli then told how her people were not fighters. "We live in peace with other siides. It is hard for me to understand that your people must even fight other tribes."

"I wish it were different, too," said Nootimis. "Maybe someday peace will come to us, but even the Fifth Fire of our ancient prophecy tells us that a great struggle will come to all the people of the earth. My hope is at least a few among the pale skins and us, too, will be wise enough to make peace."

And so it was that Waban gave birth to a baby boy just as the mosquitoes hatched in ponds and shallow pools. Her people had already moved to their summer home near the coast. "From where the first light of day wakes us," Nootimis said. "That is why we call ourselves the Wampanoags, the people of the dawn."

As Tuuli washed the caul and blood from the baby's head, he screamed and kicked his skinny legs even though she was as gentle as could be. When she handed the tiny boy to another woman who was waiting to wrap him in a deerskin that was stuffed with soft mosses, she noticed that his eyes both focused toward his nose instead of straight ahead. After he was warmly swaddled, Waban took him into her arms. He continued screaming until she cooed soft melodies to soothe him.

Come, sweet boy,
Into my arms.
This day welcomes you.
I, your mother, welcome you.

You, conceived of pain and hatred
Bring joy to my heart.
I name you Wewes
For the owl that called when you were born.
Come to my breast,
Sweet boy.
Dear Wewes.

Tears sprang from Tuuli's eyes to hear such a loving song. To see how Waban cared for her son. She missed Lásse. She'd held him for too few days. She hoped better for Waban and grew impatient for Hánas to return.

50

Strapping her baby boy to her back, Waban led Tuuli toward the town. "I wish you would stay with me and not return to this evil place," she said.

Tuuli stopped at the side of the trail. "You know that if Hánas doesn't return, I still need to get on a ship and go back. My own people are as threatened as yours. I need to be with my people to fight against the strangers' message."

"Let's rest awhile," Waban said when Wewes fussed. "He cries when he's hungry. We don't want him bringing attention to us now that we are so near the town." They stepped off the trail and hid themselves in a copse of hazel. Squirrels skittered away. Small birds sang from the trees, so high they could not see them. A bold raven lit onto the top of a nearby tree. It looked down at them and then flew off.

Tuuli poured ground cornmeal from a pouch onto her hand. She licked it slowly. When Waban was done nursing, she took meal from the pouch, too. "Tuuli, you need a shelter for the night and bad weather," Waban said. "We'll find a secluded spot and make you a small wetu."

They crept closer to the town and then scouted the woods off the worn trails for a good place. They found one in the hollow made when a huge tree tore from the earth during a windstorm. Its root mass had pulled a lot of soil with it when it fell, making a small cave. "We just need to make half a wetu," Tuuli said. "To cover the open area and make an entrance."

"Bears like to hibernate in hollows like this, too. Maybe you'll have big furry visitors to keep you warm if you stay here for the winter," Waban said as she spread fresh fir boughs on the bottom of the hollow.

"Even though the bear is my brother, I'm not sure I'd like that." Tuuli smiled as she imagined herself curled up with Guovza.

"Why not? Do you think bears snore?" Together, they laughed as they cut saplings with the knife Tuuli had taken from the Kron's cupboard. Then they made long slices in the bark of the yellow poplar. Its top layer curled back, making it easy for them to peel it from the tree. Not having enough bark, they found a wetland where cattail reeds and marsh rushes grew. They picked these and wove them into mats to finish the walls and cover the underside of the tree roots that made up half the roof. A raven kronked from a treetop.

"Do you think he sleeps too much?" Waban asked. Her son had not wakened once while they were making the shelter. "He should be hungry by now."

Tuuli wondered the same. Her Lásse had wakened often and eagerly took to her breast even when he was just a few days old.

"I'll go to the river for quahogs. You rest with Wewes and be ready to feed him if he wakens."

Tuuli collected rocks and made a fire pit after she'd found enough clams for their meal. After she got the fire going, she tweeted like a bird—a signal she and Waban had agreed upon—and waited for her friend to find her. Together, they wrapped the clams in seaweed and steamed them. When their meal was ready, they scooped tender meat from the shells into their mouths.

As they snuffed their cooking fire, Waban hushed Tuuli and held a finger to her lips. Then Tuuli heard it, too. Soft footsteps. A snapped twig. Tuuli put her ear to the ground. Someone was coming. And that someone was no longer on the beaten path, but making his or her way through the brush—stopping once in a while before moving on. Coming closer. From the faint sounds, Tuuli could picture that person studying the ground for crushed grasses. For leaves that had been brushed from their branches. *Why weren't Waban and I more careful?*

They held their breath. Waban gently put a hand on her baby's chest, ready to soothe him if he awoke. They dared not move. Maybe the person would veer off before finding them. *Not much chance of that*, Tuuli thought. The smoke from their fire still wafted in the air. She held her knife ready at her side.

Waban padded her hand with seaweed and grasped a hot stone with it. The evening birds stopped their singing. Stopped flitting from tree to tree. Even the waves of the cove faded and no longer lapped the shore. In the silence, they waited.

A raven winged its way and roosted on the top branch of a tree close to them. A hare zigzagged its way to the shore. A soft tune broke the stillness. A willow whistle? A tune like Poppi used to play when the morning dawned? Then Tuuli heard the throaty call of the male willow grouse. Sweat broke on her brow. She stood. Waban tugged at her skirt and whispered, "Stay down!"

Tuuli clicked with her tongue—imitating the sound of a reindeer walking. The clicking sound came back to her from a thicket nearby. The branches rustled.

"Aiko!" Tuuli ran to him. They embraced silently.

"You are a hard person to find," Aiko murmured. "Hánas told me that you were staying with the gunsmith and his wife. But when I went there, they said they did not know where you'd gone. I have been so worried wondering what happened. I spent many days scouring the village and woods looking for you."

"It is good to see you! You came! How? When? How is Lásse? Is Hánas with you? Tell me everything." Tuuli tried to ask all her questions at once.

"I have much to tell you," Aiko said. "But I don't carry much good news."

Waban and Aiko greeted each other. Then Tuuli led the way to their tree root shelter. As Aiko told his story, Tuuli stopped him often so she could change his words into those that Waban could follow. As she did so, she remembered how she'd called Hánas a *broken branch* so long ago because he had changed the Saami into the words of the strangers and back again. How long and how many twists her life had taken since then!

"When Hánas took you to the ship and sailed, I stayed hidden with the butcher and his wife. The next day, the good man bought a milking she-goat so we could feed Lásse. The poor baby missed you terribly and cried most of the day. He refused the milk until the next day when he was very hungry."

Tuuli clasped her hands over her heart. "Oui-ma. Oui-ma," she keened, and tears slid from her eyes. Waban held her close and joined her voice to Tuuli's.

"Meanwhile, the town was in an uproar looking for you. The king was said to have bellowed his anger. He had been eagerly expecting to enjoy a great celebration of burning a witch, but she'd escaped. In a rage, he sent every able-bodied man out to the forest, along the paths, and to search every house. When they came to the butcher's, his wife said the baby was her daughter's and rocked Lásse close to her breast. It's a good thing Hánas got his boat under way that first night, because the searchers even boarded all the ships looking for you."

"I didn't deserve to be burned alive! All I've ever wanted to do is help people!" Tuuli cried.

"We spent many days on the way to your siide. We stayed off the main trails that the searchers would be on. The goat wasn't cooperative about traveling so far each day. We stopped often for her to eat and for Lásse to suckle the cloth I soaked with the goat's milk. I had to find fresh mosses to tuck around his bottom. Whew! I never thought that caring for a baby was so much work, but he was a good boy and didn't cry much after that first day."

Wewes awoke and started to cry. Waban took him to her breast. Tuuli's heart tore at the sight of mother rocking her son and looking into his face while he nursed. Aiko stopped, held Tuuli to him, and sang a soft joik.

Someday,
Someday,
You, too,
Will hold your baby.
Hold your Lásse.

"Tell me more," Tuuli said.

"It was full summer when I reached the far north and found your siide. When I placed Lásse into Siru's arms, at first she yelped because she thought it meant you had died. When she heard your story, she was as mournful as if you had, because of the cruelty you endured. She cradled Lásse with the tenderness and love that any mother would have for her own child. All the women clamored around. They all promised to be mothers to him until you return."

"How did my people treat you? Did they know you're the banished one?"

"I think some might have guessed, but no one asked my name. They invited me to their campfire and shared their food generously. They asked me to find you and bring you back. You are more important to them than worrying if I was the banished one. When I left, they packed food for me. And wished me good travels, and to return.

"It took me a long time to earn passage on a ship to come here. As it was, I only had about half of what I needed, but I agreed to work the sails and clean the decks for the rest of my passage."

"And what about Hánas? Why hasn't he returned?" Tuuli asked.

"His father suspected Hánas stowed you on his boat. He was red with anger and confronted Hánas when he returned. He was afraid his trade would fail if others suspected the same—and it has. His business is very poor. Sailors on board the ship Hánas took you on confirmed you were there. His father kept Hánas tightly guarded in the warehouse and at home. He no longer sent him on trading ships across the ocean. He has also asked other shipowners not to take his son aboard."

Tuuli felt a pang of anger. And of guilt. She had caused much trouble for her people and for Hánas. How would she ever get back to her siide to fight against the strangers?

"For a long time, I looked for Hánas before I left. Then I heard he escaped from his father, who has disowned Hánas and offered a pouch of money for anyone who captures him. Many rumors persist. One is that he was caught by the king's men. Both his legs were broken so he could never escape again. And then there is talk that he crossed the Baltic waters to a small fishing village far away. Some say he went to Gothenburg and boarded a ship that would sail for the colonies."

Tuuli clasped her hands together. Was it possible Hánas was coming for her? "When I go back," she said, "I will hold my Lásse next to my heart and never leave him again."

51

Soon after Aiko arrived, leaves turned from green to golds and reds. Squirrels dashed from tree to tree collecting acorns and hazelnuts. Flocks of geese and ducks flew south. In the mornings, thin layers of ice covered shallow ponds. Whaling ships arrived and pulled down their sails, safe in port for winter.

They lived with Waban's people. Aiko helped them make clubs to replace the weapons of the Wampanoags that had been confiscated. They used the muskets that had been hidden as well as the clubs when they raided small homesteads on the outskirts of the forests to get more muskets and gunpowder. Talk around the campfires was all about Metacomet and the war he was planning against the settlers.

Aiko also went often to the settlement to learn what ships had come into port and to gather information. "In the town, they talk of boats lost in the deep waters. Many, many," he said.

"It can't be. Hánas must come back." Tuuli twisted the ends of her long braids. Tears swelled in her eyes.

Aiko put his arm around her shoulder. "The women all worry when their men go out to hunt the whales or to bring trade goods across the big waters. The cold deep waters of the Atlantic are dangerous, especially in a storm. Some never return."

"How will we ever return, if the danger is go great?"

"Right now, I am glad to be with other people. It wasn't so good for me to wander alone all the time. Now that I know you are safe, I am content to stay here. I am in no hurry to return to a life of a castout wanderer. I could make a life here. Is it so bad for you?" asked Aiko.

"The Wampanoags have been good to me, too, but I want to return to my baby boy, my Lásse. I always wonder, who is holding him now? He must be walking. How many teeth does he have? Will he fit in with our siide, or will he always yearn to learn about the towns of his father? I need to be with him."

"I think I know your pain. The first day I was cast out, I climbed to the top of a tree and watched my siide go about daily chores and enjoying each other. I was dreadfully alone and sad. But now I have seen enough to know that life for our people is changing and will never be what it was for our ancestors. The Wampanoags have been good to me, too. They are much like our people. With them, I am not banished."

"I am glad of that," said Tuuli, "but the Coat People are not so welcoming. With them, it is much like how the strangers treated us at home. They look for any excuse to tie our arms behind us. To burn us. To kill us."

"You are right. We are more like the people of the forests."

"From Waban's people, I have learned much more about new plants. Those that heal. Those that are good to eat. Some are very much like the ones we already knew about."

Tuuli thought about it. Aiko had always been good and gentle with her since he had helped save her from the cold that crept to her heart. She asked him now, "Do you remember the first time we met? We were both alone in the wilds of the north."

Aiko linked his arms in Tuuli's. "How could I ever forget? I was so sorry I tried to trick you that I made a promise to myself on the last day when we hunted for healing roots and leaves. I vowed to always find a way to help you whenever possible."

"And you've done that. How could I ever have imagined the two journeys I've had to take? Journeys the wind whispered to me. And you, too, told me my journey would not be over after I returned to the gathering of siides."

The little fire on which they roasted a fish sputtered. Aiko added more wood. The flames leaped and warmed them. They told each other the story of their first meeting. The shades of the night danced across their faces as the flames wavered in the dark.

One morning, the whole Wampanoag village awoke to the thunder of a cannon. Aiko, Waban, and Tuuli hurried to the shore to see what was happening. In the distance, they saw a ship nearing port. The main sail was down. Other ragged sails flapped in the wind. The boat listed to one side, but it still managed to flounder toward shore. The banner it waved was blue with a gold cross. Sweden! Could it be?

Tuuli started to run toward the landing, but Aiko held her back. "I should have warned you. It is not safe for you to go to town. The townspeople look for you. They call you thief and witch. The gunsmith says you and Waban stole many knifes, muskets, and silver from him. His wife says the two of you are wicked—evil. The cooper's son says you healed his foot with a spell and witch's potion. They all call for you to be brought to your death. There is a noose waiting for you in the center of the town."

She struggled against his hold. "We took one musket and one knife. I just made an ordinary poultice for the cooper's son. Why is this happening to me again?"

"We are nothing to them. They have all the power. Do not show yourself. I'll go. I'll bring back news."

"Then go. Go. I must know. I sing for Hánas's return. My misery will be half over if Hánas is on that ship."

But Hánas wasn't on that ship or on any other coming into port. Great storms blew up gigantic waves on the big waters through all seasons. The harbormaster scratched a list of ships that never had arrived on a board near the docks. It grew longer with each storm.

52

WABAN'S PEOPLE PREPARED THE FEAST FOR their last day before moving to the forest for the winter. Tuuli watched the children play ball and joined in dancing. Laughter filled the warm autumn air. She even brought out her drum to tap a rhythm for the circle dance. As she tapped, the wind swirled and churned next to her ears. "What is it, Wind?" she asked.

> *Take care.*
> *Be strong.*
> *A journey awaits.*

Tuuli brushed the wind from her ear. Of course a journey awaited. She needed to go back to Lásse and her people.

Just as the dancing and games were over and the campfires burned low and the sun sank in the sky, a horde of men on horseback rode in. The men carried muskets. One jumped off his horse and pointed at Tuuli. It was Alden Cooper. "It's the witch," he said. "Take her prisoner!"

A huge skirmish arose. Indian against settler. Muskets roared. Hot rocks thrown. Horses reared. Aiko grabbed Tuuli by the hand and ran for the river. They dove in, but the current was strong, and Tuuli was caught by a townsman on horseback before they even got halfway across. He pulled her up, laid her belly down across his horse in front of himself, and galloped away.

Tuuli paced the rough board floor of the little hut where she was imprisoned. She winced at each sound that came to her ears from outside. She could hear the guards outside the door talking, muttering. Sometimes their barking laughter frightened her until cold sweat drenched her. She was always afraid one or more of them would push open the door and brutally beat her or worse. In the morning, the sentries would take her to the town to be hanged in the commons for all to witness. Fear made her chest squeeze tight, and a ball of bile stuck in her throat.

The wind could not speak to her, could not comfort her through the thick walls. It had spoken to her before the militia had ridden into the celebration. It had said, *Be strong. A journey awaits.* What did that mean? A journey to the gallows. Her drum was in her wetu in the Wampanoag camp. She didn't know if Waban and Aiko were alive and unharmed. Everyone had been defenseless. Had they been butchered after she was taken away?

Tuuli wished for the root that she could chew so it would send her to the spirit world before the Coat People could shame her in the gallows. Even more than that, she wished she'd never left her people. And even before that, she wished that she had destroyed the white fawn as soon as it was born.

Outside the hut, the wind howled and tore through the trees with an unnatural suddenness. Through the cracks by the door, Tuuli saw shards of pale light. She shivered. Morning was coming. The guards would bring her to the gallows scaffolding soon. Yesterday, after she'd been captured, they had stopped in front of the structure and told her to look at the last place she'd be standing.

The wind blew more fiercely, and then it calmed. Then she heard a great flapping of wings and the coarse *kruuuuncking* of many ravens filling the air. The guards cursed and yelled. They shrieked in terror. Again. Silence. Then an eerie howling arose and reverberated in the woods surrounding the hut. Howling wolves raced closer and closer. The uproar grew. Tuuli imagined the fight outside. The men yelled. Cried. The wolves growled and snarled. An angry wind wailed. And the ravens returned.

As quickly as it had started, it ended; all was quiet. Tuuli dared open the door a crack. The guards were gone. Aiko limped out of the woods, and Nootimis followed. She took Tuuli into her arms and stroked her hair. A bear left the forest and circled the small hut three times, then disappeared among the trees.

53

THE GUARDS FLED TO THE TOWN. They nursed their bruises, bites, and scratches. No one asked about their prisoner. No one waited, wondering why the hanging wasn't taking place because King Philip's War—the war between the Coat People and the Wampanoag—had begun.

Aiko, Tuuli, Waban, and Wewes fled the battles. They walked away from the flames of warrior fires and the noose awaiting Tuuli. Waban carried Wewes on her back. She swung a sack filled with seeds. Tuuli bundled her drum with her knife and felt her way with Poppi's walking stick. Aiko carried a flint and a pouch of corn and salted meat.

They walked away from the rising sun toward the setting sun. They walked until their feet were sore. They heard the owl *hoo-o-o*. Critters scampering. Watched fox kits play in the sunlight. Each night, they looked to the sky at a speck of light, comforted by the seven stars of the Great Bear guiding them to unknown lands.

They plucked eggs from nests, dug for roots. Picked berries, and steamed a turtle in its shell. They walked until the wind whispered to Tuuli and a raven called from a high treetop. There sheer rocks lined one side of a river and slopes of black stone tied shore to the waters. A twisting river murmured peace. Bird melodies filled the air. Beavi warmed their tired shoulders. A gentle doe nibbled grass. It was there they stopped. It was there they would make a home for Wewes.

Tuuli held her drum high. On bended knee, she gave thanks. Thanks for life. Thanks for escaping the noose. They all dipped their feet into the river's clear water, washing away the soils of a long journey. They sang with the winds. They sang to journey's end. The wind whispered, *This is home.*

※※※

"Boozhoo." A young boy popped out from behind a willow tree. A pretty little girl with long braids followed him.

Surprised and not knowing what to say, Aiko and Tuuli said, "Boochew."

The boy and girl giggled. "Boozhoo," they said again.

Waban repeated, "Boozhoo."

Chuckling, the boy took the girl's hand, and they disappeared into a thicket of willows.

"There are people nearby," Tuuli said. "I had hoped we would find a land with no one to bother us. No one to burn drums. No one with black books."

"The children seemed friendly." Waban spread a fur on the ground and set Wewes on it. Then she untied the pouch of seeds from her waist.

Tuuli heard the soft footsteps first. "Many are coming," she said. Waban picked up Wewes and held him close.

The young boy appeared first. He grinned as he pointed to Aiko. Five, seven, nine people followed him. They wore deerskin clothes. Their hair was long and dark. Best of all, their eyes shone with kindness. "Boozhoo," they greeted.

"Boozhoo."

It was only one word, but they also offered baskets of dried fish, a sweet brown sugar, and a grain they called *manoomin*. Waban, Tuuli, and Aiko warmed in the welcome.

> *Then the men of manoomin*
> *drew long knives.*
> *A gasp from Waban.*
> *A cry from Tuuli.*
> *But the men chopped down saplings.*
> *Bent them into frames for shelter.*
> *Wigwam, the women said*
> *as they gathered reeds from the river.*
> *Tuuli wove mats with the women.*
> *Aiko and the men tied bark to cover the wigwam.*
> *Waban cradled Wewes.*
> *Children dug clams and threw them onto shore.*
> *Done with labor,*
> *they splashed in river.*
> *Cooling. Laughing.*
> *Then they built a fire.*
> *Steamed clams.*
> *Ate and sang.*

When Waban entered the wigwam, she said, "It is snug like our wetus. It'll be a good home. Keep us warm in the cold season."

Everyone rested by the fire, eating clams and sucking on the sweet brown maple sugar. Then a man named Youngblood brought out a drum and gently tapped a rhythm. Aiko nodded to Tuuli. She unwrapped her drum and repeated the rhythms. The children grabbed the hands of their mothers and fathers and began to dance in a circle. Waban and Aiko followed their steps, and soon, Saami, Wampanoag, and O-chib-wa smiled and danced the circle together. No words were needed. Just drums and dance.

※》》》《《《

Their new home was a place of shelter and abundance. Besides the berries and roots, there were deer, birds, and fish. Waban planted her beans, squash, and corn. They made one canoe Waban's way by slowly burning the insides of a tree trunk and scraping the ashes out with a clamshell. They made another out of birchbark with the help of their O-chib-wa neighbors.

In the mornings, they watched gray mists rise from the waters,
blurring the line between river and land.
Pink crept into the skies, outlining ragged cedars along the shore.
They sang their song that beckoned light for each new day,
welcoming Beavi.
Each dawn, Tuuli whispered enchantments
to spider webs glistening in the early sun.
She whistled them to the red-winged blackbird
whose breath puffed in a little cloud in the chill of the early hours.
While the chickadees and sparrows sang,
she united her song with theirs.
"Home," she whispered.
"Bring me home to Lásse."

54

SEVERAL MOONS PASSED. THEIR FRIENDSHIP WITH the O-chib-wa village strengthened. Youngblood came often to help Aiko catch fish in the river. During the first leaf-falling time, he paddled with Aiko along the lakes where the manoomin grew and taught him how to knock the ripe grains into the canoe. Both Aiko and Tuuli noticed that Waban smiled shyly each time Youngblood was near. And when Youngblood brought fish or a piece of roasted venison, he always presented it to Waban.

At one such visit, Youngblood strapped Wewes's cradleboard to his back, and, taking Waban by the hand, they set out for a walk in the woods. Aiko watched them go and then invited Tuuli to sit with him at the fire. "Have you thought about taking a man to be with you? To share your bed?" he asked.

"I watch Waban and Youngblood and think about it. After how I was used by the strangers, I try to forget the pain, but it's still a strong memory. I wonder about my child, too. I hope he will never be cruel like the one who left his seed within me to make the boy."

"You suffer so worrying about Lásse. I know you miss him. He should be in your arms. Siru and your siide are teaching him to be good and kind. He will be taught the ways of a noaidi."

"I have no doubt about that, but I am his mother. I yearn to hear him coo. To watch him grow. When I left him to flee the burning, I felt like a she-wolf whose leg is caught in a snare. To be free, she must chew off the trapped leg and leave it behind. I escaped the fires of the strangers, but I had to leave a part of me behind. That pain is greater than having my leg ripped off. My heart aches for Lásse every day. I will be that wounded wolf, missing a part of me, until the day I return."

The two remained quiet as Tuuli wept. Aiko held her close and softly crooned joiks into her ear. When Tuuli's tears came no more, he broke the silence. "Tuuli, I want you to know that being with a man does not have to be shameful and painful. Would you let me show you? I will stop if you ask, but I want you to know that joy is possible with a man."

Aiko lightly brushed his lips across her cheek. Tuuli shivered, not from the cold but from the softness of his touch. Together, they became silent. Aiko lightly moved his mouth to her ear and let his breath whisper to her. Tuuli felt a tingling all the way to her toes. She dared not move. His whispers and his breath excited her in a way she'd never felt before.

Slowly and gently, Aiko let his lips and fingers talk for him. Telling Tuuli the story of soft joinings, soft strokings, and tender embraces. He ran his hand along her backbone and let his fingers explore the recesses of her throat. They held their hands together, palm to palm. Her fears calmed as his hands moved across her body and to the parts where she'd only felt pain. But not this time. An awakening stirred in her. Waves of pleasure rose. She returned his kisses. She whispered in his ear. "Yes."

Her skin welcomed each touch. Aroused, she held him to her and answered all his moves with her own rhythm. The hooting owls of night. The skittering of rabbits. The rustling of dried leaves. The fox hunting food. The fire crackling. A shooting star in the dark sky. All went unnoticed as Tuuli held Aiko to her. He had been right. A man and a woman together could be joy. Pleasure. Soft. Tender. A breeze lightly blew.

Later that night, when Aiko's quiet snores made her smile, she ran her hands over her whole body, the curves of her breasts, the sharp bones of her hips. The deep warmth. Her soft thighs. The muscles of her legs. She licked the saltiness of her own arms.

When she fingered the indent of her navel where her own mother had tied a knot after severing their connection, she remembered cutting her own son loose and tying his cord. Tears spilled from her eyes again. She'd cuddled Lásse for too few days. Siru would be cradling him now. A deep wave of sadness swelled within Tuuli, so she reached for Aiko. She rocked him close to her and tasted his salt as she kissed his face. Even as she held him, deep sorrow overcame her.

Wewes had been irritable for several days. No amount of cuddling or rocking comforted him. One morning, he trembled constantly. Tuuli and Aiko made potions from roots and leaves. The O-chib-wa healer made a compress for his chest. Nothing helped. Wewes weakened and died the next day. Waban keened as they placed his tiny body into a hollow in the soft earth. She cried as she helped Youngblood, Aiko, and Tuuli carry rocks from the river to build a cairn over his grave. Tuuli held her close and wept with her. She, too, lamented each day she could not hold Lásse. But deep within her belly, she felt the stirring of new life.

When the loons came to live nearby the following spring, their laughing and flapping wings filled the air. Day by day, the cold gave way to warmer days, but the nights were still chilly. Youngblood and two youngsters taught them how to tap maple trees and catch the running sap. They took turns singing their own songs as they passed smoked venison and dried berries back and forth while boiling the sap down to a sweet syrup. Aiko whittled willow whistles for the children. Then he taught them how to blow simple tunes.

In midsummer, Tuuli lay on her bed. "It is time," she said. Aiko ran to the O-chib-wa village to tell the news. Several women came back with him to help Waban with the delivery.

When pain racked Tuuli's body, Waban held her close, taking in her myriad scents. The cedar of the forest that she'd layered for her bed. The chamomile she washed her hair in. The intense musk of her laboring body. The women gently pressed her belly. Outside the wetu, Youngblood beat a calming rhythm on his drum, and Aiko sang for an easy birth.

Tuuli felt the pressure of her baby ready to be born. She pushed. And Waban held her hands out to receive the baby. Placing the baby over Tuuli's heart, she said, "It's a boy."

Later that evening as she nursed the pink and wrinkled little one, Aiko said, "Niilo. Shall we name our son Niilo?"

Tuuli smiled and sang a joik.

Niilo. Niilo.
Son of our flesh and bone.
May your branch find your way.
Back to our tree.
Back to our people.
To the home of my heart.
Baiki.

When the summer waned and the leaves turned red and gold, the O-chib-wa took them to gather manoomin. At the rice camp, Tuuli and Aiko helped parch the grains by stirring constantly so they wouldn't burn. Then Waban and Youngblood took turns dancing and twisting on layers of rice in a shallow pit. When the chaff loosened from the kernels, Aiko and Tuuli held corners of a deerskin as manoomin was poured onto it. The breezes lifted the chaff and blew it away, leaving the food that they'd all eat throughout the winter.

55

Each summer, as Niilo grew, Tuuli, Aiko, and Waban showed him where to hunt for blueberries, raspberries, blackberries, cranberries, and wintergreens. They got their feet wet in low bogs, and they climbed up high crags in search of colorful berries. Each day, loons called to one another across the rippling river. They laughed and swam, stretching their necks and showing off their beautiful feathered necklaces.

After rainstorms, they followed ancient forest paths looking for mushrooms—the delicate gift of rain. The forest smelled damp and rich. The fragile caps hid beneath leaves, under pines, enlaced with forest flowers.

When he was old enough, Niilo made friends with the O-chib-wa children. "Sakima," a brown-eyed boy said, pointing to himself.

"No, not Sakima. Not chief." His sister laughed. "He's Little Duck. I'm Dancing Star."

Her brother answered, "But I call her *Girl Who Talks Too Much*!"

The children threw a ball made of deerskin and stuffed with mosses high in the air for each other to catch. They raced from one tree to another. They challenged each other to pick the most clams.

They peeked into bird nests to see the babies spread their beaks wide, waiting for food. They imitated birdsongs, dared each other to climb the tallest trees or to creep close to a skunk or porcupine. When they snitched honey from beehives, they had to spend the next two days daubing mud from the river onto their many stings. The wise O-chib-wa healer who helped them smear themselves with mud said, "Beware of sweet things. Sometimes they hide sorrow."

Niilo easily learned the language of his playmates. He translated words for Aiko and Tuuli so they could learn, too. Together with the O-chib-wa, around cooking fires, the women stitched boots and clothing while the men wove mats and baskets. They shared the fish they'd caught and the berries they'd picked.

In the evenings of waning light, Aiko taught Niilo how to sizzle mushrooms with savory fats and wild onions over an open fire. Then they dried the rest of the mushrooms before hanging them in a sack next to dried berries to save for winter. Tuuli and Aiko also told Niilo stories of his people.

"We lived with the reindeer. We tied antlers on our feet to glide on frozen lakes. It was dark in the cold season, and yet the sun never set in the warm." Aiko and the O-chib-wa wise man taught him about plants and roots that would heal a gash or take away a fever. Tuuli held him close and told of the family of noaidis he was born into. Of the Mount of Four Winds. Of the family she'd left behind. Of Poppi. Of his brother, Lásse. And the sacred bear. He sang joiks with them. Joiks of happiness. Joiks of healing. Of mourning.

Each time Tuuli climbed a hill, she faced each of the four winds one by one. She held her hands above her head and listened. The wind whispered to her—gentle murmurings, but it was never a whisper of return. Aiko watched from a distance. Always she held her head low and shook her head when he asked, "Is it time for you to leave?"

"I always wish so, but I'll wait until Niilo is older and strong enough for the long walk."

Tuuli was filled with hope when she saw how Niilo held the drum and felt it vibrate. He tilted his head to listen to the wind but heard nothing but the leaves of trees tremble. Tuuli taught him about báiki: how she carried her people and their story within her heart even though she was far away. When Aiko and Tuuli told stories of their people, Niilo repeated them until the sun's heat left the rock and it was time to sleep. Each night, Tuuli tucked her drum on her side. She felt its vibrations and fell asleep thinking of home.

Each day, after the fish had been caught and the berries picked, Aiko and Niilo made a bead from the white birch. They cut a three-sided strip of bark. Laying two pine needles at the wide end, they rolled the bark around the needles. As they rolled each bead, they told the story of their day. With a hot rock from the fire they heated the bead until juices from the bark bubbled. When it cooled, the sap stuck fast, forming a perfect bead.

With care, they poked a length of sinew between the two pine needles. Pulling the needles, they threaded the line through the bead. At night, they fingered the beads—one by one—and told the story that was wrapped within.

This bead for the day Tuuli found the forest orchids.
This is for the great fish, the sturgeon that got away.
We made this the day the wolves and their pups played on a sunny hill.
This bead is for the night
we watched the lights of the north flash and weave across the sky.
This, for the butterfly Niilo freed from a silken web.
And this for when Aiko answered the hoo-o-o of the owl.
A memory for each day.
A bead for each memory.
A necklace of memories.

The rowan trees hung heavy with red berries when, one morning, Aiko couldn't rise from his bedding. His whole body shook, racked by fever.

Tuuli and Niilo carried waters from the river to bathe his forehead, cool his body. They crushed healing roots for him to chew and made potions for him to drink. Niilo ran to ask the O-chib-wa wise man to help. They smoothed honey from wild bees onto Aiko's tongue when he could eat no more. Tuuli beat her drum and called for the fever to subside. The wise man packed poultices on Aiko's feverish chest and chanted songs of healing. They sat at his side when the morning light broke through. They shaded his eyes in the brightness of noon. They held his hand as the loons sang their last songs of the night.

When a raven alit high on a treetop, Tuuli said, "The raven is your brother in spirit."

"Yes." Aiko nodded. Tuuli placed her drum in his hands. Eyes closed, he tapped the drum and sang, his voice but a rasp. Weakly, he whispered, "The prophecy of the Fourth Fire that Nootimis told is not ended. Just as the Coat People changed the lives of Waban's people by taking their hunting lands and demanding they convert to a new god, the same will happen here. The Coat People will come like hungry mosquitoes in the spring."

Tuuli spread honey over his lips. Niilo sang a joik. Aiko sang, too. A new song.

My journeys are over.
Soon I walk in spirit with my ancestors.
Jabemeahkka awaits.
We have had a good life together.
We are like the Wampanoag and O-chib-wa.
We live in harmony with the land and waters and all the forest creatures.
Go back, Tuuli.
Cross the big water filled with perils.
Go home.
Our lands and ancient ways are threatened.
Our people need you.
Join Lásse and Niilo together.
Hold Lásse to your heart.

More ravens gathered, filling the treetops. When a wolf howled in the deep woods, Jabemeahkka came to guide Aiko to the other world. Tuuli and Niilo sang mourning joiks all day and night. With Waban and Youngblood, they built a great fire and watched as the winds whisked ashes from the fire and swirled them to the skies. They scooped a few of his remains into a pouch. They buried the rest next to Wewes and then carried rocks from the river to cover his grave.

The loons flew south, and the bears found their winter dens.

"When the loons return, we will go to the people of the first light. Waban's people. From there, we will find a boat to take us across the big water," Tuuli said to Niilo. "It is a dangerous journey. The deep ocean swallows ships and all those within." And then she told of Hánas and how he never returned.

Niilo nodded and said, "We will go, Mother. I am as old as all the fingers on one hand. I am big and strong enough to walk long days. I want to know my brother, Lásse, too."

All winter they waited. Touching the beads, Tuuli sang songs of memory—Waban with the sun on her face. Aiko sipping nectar from clover. The beads whispered of rainbows, of evening breezes, of sweet rains, and of wobbling fawns.

The days lengthened. Icicles dripped. The sun strengthened. Sap from maple trees ran freely. The loons arrived. Tuuli and Niilo walked the trail to the O-chib-wa camp one last time to say good-bye to Waban, who had joined herself to Youngblood. They thanked Little Duck and Dancing Star and all the others who'd given them the gift of friendship, manoomin, fish, and maple sugar. It was difficult leaving those who had welcomed them to their land and been so good to them.

On the path back, they saw pink moccasin flowers blooming. They picked wintergreen berries. They climbed a high cliff overlooking the winding river they'd lived by. The forest with its twisted trees fringed the land with fragile green. An eagle soared overhead. Butterflies and spiders awoke to the sunshine. Mother and son sang a final song while standing on a patch of lichen next to two pines that were rooted in rock.

Báiki calls.
Home of my heart.
Home of my sons.
Home of my people.

They washed themselves with three dippers of cool water from the spring. They drank deeply from the fourth. Tuuli combed her tangled hair and cut her ragged nails. She slipped on her birchbark shoes. Niilo did the same.

Then they picked up their packs full of dried fish, wild rice, berries, and Aiko's ashes. Tuuli wrapped her drum in Gabba's pelt.

Niilo tied the birch bead necklace around Tuuli's neck and then handed her Poppi's walking stick.

At last they stood on the ancient glacial rock that had been their home. They thanked the forest and the waters. And then turned to the east, to the rising sun—the direction they must go.

56

Just as Tuuli and Niilo set on their path, Waban and Youngblood hurried to them.

They each carried a bundle on their back and a pouch at their side.

"Waban misses her people. We will go with you," Youngblood said simply.

Tuuli hugged her friend. "Leaving you was making a big empty spot in my heart. I am so glad you're coming with us."

Youngblood carried Niilo over the rockiest and most difficult paths. Waban discovered she was with child. She tired more easily, so the journey took three changes of the moon. By the time they reached the land of the Wampanoag, they were sore of foot and weary of constant walking.

As soon as Waban, Youngblood, Tuuli, and Niilo entered the Wampanoag village, the people burst into singing and dancing. Tuuli joined the drumming. Waban and Youngblood danced. Niilo played a stick-and-ball game with the children. And then a feast was set roasting over the fires.

After the children were put to bed, the people began to tell what had happened in the six years since Waban had left. The news was bad. The war had been brutal. The settlers had won. Metacomet had been betrayed and shot. His body quartered. And beheaded. His head remained speared by a pike and still hung at the fort these many years later. It was a stern warning to all who dared rebel. His wife and son had been captured and taken away on a ship as slaves. Nootimis had passed to the next world. She had been burned trying to save her people.

A damned bloody war.
So many dead.
Butchered.

And nothing had changed. The Coat People still pushed farther and farther into the lands of those who lived with the earth. Toward the lands of the O-chib-wa.

57

AFTER FEASTING AND RESTING WITH WABAN'S PEOPLE, they went to the docks to find passage across the ocean. It would be two or three weeks before a ship sailed for Sweden. Tuuli and Niilo were given free passage if they would work in the galley cooking and on the decks.

Saying good-bye to Waban and her people was as hard as it had been to leave the O-chib-wa. "I wish you would be here for the birth of my baby," said Waban, "but I know you are eager to return to your people, just as I was to return to mine. I will always think of you as my sister."

"And you will always be a sister in my heart, too," said Tuuli.

On the ship, Tuuli and Niilo rocked with the waves rolling high and endlessly. They scoured away the vomit of sick sailors. They emptied slop buckets into the roiling ocean. They hefted water onto deck. They scrubbed and scrubbed. And mended torn clothing.

They pulled the ropes of the sails with all the hands on deck in stormy weather. The work was hard. The men were fierce and coarse. When the sailors got drunk on foul-smelling rum, they demanded more work from Niilo and Tuuli and whipped them with leather straps.

Tuuli and Niilo slept on musty tickings in the damp, dark bowels of the ship. Exhausted after hard days of work, Tuuli was glad to be far away from the crew. She kept a knife at her side, but no man came to her at night in the seeping and fetid quarters.

They paid their way
with welts and work.

58

Stepping off the rotten ship, Tuuli dared not raise her drum rejoicing. At first, they wobbled on the wooden pier. Niilo laughed. "I can't get used to walking on solid ground."

Tuuli dared not raise her face to the sunlight even though, after such a long time, she didn't think anyone would recognize her. Their clothes were so ragged and dirty from the long voyage that she wanted to hurry out of the town without calling any attention to herself. She steered Niilo away from the castle.

Tuuli led her son away from the ocean. They stayed off worn paths and avoided towns. They walked with the sun to their backs. The wind blew gently as they headed for the land of reindeer and the land of Saami. Northward. Northward they went. Every day, as they got closer to their people, Tuuli felt a quickening in her heart and an eagerness quickened her step. In the evenings, they stopped and made their beds surrounded by trees. "Just smell the earth. Look at the flowers. Look at the trees. We're close to our Saami," she said to Niilo. "Your people, too."

One evening when they were far from the shores where castles and ships were found, Tuuli took out her drum and tapped it with her thumb. It awakened as if from a long sleep, and sweet sounds rever-berated among the pines. While drumming, she recited grandmothers and grandfathers of eighteen generations of family noaidis. The wind blew, welcoming her back. She told Niilo again of Lásse. Of the rein-deer. Of the Mount of Four Winds. "We will bring Aiko's ashes there and swirl them to the winds," she said.

> *They shed what had been.*
> *Step by step,*
> *they became one with the drum.*
> *One with the wind.*
> *One with the land.*
> *With the bear. The deer.*
> *One with their people.*
> *The Saami.*

59

At the last afternoon of the autumn gathering of siides, the wind whispered to Lásse. *They are coming.* He shook his head. What did it mean? More strangers? "Hold still!" Siru scolded him. Her voice brought him back. He grasped the reindeer's antlers more firmly, holding its head in place. "That's better," Siru said as she continued to milk into a carved bowl. Lásse watched her squeeze each teat with her one good hand. Not a single squirt missed the bowl.

The wind swirled and whispered again. *They are coming.* Lásse looked around. "You can let go now," Siru told him. "It's a good thing I'm finished. Sometimes you're as helpful as a puppy chasing its own tail." She smiled and reached to pat his cheek. He'd grown so much since Aiko had first laid him on her lap. Each year when the lake ice cracked open, showing dark waters, she'd bitten a mark onto her waist pouch. Ten marks. He was as still not as old as she and Tuuli had been when the strangers came to their siide, but he had grown tall and strong.

A slick black raven flew overhead and perched on a treetop. "That bird again," she muttered. *Kronk. Kronk.* A feather sluffed and floated downward. Lásse caught it and stuck it in his hat. Then he picked up the milk bowl. As he walked with Siru to their *lavvu*, he said, "You told me that my mother talked to the wind."

"The other way around. The wind talked to her." Siru stopped. "Is that what's happening to you when you look like you're in another world? Just now when we were milking?"

"Yes. It's happened for some time now, but at first I just heard murmurs. Now I think I can make out what it's saying."

"And what does it say?"

"It says, 'They are coming.' I remember when you told me that my mother heard the wind warn about strangers coming. They've kept coming. They're as pesky as spring mosquitoes. I've had enough of them. The cold season is coming on. Why would they come now?"

A chill ran up Siru's back to her neck. She had never told Lásse that his father was a stranger. How could she? Shaking memories of that long-ago time, she just said, "Vuoi. Vuoi. How would I know? First Tuuli. Now you." Then she scolded, "This wind listening is dangerous. The time of noaidis is over. The strangers say, 'No more drums. No more chants. No more calling upon our ancestors. No more rituals. No more this. No more that.' I worry enough for you. Don't tell anyone about the wind whispering to you. Just agree with everything the strangers say, or they'll put a fire to your feet."

Kronk. Kronk. The raven flew from treetop to treetop.

Siru nudged Lásse forward so he'd quit watching the bird. "Come. We need to finish our boots for this winter."

"What do you mean *we*? You know you're going to make me do all the cutting and stitching," Lásse teased.

"Yes, you have two good hands. My good one is tired from milking, but it's not so tired I still can't give you a good *get-going* pat on the behind."

"Ooooh, now I'm afraid," Lásse said as he scampered ahead.

60

AFTER LÁSSE FINISHED THE LAST STITCHES in the four boots he'd made and Siru had given her nod of approval, they made a pouch for the milk, tied it shut, and hung it on a branch to clabber. That night, a sharp chill stabbed the air. Lásse pulled his robe tighter around his shoulders. Red embers from the small fire his siide had built to roast a willow grouse slowly faded. Snores from all the lavvus told him that he was the only one awake.

Nights were longer now. Beavi showed for shorter times each day. The snows would come soon. The falling-leaf gathering was over. The celebrations ended. Courtship races had been run. The herders had already packed and were ready to follow their small herd of reindeer when they migrated to the winter grounds.

Lásse wished Siru were awake. He'd ask her to tell again of when their siide numbered many more and the herd was much larger. That was before the strangers came. Before his mother had been taken away. Before the strangers threatened death to those who followed the ways of their ancestors. He wanted to be a noaidi and had sat at the feet of those during the gathering of the siides. They had talked in whispers.

Of times gone past. Of who had followed the words of the strangers. Of how to resist the new ways. Of Poppi. Of Tuuli.

The wind was quiet. The raven that had followed them during the day was gone. Lásse breathed deeply in the night air. He listened to the sounds of the night. An owl softly hooted. The deer shuffled. His little dog woofed in her sleep. And now, other sounds. A branch snapping? Footsteps? A stumble in the dark? Soft voices? He groaned to himself. The strangers again!

Kronk. Kronk.

The raven again! Why was it flying in the dark? And why were the strangers coming now? Were they searching for drums now while several siides were all together? He detested the strangers! They'd taken his mother and burned the ancient drums.

Kronk. Kronk.

They were closer now. Two figures wavered in the shadows. He could hear them talking. Saami words! Saami voices! He built up the fire and wished there were some grouse left to offer. Whoever they were, they must be hungry, traveling so late. He left the fire and went to his lavvu to get the basket that held dried fish and venison he and Siru had put aside for the migration.

No one tended the fire when Tuuli and Niilo entered the camp. Tuuli called out to awaken the people. Sleepers wakened to the voice. They crept out of their lavvus to see who had entered the camp. In the dim light of the campfire, it was difficult to see.

"*Bures, bures,*" Tuuli and Niilo said.

Light from the flames and shadows from the dark danced across the faces of the newcomers as they approached the fire. The rich sap from a log sputtered. It crackled and sent forth a tall lick of flame that illuminated the newcomers. Tuuli said, "We come looking for our siide."

"Who are your people?"

"The Many Rowans Siide."

"This is Many Rowans. Welcome."

"Who are you?" asked one of the herders.

"I am Tuuli."

"Tuuli? Poppi's Tuuli? Come closer to the fire so we can see you." Many talked at once. "It is possible? Are you really Tuuli?"

Siru tumbled out of her lavvu and hurried to Tuuli. The two hugged and hugged and hugged. At last when Siru let go, Tuuli asked, "Where is Lásse?"

At that moment, Lásse stepped forward carrying the food basket. Siru said, "Don't you recognize your own son?"

Lásse put down his basket and said, "Are you my mother? Tuuli, my mother?"

It was as if the stars, the moon, and the world stood still. All the grandmothers, the grandfathers, the herders, the mothers, sons, daughters, little children, and even the dogs stood still. Watching. Watching as mother and son embraced for the first time in the passing of so many seasons, so many moons, so many births, so many deaths. After a night owl passed on silent wings, Tuuli unwrapped her arms from around Lásse.

She held his hand. And Niilo's, too. She joined them together as she said, "Son Lásse. Son Niilo. Brothers."

61

Tuuli inhaled deeply, drawing in the air she hadn't breathed for so long. The fragrance of damp mosses, moldering leaves, and pungent saps filled her lungs. "Look," she said to Niilo. She pointed to the seven stars of the Great Bear. "He guards us here, even as he did through all our journeys." By now, everyone had wakened. They piled out of their skin tents. A little red pup ran to Tuuli and begged to be picked up.

Dizzy with joy, Tuuli dropped to her knees. The puppy licked her face. She laughed. Her son! Her people! Tuuli had returned. She was with Lásse. She could not keep her eyes from studying his every smile, every gesture, every glint of his eyes. This was the infant she'd held to her breast, and now he was as old as all her fingers on both hands. He was no longer an infant, so tall he came up to her shoulder. She thanked Siru and all her people over and over for keeping her son safe.

A myriad of stars and the moon gleamed above. Campfire flames danced. The night was awake. Everyone bustled to bring dried meats, berries, and mashed roots. Breathing crisp air, hearing the crackle of the fire, the people of the Many Rowans siide as well as all the other siides gathered to watch as Tuuli savored every mouthful. Biting into a bit of smoked venison, she said, "This is the taste of home." She had dreamed so often of this return. And now it was real.

"Come to our lavvu," Siru said. "You must be tired from your long journeys."

"Sore feet? Yes," Tuuli said, "but I am so happy to be here, I won't be able to sleep until I hear about all that has passed."

Niilo sat with Lásse. "Brother," they said to each other.

"Tell me everything," Tuuli said.

"We have no good news."

"We are but a shadow of who we were when you left," Siru said.

"More forests are cut. More lands plowed and planted. Waterways have been dammed and the course of rivers changed."

"The taxmen who come from the king take more furs."

"Those with the black book swarm our lands, too. They look for drums. They burn siides. They tell us our joiks summon the evil one. We are forbidden to sing."

"The strangers have scattered so many herds, the wild deer are scarce."

"Many of our people have died. Some have left with the strangers. Some stay but no longer carry on our ancestors' ways. Utsí left. We haven't seen him for many gatherings."

"Your father Beto came. When he heard that the king's men were looking for you to burn you at the stake, he searched the woods hoping to find you before they did. When he didn't find you, he came here. He held Lásse. Cradled him. Sang to him. But his heart weakened. Jabbemeahkka came for him just two cold seasons ago."

"We have no noaidi. No one from other siides wanted to join us because of threats by the strangers. We have worried about you and are glad you are back."

Tuuli listened. Then she unwrapped her drum and softly tapped it as she sang the story of the many seasons she had been gone. A song that told her story.

Men took me on their horses. You saw them that frightful day.
They violated my deepest being.
Lásse is my son of that seed.
Lásse, who I held to my breast for too short a time.
Look at him now. Ten gatherings later.
How I cried and pulled my hair and beat my chest
crying out for my baby. Wondering how he grew.
Wondering if he'd ever call me "Mother."

Lásse took both of Tuuli's hands in his and said, "Mother."

They took me to a land of kings and castles.
I was scorned by the many. Called a witch. An evil one.
Condemned. They set a fire to burn me to death while all watched.
Aiko. Yes, I say his name. The Banished One among our people.
Aiko saved me from the fires.
He brought me to Hánas, the Broken Branch of our people.
The king ordered hundreds to scour the land for me. So a plan was made.
Aiko brought Lásse here. Hánas hid me on his father's great trade boat.
We rocked among the waves for two full passings of the moon and more.
We crossed the deep waters to a place called Mass-a-chu-setts.
Hánas promised to return the following warm season.
If it was safe, he would bring me back to you, my people, and to Lásse.
But he never returned. Perhaps he is no longer of this earth.
In the New World, there are people like us.
The Wampanoag—people of the first light—and
the O-chib-wa—people of food that grows in water.
And others.
People who live with the earth, the animals, the stars, the sun, the moon.
They, too, have many gods who care for them.
They, too, revere those who have gone before.
But there, across the big waters, are the pale-faced people who snarl at our ways.
Just like here.
They tell us our gods are not gods at all.
They are cruel there, as they are here.

They are called the Coat People.
They of pale skin.
Aiko crossed the waters to find me.
In Mass-a-chu-setts, too, I was cursed.
Cursed for having healed a young man. Cursed for being different.
Accused of what I did not do. Condemned again.
A noose was readied for my neck.
I was imprisoned.
Awaiting the day of my hanging.
Then a war between the Coat People and those who are like us broke out.
My watchers ran to fight, forgetting about me.
We, Aiko, Waban, and her son escaped.
We followed deer paths, scaled mountains, sloshed through wetlands,
skirted lakes.
Endured mosquitoes, rains, sore feet, blazing sun, and cold, cold nights.
But then we found home by an ancient river surrounded by cliffs, tall trees.
A land of many waters.
Lakes abounded with fish and a food the people called manoomin.
The forests held deer, rabbits, squirrels, birds. Berries, roots, leaves.
We planted corn and squash. We lacked for nothing.
Guovza, ravens, fox, and wolves lived in the woods nearby and kept us safe.
That is where Niilo was born,
after Waban's son was taken by their Great Spirit, it was just Waban,
Aiko, Niilo, and me.
Aiko and I taught our son about all of you. All our ancestors.
But one day, the raven called Aiko to enter the spirit world.
It was time for us to return.
To find Lásse.
To be home again.

When she was finished, her people murmured. "Is it really true," they asked, "that you traveled so far and found people with the same fears and who suffer the same mistreatments as we endure?"

"Yes," Tuuli said. "Sadly, yes."

$\ggg\!\!\!\times\!\!\!\lll$

In the morning, a mist hung low. After Tuuli and Niilo finished eating a stew of fish, Lásse said to Niilo, "Come, brother. Come see my pet deer and help me care for her. I'm hoping she'll give birth in the spring. If she does, the fawn will be yours."

Niilo looked to Tuuli. She nodded that he could go. Then she watched as her two sons ran together, side by side. Tears gathered in her eyes; joy swelled within her. She heard the drum. Her heart beat with it. The wind whispered as she sang.

> *Báiki. My home. My people are here.*
> *My journeys are over.*
> *Báiki.*

AUTHOR'S NOTE

TUULI IS A FICTIONAL CHARACTER SET IN THE 1670S. In the story, when she returns to her people, King Karl XI is still ruler of Sweden; suppression of the Saami culture continues throughout his reign. When he dies in 1697, his son Karl XII follows him to the throne. He is even more fanatical about eradicating the noaidis, the drums, and the rituals of the Saami and confiscating their lands. During the period of witch hunts, anyone who sings joiks, beats drums, or takes part in any Saami rituals is found guilty of witchcraft and sentenced to death. In the lands of Arctic Norway, it is reported that at least 175 Saami were burned or hanged as witches. It is not known how many more in Sweden met death in this way, too.

Tuuli's return put her into the midst of fervent persecution and confrontation of all indigenous Saami religions with a focus on destroying the drums. Very few drums from that period survive. Some are displayed in museums. In 1688, a Swedish bishop traveled through the lands of the Saami. All who did not hand over their drums were threatened. The constant pestering, mistreating, scattering, and burning of herds and villages continued into the next two centuries.

Tuuli's desire to save her people and preserve their ways was met with strong resistance from the governments of Sweden, Norway, and Russia. Finland was under Swedish rule at the time. Each nation claimed the lands to their north where the reindeer roamed freely. The nomads who followed the deer were considered subhuman, dirty pagans, and were suspected of invoking evil spirits through their drums and songs.

Tuuli's story could have been set anywhere in the New World from the northernmost tip of North America to the southernmost tip of South America. Newcomers to this world claimed these lands for their kings and for their religion, also. Systematic genocide was used in some places. Torture, burnings, and hangings were used to subdue the people and force them to give up their beliefs and way of life. Enslavement and beatings were common as well as the destruction of any written, artistic, or symbolic works of the native peoples. Tuuli's heart was with her people, but the forces she was up against were larger and stronger.

GLOSSARY OF SAAMI TERMS

Ag'gja	Father
Báiki	The home you carry in your heart wherever you go
Beavi	Sun
Bieg	A folklore monster who creates huge storms when anyone trespasses onto his lands
Bures	Hello
Gabba	White—the name of Tuuli's fawn
Goahti	A wooden-framed skin- and bark-covered winter shelter
Guovza	Bear
Jabbemeahkka	Goddess of death
Kah!	An exclamation
Kulta	Tuuli's little red dog
Lavvu	A portable conical shelter of saplings covered with skins, much like the tepees of the plains Indians. Used during migrations.
Noaidi	A spiritual man or woman who has mystical skills
Ruusu	Tuuli's old pet reindeer
Saami	The Arctic people of Norway, Sweden, Finland, and the Kola Peninsula of Russia. (Alternate spelling: Sámi)
Siide	A group of families who live together and migrate with the deer
Stallu	A monster in folklore who captures young women to be his brides
Vuoi	An exclamation of joy, surprise, satisfaction

GLOSSARY OF SWEDISH TERMS

Dotter ar mörken	Daughter of darkness
Drick	Drink
Du är ganska	You are pretty
Gott	Good
Gris	Pig
Häst	Horse
Håxa	Witch
Inte i mitt hus	Not in my house
Ja	Yes
Jaga djävulen ur	Chase the devil out
Kaffe	Coffee
Kom, Komma	Come
Kung, Kungen	King
Kungen Karl	Fifteen-year-old King Karl of Sweden at the time of this story
Kyckling	Chicken
Ledsen	Sorry
Med barn	With child
Mer kläder	More clothes
Nej	No
Nu	Now
Rena den själ	Cleanse your soul
Slott	Castle
Smutsig	Filthy
Sømn	Sleep
Tvätta	Wash
Unge	Baby
Vänd dig om	Turn around
Varför?	Why?

GLOSSARY OF OJIBWE TERMS

Boozhoo   Greetings

Manoomin   Wild rice (There are many alternate spellings for this word.)

GLOSSARY OF WAMPANOAG WORDS

Cone   Sun

King Philip's War   Started in 1675 in an effort by the tribes around the area of today's Martha's Vineyard, Cape Cod, and Nantucket to preserve their traditional way of life and to keep their hunting lands. It was also in retaliation of the execution of three Wampanoag Indians. The war lasted less than a year. The Wampanoags suffered a great loss of people. Survivors fled to other tribes for protection. Those captured by the colonists were often sold into slavery.

Metacomet   Grand Sachem. Called *King Philip* by the colonists. He led his people into the war to stop Puritan expansion into their hunting lands. He was shot in the heart by a Wampanoag man who'd converted to Christianity. As a warning against further insurrection, his body was cut into quarters and hung in trees, and his head was mounted on a pike at Fort Plymouth. His right hand was given to his slayer as a reward. His wife and nine-year-old son were captured and sold into slavery in the West Indies.

Mishoon   Dug-out canoe

Moccasin   A shoe/boot made of deer or moose skins

Nanabozho   The Great Spirit/Creator of the tribes of the Algonquin Nation

Nootimis   Sachem for the band of families that take Waban and Tuuli in. Means *oak*.

Prophecy of   Seven prophets appeared to various tribes of the Algonquin
Seven Fires   people. Each revealed a prophecy or *fire*. The Fourth Fire predicted the coming of pale-skinned people. The Fifth Fire told of a struggle between those who accepted the ways of the pale

skins and those who continued with the old ways. These two Fires were occurring at the time of this story.

Sachem	A leader who makes decisions for his/her people
Shennucke	Squirrel
Waban	Name meaning *wind*
Wampanoag	Means *People of the First Light* or *People of the Dawn* because they lived on the eastern shore and received the first light of day before others. One of the Algonquin tribes that live in the present-day area of Cape Cod, Martha's Vineyard, etc.
Wamsutta	Grand Sachem before Metacomet, his brother
Wewes	Waban's son fathered by gunsmith Kron. Means *owl*.

ACKNOWLEDGEMENTS

MY LOVE OF STORY BEGAN WITH WELL-WORN BOOKS, discarded from libraries, that my mother rescued and shelved in wooden apple crates, and then stacked and lined along one whole upstairs wall. On lazy mornings I just reached for a book while staying snug in bed and read to my heart's content. I am grateful to my mother and father for fostering my love of reading and writing.

As a child I was introduced to the world of shamanistic magic and healing by the Ladies of the Kaleva who held a camp each summer and read Finnish epic poems to us campers from *The Kalevala*.

Later on I was inspired by the poetry and *joiks* of Norwegian Sámi Nils-Aslak Valkeapää through his recordings and book *Trekways of the Wind*.

I am grateful for the patience, understanding, and support of my husband. I am also indebted to my first writing teachers: Milan Kovacovik, Maryanne Weidt, Bart Sutter, Mara Hart, and several teachers at the University of Minnesota's Split Rock Arts program.

My deepest appreciation also goes out to the following:

Gary Miller, who offered up excellent advice as well as encouragement.

Tim Jollymore and Peter Rennebaum for their suggestions and reassurance.

Marlene Wisuri of the Sámi Cultural Center of North America in Duluth for her commitment in providing a home for all of us seeking to know more about the Sámi culture.

My writers' group for their critiques, especially Ann Treacy who never said no when I needed something read and re-read.

Hanna, Alicia, Athena, and the whole staff of Beaver's Pond Press who helped bring my dream to reality.

ABOUT THE AUTHOR

KATHARINE JOHNSON LIVES IN NORTHERN MINNESOTA with her husband and the woodland creatures, large and small, who come into their yard to browse or snitch seeds to fatten their bellies. Her previous publications are: "Company's Here" in *Ladybug* magazine, "Ada," "Forgiveness of Sins," and several poems in anthologies.